For Westley and Buttercup, the couple that started it all for me.

Queen of Whispers and Mist

Meg Anne

Cover Art by Story Wrappers

Edited by Mo Sytsma of Comma Sutra Editorial

Proofread by Dominique Laura

She's the kind of queen that knows her crown isn't on her head but in her soul.

— ADRIAN MICHAEL

QUEEN OF WHISPERS AND MIST

AUTHOR'S NOTE

Queen of Whispers and Mist contains mature and graphic content that is not suitable for all audiences. Such content includes murder, kidnapping, explicit violence and gore. **Reader discretion is advised.**

A detailed list of content and trigger warnings is available on my website.

CHAPTER 1

RONAN

*T*he last time he died, Ronan was struck by how loud death was. This time he was taken by the silence. That's how he knew it was real.

At least he thought it was until the collective inhale of the crowd transformed into ground-shaking shouts. That was the moment he registered the answering tremors beneath his ribs and recognized them as the thundering beat of his heart.

If Shadow slit his throat, it should be sluggish and slow, not racing.

And there should be pain . . . right? Or was the lack of pain significant? Suggesting perhaps that she cut so deep he died instantly?

Why was dying so confusing? It always seemed such a straightforward affair from the other end of the blade.

"What are you playing at? Finish it!" Erebos's enraged shout rang out.

The crowd's bloodthirsty cheers grew louder, echoing the High Lord's order.

"I forfeit." Shadow's voice was nearly a whisper by comparison, but it cracked through the arena like thunder.

Only then did he finally understand. Even with all the evidence he'd already gathered, it wasn't until he heard the defeat in her voice that the pieces clicked into place.

She couldn't go through with it.

She couldn't kill him.

For the second time in less than a month, Ronan had walked into a battle expecting to meet his maker and found himself still breathing on the other side.

His eyes snapped open to find Shadow's head bowed over him, her arm hanging limply at her side while her chest heaved. Her expression was haunted; clearly the decision hadn't been an easy one for her.

There were so many things he wanted to say to her, questions to ask, thanks to convey, but the best he could manage was a rasped, "Kitten..."

Her gaze found his, and what he saw reflected at him left him speechless.

The intensity of his shock mingled with his relief, rendering him little more than a boneless puddle in the dirt. He'd wanted to believe her feelings for him would weigh into the outcome, but hope was a painful and dangerous thing, so he hadn't allowed himself to give in to it.

Instead, he'd prepared himself for the worst and resigned himself to death once more. This time, at least, he'd felt as though his demise served a greater purpose. There was comfort in that, if little else.

"Ladies and gentlemen, we have our winner!" Dmitri's voice boomed throughout the arena, shattering Ronan's illusion of privacy.

There was a barely perceptible lull before the crowd went utterly wild. Shadow's words had already ignited their interest, but the Peacock's announcement transformed their excited cries into wildfire. There wasn't a person in Glimmermere who wouldn't know what had transpired in the arena within the next twenty minutes.

Ronan ignored all of it, focusing instead on the woman he'd been ready to sacrifice everything for. She held his gaze, unblinking, conveying thousands of unspoken words through her multihued irises —none of which he understood beyond the unsettling certainty she was saying goodbye.

"What is it?" he asked, his voice still little more than a harsh whisper. His body was so shot through with adrenaline that he trembled as he lifted his hand up to cup her cheek. "What aren't you telling me?"

Before she could answer, Shadow was pulled off him by two of the High Lord's men. She could have fought them if she wished, but she didn't. Instead, she allowed them to whisk her away without so much as a backward glance in his direction. The slump of her shoulders told him everything he needed to know.

Nothing good awaited her at the end of this forced walk of shame.

"Wait, I—" Ronan staggered to his feet and tried to go after her.

If she disappeared now, the moment between them would be lost. The next time he saw Shadow, assuming he was lucky enough to see her alone again, her wall would be back in place. Trapping her on one side and him on the other.

Even before she lost her memories, vulnerability of any kind was in short supply from the Forsaken queen. There was no way she'd willingly bare herself like that again anytime soon. Least of all to him —the man who'd basically stolen her win out from under her.

Not that it had been his intention, but she couldn't know that. They never got around to speaking about his motives for joining the competition.

Or hers, for that matter.

He never did make sense of it. Her rationale for joining the contest. She was Erebos's champion in all but name, so was it just the official title she was after? Or something else?

And if so, *what*?

This was hardly the appropriate time for him to try to solve the enigma that was Shadow, but he couldn't help but think the answer to that question was imperative to his own mission. How could he help her if he didn't understand her?

Ronan took two running steps, intent on following the guards as they bodily pulled the High Lord's assassin from the arena, but stopped when chants of his name echoed through the stadium. The chorus of 'Butcher's was much more enthusiastic than he'd heard thus far in the competition, the crowd finally won over now that he'd been declared the official winner.

There was nothing he could do about it. Not with all these eyes on him. He had to continue playing the game, at least for a little while longer.

Inwardly resigned, with his persona's cold-blooded mask firmly in place, Ronan turned away from Shadow's retreating figure to look toward the dais where the High Lord and his flock stood. Erebos's gaze found his, and true amusement made Ronan's lips quirk upward. Behind the regal façade and slight smile, fury burned in those jade orbs. This was not the outcome Glimmermere's leader wanted, but he was handicapped by rules of his own making. Forced to honor a man he'd intended to see slaughtered before his very eyes.

Good. Ronan shared his disappointment. Not because he was still breathing, but because Erebos was. Maybe he could solve that little problem during his hopefully brief tenure as the man's champion.

After a slight nod from his liege, Dmitri rushed down the narrow flight of stairs connected to the stage, taking them two at a time. Reaching Ronan's side, he took his wrist in a surprisingly strong grip and lifted his arm high into the air.

"People of Glimmermere, it is my most humble honor to present to you, Empyria's newest protector, the High Lord's Champion."

Ronan found it telling that his identity was now dependent on the other man's. He was no longer Ronan or the Butcher, but the High Lord's Champion. No longer a person in his own right, but the High Lord's shiny new possession. Much like Shadow was.

In Elysia, he was known as the Shield, but he'd never stopped being Ronan. He'd never been reduced to existing solely as Helena's plaything, which was why the distinction was so notable now. Instead of empowering, his new title was demeaning. One of ownership rather than respect.

No one's existence should hold value only because of their ties to someone else.

Unaware of his dark musings, the crowd erupted into a new round of cheers while Ronan was forced to endure it. He was more thankful than ever he'd entered the contest as the Butcher. At least this way, the mercenary wasn't expected to do something as polite as smile. Which was for the best, really. Any attempt at forcing his lips up in a believable display of pleasure wouldn't be mistaken as anything other than the grimace it was. Then everyone would know he felt none of the pride he should have for such a perceived honor.

Issues with the title aside, why should he?

Truth was, he'd lost this contest. There was little doubt in his mind he could have ended it and won for real, but that had never been the game. Not for him. The only reason he was standing here at all was that Shadow couldn't take his life, and everyone knew it.

Though, from the audience's cheers, no one seemed disappointed in the outcome. If anything, the drama only seemed to spur on their enthusiasm.

Tipping his head so Ronan could hear him over the roar of the crowd, Dmitri murmured, "Come with me." It wasn't a request but a coldly delivered command.

Ronan followed his lead, trailing after him in the opposite direction Shadow had been taken, something inside him protesting each step that took him farther away from her.

Soon. Bide your time. Make the best of this opportunity. Learn your enemies so when the time comes, you're ready to destroy them.

The reminder went a long way to easing the storm raging through his veins. So much had happened in the last hour. Bast. Loren. The games. Certain death. Shadow's choice. Winning. Any one of those things was a mindfuck. All of them back-to-back? He was just lucky he remembered his damn name.

The only way to cope was to focus on the present moment. Anything else was impossible.

Instead of leading him up to the stage, Dmitri escorted him through an archway that turned into a series of tunnels. When the Peacock smacked a random brick set into one wall, causing it to swing open, Ronan could only assume they were taking a secret passage to the palace.

It didn't surprise him that Erebos had a way to move through the

5

city unseen. Helena had similar passages throughout Tigaera, which granted her the flexibility to walk about freely when she didn't want to risk being caught in public. In his tenure as her Shield, he quickly learned that rulers couldn't be amongst their people without garnering unwanted attention or demands on their time. It was rare to go more than a few steps without being stopped.

Given his new celebrity, herding Ronan from the arena to the palace without being waylaid by overzealous townspeople would be impossible. So, while the warrior in him balked at the notion of venturing into a darkened corridor with someone who was essentially his enemy, he understood the value of such a walkway. This route ensured they could get him where they wanted him as expediently as possible.

His suspicions were confirmed when, without a word, the Peacock led him through a dank underpass that opened up into a receiving chamber of sorts. The lack of furnishing immediately stood out. While the checkered black-and-white marble floors were polished to the point Ronan could make out his reflection as clearly as if gazing into a mirror, the blood-red walls were practically macabre in their nudity. With only a handful of wooden benches—albeit intricately carved ones—lining the space, there was little to detract from the sheer majesty of the three figures standing in the far corner of the room.

Which was likely the point.

Three sets of eyes fixated on him the second he set foot in the room. After sparing a second to acknowledge the other two members of the flock and finding nothing friendly in either of their expressions, Ronan met Erebos's gaze head-on.

Now that Dmitri was present, the only member of the inner circle notably absent was Shadow. The realization had the little hairs on the back of his neck standing on end.

She should be here.

On the heels of that thought came another, more sinister one.

Unless her actions today mean she's fallen out of favor with her liege and must now be punished.

Mother's tits. What sort of danger have you gotten yourself into, Kitten?

"I suppose congratulations are in order," Erebos drawled, breaking their silent standoff. The words were innocuous enough, but there was no mistaking the anger threaded through them.

Ronan found it interesting that even now, in a room filled with only those loyal to him, he continued to play the role of magnanimous ruler. Erebos could probably gut him here and now and his flock wouldn't raise an eyebrow or breathe word of it . . . so why the fanfare?

"Have you explained the terms of his prize?" The High Lord's eyes flicked to Dmitri.

"Not yet, my liege."

With a long-suffering sigh, Erebos returned his attention to Ronan. "As per the terms of the contest, along with your position as my Champion and all the perks it affords you, you are entitled to one boon."

"A boon?"

Ronan was familiar with the custom, but it brought him great joy to force Erebos to spell it out for him. Anything he could do to undermine and annoy the man was a blessing as far as he was concerned.

The blond man's lip curled up in a sneer. "You are allowed to make one request of me at tonight's ceremony. Whatever you desire, if it is in my power to give, it is yours. Think hard, Butcher, and make it count. It will be your only chance to make such a request of me."

Before Ronan could respond, Erebos raked his gaze over his face and continued. "I can see the idea intrigues you. Make no mistake, you may have won, but there's all manner of ways for a man such as yourself to disappear in the line of duty. Your presence in my life is a temporary annoyance at most. One I intend to rid myself of at the first possible opportunity. All you've proven today is that you're a stubborn fool. Luckily for me, I happen to know just how easily fools can be dealt with."

Ronan listened to all of this without a word. There was nothing he could say right now that would make a damn bit of difference. He needed to think carefully about his boon, knowing that the phrasing was every bit as important as the request itself. He had an idea of how he could make the best of this final night of freedom, but in order to ensure it came to fruition, he needed to word his request in such a way Erebos was honor-bound to grant it.

Part of him had expected Erebos to off him here and now, but Ronan was starting to understand the man's methods. Everything he did was a performance. A way to build political capital he could cash in at a later date. If Ronan went missing before tonight's ceremony, there'd be no escaping the murmurs. *That* was the real reason Erebos continued to play the game. But there was an expiration date on his participation. Once the eyes of his people were no longer on them and they were out from under the spotlight of this contest, Ronan would be under no such protection.

He needed to make the best of his reprieve.

"You're free to go for now, Champion." There was a noticeable bite to the word, as if it pained him to use the title. "I'll see you tonight. Oh, and do take great care that you do not do anything in the meantime to embarrass me. You're mine now. Everything you do or say will reflect upon me. I take great pride in ensuring nothing tarnishes my sterling reputation."

Ronan nearly laughed at the absolute ego of it all, especially since he had little doubt that brainwashing factored into the man's methods. But somehow he managed to keep his face impassive as he nodded.

"Good. Dovina will meet you upon your return and escort you where you need to be. Enjoy these last minutes of anonymity, Butcher, for after tonight, life as you know it will never be the same."

CHAPTER 2

RONAN

*E*xhaustion weighed down his steps as Ronan staggered up the stairs to the little room he shared with Bast. Pushing open the door, he stiffened in surprise when he found two weapons trained on him.

"*Merde!*" Sebastian fervently groaned, lowering his slingshot. "Put the crossbow down, Loren. It's just Ronan."

Loren eyed him slowly from head to toe before eventually doing as he was told, setting the crossbow aside and picking up an empty travel bag. It would seem Ronan had interrupted them in the middle of packing.

"Thanks for the warm welcome," he grunted, giving each man a wary once-over as he stepped inside and kicked the door shut behind him. "What did I do to deserve it?"

"We thought you might be one of the High Lord's men, come to take out the trash," Bast answered with a bitter laugh.

With the way the trial losers had all gone missing, that was a fair assumption. Although even if they hadn't, anyone who'd aided Ronan would be marked as an enemy. There was little doubt in Ronan's mind what Erebos would do to Bast or Loren given the chance. Glimmermere was no longer safe. Not for them.

"Why hang about then?"

"We needed to gather supplies before heading out of town," Bast replied, taking a seat as Loren knelt down and resumed tossing items into a rucksack.

"We leave at sundown," Loren added.

Ronan flicked his gaze out the window, taking in the burnt-orange and coppery tinge of the sky. The sun was nearly set; there were perhaps another twenty minutes at most before the soft purple of dusk would replace the vibrant colors. It was a smart play, using the cover of darkness to make their escape.

"I take it you'll be heading for the border?" he asked almost absently as he claimed one of the seats at their rickety table.

Sebastian nodded. "There's a place I know of in the western mountains. I stayed there once before."

When Ronan's full weight hit the chair, it sharply tilted back and to the left, one leg shorter than the others. He scowled but didn't bother moving. The other seat wouldn't be any better. This furniture had not been crafted for a man of his size. Then again, this entire room was an afterthought. A way for the shop owner downstairs to make some extra coin. It was never intended to be used as a full-time dwelling.

With a slight jolt, Ronan realized this was likely the last night he'd spend in what had become a safe haven. Surely Erebos would expect his Champion to reside in the palace where he could keep an eye on his comings and goings. The only upside of the move was that he'd be closer to Shadow.

Completely unaware that Ronan's attention had wandered, Bast had continued prattling on. Thankfully, he didn't seem to require any sort of response. He was like this sometimes, not really seeking conversation as much as an audience to talk at. Sebastian Villehardouin, one man show.

Ronan's lips quirked up. He was going to miss the windbag.

"Anyway, Brillergarde should be safe enough until we can make arrangements to get Loren back home."

Realizing this was his cue, Ronan prompted, "And home is?"

"Knightsgrave," Loren answered, standing and hefting the now full bag over his shoulder.

While still not entirely familiar with Empyria's layout, Ronan knew Knightsgrave to be in the south, protected in large part by a treacherous mountain range known as The Crags, which ran diagonally through most of the continent. To cross them would likely require a guide familiar with the dangerous terrain. From the bits of gossip Ronan overheard in the marketplace, most travelers opted to go around through Brillergarde or Darkhollow—the neighboring realms—where passage was more forgiving. Except for those few brave souls who preferred to travel by sea along the southeastern coast.

Realizing the journey ahead of them was long, Ronan appreciated their choice to remain in town a bit longer and ensure they'd have what they'd need in the days to come.

Letting out a soft grunt that wasn't so much approval as acknowledgment, Ronan returned his attention to Sebastian, who was still wearing his bloodstained clothes from earlier. Through the torn bits of fabric he could make out smooth, unmarred skin, meaning the men must have stopped by a healer on their way here.

"I must say you're looking well, considering the state you were in when I saw you last."

"Well? I wouldn't go as far as that. A little less holey, perhaps," Bast said with a smirk.

Ronan shook his head at the terrible pun, but there was no denying the relief he felt seeing the other man back on his feet and up to his usual antics. He was no stranger to the horrors of battle, but one never truly rid themselves of the ghosts of their fallen comrades. He was thankful he wouldn't have to count Bast among them.

"I'm just lucky Loren has a few contacts in town," Sebastian continued. "They had me patched up in no time."

"Perks of the job," Loren said with a self-indulgent smile. "Any hero worth his headlines has a healer in every port."

"I'm sure healers aren't the only thing you have in every port." Bast's voice had a knowing lilt.

"Like I said, perks."

They laughed, seeming far more comfortable with each other than a pair who'd only been introduced a few nights prior. Ronan wouldn't presume to know what existed between them, but he'd never forget Loren's genuine panic when he'd seen Bast's wounds. Whatever happened in the days to come, he knew Sebastian would be in good hands.

The room lapsed into comfortable silence. There was only one thing left to do, but no one seemed in any hurry to do it.

Realizing it was up to him, Ronan stood and said, "I guess this is where we part ways."

Bast's smile slipped. "I guess so." He stepped forward and held out his hand, the same as he had the night they'd first met. "It's been a privilege to know you, Ronan. I hope our paths cross again one day."

Ronan glanced at the offering and mutely shook his head. With a little sigh, Bast started to step away, but Ronan grabbed him by the shoulder and pulled him in, giving him a tight one-armed hug. Sebastian was too surprised to react, his body rigid in Ronan's hold. After a second, Ronan cleared his throat and slapped him roughly on the back. "Safe travels, Bast. May the Mother watch over and guide you."

There was a soft hitch as Sebastian's breath caught before he returned Ronan's embrace, squeezing tightly. "We both know the journey you've begun is far more deadly than the one I'm about to embark on."

"Perhaps I can help with that," Loren said, drawing both men's attention as they released each other. "There's been some rumors flying around about your Shadow."

"*My* Shadow?" Ronan asked, trying for casual but knowing he failed.

Bast shook his head and laughed. "You fool no one but yourself, Ronan."

"What do you know?" he asked Loren, ignoring Bast's remark.

"It's okay. Ronan knows not to shoot the messenger. Tell him what you told me," Bast said, giving Ronan a look that told him in no uncertain terms to behave.

"Erebos intends to marry Shadow. A wedding is already in the works."

Ronan's heart froze before kicking into overdrive. "Wait, what? But what if she won?"

"The plan was the same regardless of the game's outcome. If Shadow won, he was going to have her abdicate her title and marry him instead."

"But his Champion—" Ronan wasn't so sure why he was hung up on the position, but it seemed to be the only detail he could concentrate on. He simply could not handle the possibility of Shadow becoming Erebos's wife.

"He was going to place someone else in her stead. The Vulture, perhaps, but no one knows for sure. These are all whispers, of course. But the one constant is that the High Lord means to be married before the end of the season, and he wants her."

Ronan's stomach churned at the thought of that snake laying hands on her. The mere thought had nausea curling in his gut. He was torn between wanting to shout his rage to the heavens or go on a murderous rampage.

As if he could sense Ronan's downward spiral, Loren placed a hand on his shoulder and offered him a sliver of hope. "If I were you, with the ability to request anything I desired of the High Lord, I would make the best of it. Think very carefully about the boon you've been given and what a man might do with such a gift." Readjusting the bag on his shoulder, he glanced out the window.

Ronan followed the other man's gaze to find that the sun had slipped past the horizon while they'd been speaking. Their time for goodbyes was up.

"Sebastian," Loren said gently, "we need to go."

"Yes, of course." He looked up at Ronan with a soft smile. "Finally, I'm rid of your dreadful snoring."

"And I the sight of your naked arse."

They held each other's stares with slight smiles. Without another word, Bast gave Ronan a little nod, picked up a second bag, and followed Loren out of the room, leaving him alone with his thoughts.

He walked through the now empty space, mind racing. When he was nearly dizzy from pacing, he sat down on the bed, cupping his head in his hands, and scrambled to devise a plan. It had always been his intent to save Shadow, to take her home if she wished, or at the very least get her far away from here. So despite the unparalleled horror he felt at learning the secret Loren shared, the only thing it changed was Ronan's timeline.

He didn't have weeks. Or even days.

He had hours.

Because there was no reality that existed where he would stand idly by and allow Shadow to shackle herself to that pompous waste of air.

If only it was as simple as asking her to leave with him . . .

He barked out a laugh. When had Shadow ever done anything the easy way? Or agreed with him, for that matter?

But what if it didn't matter what she wanted?

Ronan lifted his head, a devious smile curling his lips as his plan took shape. It was almost too easy, but the genius lay in its simplicity. The more he turned it over in his mind, the more certain he grew.

He *would* get Shadow away from the High Lord.

Tonight.

And he was going to use the craven's own rules against him when he did.

There would be no sneaking her out a secret tunnel. They'd walk out the front doors.

Together.

And there wasn't a single fucking thing Erebos would be able to do about it.

~

SHADOW

Meanwhile, at the Palace

SHE TOOK in the stone walls of her prison, the icy air not bothering her half as much as the tedium. After today's spectacular failure, Erebos had her locked up beneath the bowels of his palace.

She stopped beside a dirt-mottled skeleton still locked in its chains. "I suppose it could be worse. I could be you."

"Talking to yourself already?" Erebos drawled. "I hear that's the first sign of insanity."

The heavy wooden door opened with a series of groans and creaks. They stared at each other across the threshold, Erebos's aristocratic face betraying nothing of his thoughts.

"Well, do you have nothing to say to me, then?"

She kicked a broken bit of bone that had fallen free of its brethren. "The dungeon, really?"

"What more fitting place for a traitor?"

She swallowed, not meeting his gaze as she shrugged. What could she say to that? It was the truth.

"You disappointed me today. More than you ever have."

"I know."

"I've killed men for less."

"I know. I'm the one you send to kill them."

His lips didn't even twitch at her joke, and that's when true dread coiled in her belly. He wasn't just disappointed. He was furious. Enraged. There would be no getting out of this with an apology and a slap on the wrists.

"Why?" The word was little more than a bitten-off growl. When she didn't answer, he slapped the wall. "Answer me. You owe me that, if nothing else."

She shook her head, unable to answer the question even hours later. Darkness knows she's asked herself the same countless times already. Everything she'd been fighting for was right there within reach, but when she looked down into Ronan's crystalline blue eyes, she just couldn't do it. Stars forgive her, she simply couldn't be the one responsible for the life seeping out of them.

As the silence stretched between them, Erebos's anger wrapped around her like a blanket. Though not one meant for comfort or warmth, one that pressed in on every side, suffocating her beneath its weight.

When he finally spoke again, his voice was cruel but no less beautiful because of it, though perhaps only an assassin could find allure in the dark promise of pain. "Very well. Perhaps I can help you find some clarity."

She risked a glance at him, surprised to find that he was directly in front of her. She hadn't heard him come into the small cell. It was as if he'd simply appeared there between one breath and the next.

And this time, he didn't bother masking his fury.

"On. Your. Knees."

"W-what?"

"Do not make me repeat myself. It will not end well for you."

Shadow sank down onto the unforgiving stones without further question, the desire to please him so deeply ingrained she couldn't deny him no matter how much she wanted to. No matter what else had happened, Erebos was still the man who saved her. He was still her liege. She owed him everything, most especially her obedience.

A dark tendril of doubt crept through her mind.

Obedience at what cost? Your dignity? Your soul? Where do you draw the line, Shadow?

As if he could hear the traitorous thoughts, he gripped her by the cheeks, squeezing and tipping her head all the way back. "Do you have any idea what your actions have accomplished today?"

She'd heard the menacing tone before, but never directed at her. His use of it now sent tiny shivers of warning down her spine.

"We are stuck in this farce now because of you. Because of this pathetic act of rebellion. An act you were too weak to see through. What do you have to say for yourself?" He shook her, and she knew it was his way of telling her he expected an answer.

"I'm sorry." The words were garbled, forced out between pursed lips. His grip was so tight, she knew she'd be wearing bruises after he was through with her.

"You're not. Not yet . . . but you will be."

A shiver trickled along her nape as she held his inhumanly green gaze.

"One way or another, Shadow mine, you are going to learn your lesson. After tonight, you will never forget your place again, or you will lose it. And I promise you, you will not find me to be nearly as forgiving. Is that understood?"

"Yes, my lord."

His eyes fluttered closed, and his hold on her softened slightly. "Once we are done here, you're going to go upstairs, clean yourself up, and then"—he let out a little sigh that could have been pleasure—"and then you are going to attend tonight's ceremony at my side, where you belong. But most importantly, Shadow mine, from now on, You. Will. Behave."

"Don't I always?"

The sinister twist of his lips into that mockery of a smile told her she must have a death wish. She was well aware now was not the time to bait the bear, but the defiant retort slipped out unbidden. Even though she deserved them, his words chafed. She hated when he spoke to her like she was a child. Or worse, his plaything. She was the realm's deadliest assassin, and he had the audacity to treat her like some kind of toy.

"If you did, you wouldn't have found yourself here, would you? But no matter, this time I'm going to ensure you do."

Merciful stars, she hardly recognized him as he stared down at her. He was every inch her beautiful, dark king, but he wasn't remotely human in this moment. There was a weight to his stare she'd never noticed before. And the air around him seemed to swell and grow thin all at once, as if he was literally sucking it out of the room and drawing all of it into himself.

Finally he released her, only to run his knuckles down the side of her face with a heavy sigh. "Oh, my precious moonbeam, why must you always make me hurt you?"

CHAPTER 3

SHADOW

*E*rebos was nothing if not a man of his word. As promised, he'd delivered a lesson so thorough, she wasn't likely to ever forget it.

Two hours later, even after a visit from the palace's head healer, she was still in agony. Despite slow, ginger movements, every step was torturous. Even breathing felt as though she was being carved from the inside out. It wasn't that the healer was incompetent, or that there hadn't been enough time to care for her properly. Quite the opposite.

She hurt because Erebos *wanted* her to hurt. He'd given the healer explicit instructions. *'Heal only that which will be visible.'* Not that he'd been utterly without mercy. He'd also allowed the woman to *'deal with any internal injuries, so long as they're life-threatening.'*

Truly, he was a king among men. Her spleen and punctured lung were in his debt.

"Pain remembers," he'd hissed when she'd struggled wetly for breath, only just managing to peel one eye open to look up at him from her curled position on the blood-splattered floor.

That it did.

She could recall with perfect clarity how much pressure he'd used snapping her wrist and the exact place where his ring connected when shattering her cheekbone. Luckily for her, those injuries fell under the 'visible' category and had been some of the first to be repaired.

The rest of her, however, hadn't fared as well. Anything currently concealed by fabric was likely also covered in bruises. Her skin—what little she could stand to look at—was a mottled web of purple, red, and black. She was also pretty sure more than one of her ribs was broken and still brushing perilously against her lung, if the wheeze in her breath was any indication.

It wasn't the first time the High Lord had raised a hand to her, but it was by far the worst. She didn't blame him. She'd earned each and every beating, and today's was no exception. After what she'd done— entering the contest against his will, getting all the way to the end, and then losing . . . Suffice it to say, she wouldn't have been surprised if he'd have taught her a similar lesson even if she *had* won. The High Lord did not appreciate being made a mockery of, and that's exactly what she'd done.

Her reasoning didn't matter. Only the outcome.

Standing beside him now, her mind was oddly at peace. There wasn't room for much thinking when every waking second was spent holding her body just so. It was a blessing, really. That quiet. It kept her thoughts from drifting. From dreaming.

From hoping.

At least until *he* walked in.

And then there weren't thoughts as much as an electric current crackling to life in her brain and coursing through her entire body, sending a series of signals to her battered muscles they were helpless to ignore. The reaction was visceral, causing her to jerk involuntarily and forcing a pained hiss to escape through clenched teeth.

"Careful, dearest. We wouldn't want you to hurt yourself," Erebos cautioned.

No. We certainly wouldn't want that.

Her attention was so consumed by the red-haired warrior, the sarcastic response went unspoken.

She tracked his every movement, drinking in each detail and memorizing them to savor later. The graceful, predatory way he prowled across the room. The perfect cut of his clothes, the way they hugged his muscles, making him appear both powerful and unattainable. The vibrant bruise marring his otherwise perfect face, a tribute to the day's battles fought and won—a trophy rather than a weakness.

But the detail that stuck with her, the one that wormed its way deep inside her brain, forcing her to acknowledge it, was the way his icy gaze never strayed from his target—Erebos. One would think after the way things were left between them earlier, he'd at least spare her a glance. But he didn't even look her way. Not once. Not even to acknowledge her presence beside the man he stared down.

You great hulking fool. What in the darkness are you doing?

This was not how a Champion approached his High Lord.

Ronan's single-minded focus would never be mistaken for deference or submission. It was a blatant challenge. A taunt. One alpha male squaring off with another.

The celebratory atmosphere of the ballroom shifted with his entrance. The excited chatter morphed into curious whispers. Shadow understood the crowd's confusion. These ceremonial, high society events were filled with pomp and circumstance. For the guest of honor to casually stroll in off the street . . . it was a disruption to the natural order of their small worlds.

The conversation taking place beside her only underscored it.

"I thought he was supposed to be announced and escorted in by Dovina," Dominic asked, the general stepping in close so he could voice the question discreetly.

"He was," Erebos confirmed, his lips barely moving.

"So where is my sister?"

"Yes, that is the question, isn't it?" Erebos's voice was tight, the question clipped. The High Lord was *not* amused.

Shadow couldn't help but be impressed Ronan had managed to give the infamous Raven the slip. The woman knew everything. Saw everything. It was a testament to Ronan's skill that he found a way to circumvent her. Though, she knew it wouldn't be long before word reached the spymaster.

As if on cue, Dovina swept into the ballroom, craning her neck from side to side as she sought out her prey. The bright spots of color tinging her cheeks were the only outward sign of her anger. When she found him, her lips pressed into a tight line and her eyes narrowed.

Before she could reach him and try to regain the upper hand, Ronan's voice rang out, effectively shutting up every other person in the ballroom.

"I've come to collect my boon."

Dammit, Ronan, when are you going to stop collecting enemies the way other men collect notches in their bedposts? Was pissing off the most powerful man in the realm not enough for one day? You had to go for the entire trifecta? Is it that you simply have no sense of self-preservation, or do you really just yearn for death? And if that's the case, why couldn't you have clued me in earlier so I could help you out with that instead of going on to make such a complete spectacle out of myself?

There was no helping him now. He was going to pay the price for making fools of the High Lord and his court. Still . . . she couldn't help but be amused by his antics. The man knew how to make an impression. First day—no, not even day—first *hour* on the job, and he'd already pissed off Empyria's elite.

Erebos stiffened, his lips curling up in a tepid smile that did not remotely reach his eyes. Though his voice remained deceptively light as he called out, "Well, yes, that is quite the point of this little gathering."

Titters rippled along the room, the crowd's confidence returning at the High Lord's playful volley. They thought this was planned. A little performance for their amusement to echo the day's dramatics.

Idiots.

"He's like a groom on his wedding night, isn't he?"

More laughter.

"What is it you seek, Champion, that's made you so eager you can't even wait"—Erebos tilted his head toward Dmitri, who supplied an answer to the unspoken prompt.

"Twenty minutes, my liege."

"Twenty more minutes?" Erebos finished.

"Well, you see . . ." Ronan tossed him a smile that, were it a blade, would cut to the bone. "It occurred to me that time might be of the essence, and after a day such as today . . ." He shrugged casually, and the crowd chuckled at his unexpected reference to nearly having his throat slit.

Erebos's smile tightened. Shadow knew it must be killing him to learn his loyal citizens were so easily wooed by a roguish grin and impressive set of muscles.

"I was simply loath to waste a second of it."

"Is that so? Very well, you have our attention. What is it you desire as your reward, Champion?"

Everyone, including her, held their breaths as they waited to find out what the High Lord's new Champion would do or say next.

They were not disappointed.

Without missing a beat, Ronan lifted his hand and pointed directly at Shadow, finally shifting his gaze from the High Lord to the woman at his side.

"Her."

EREBOS

THE RINGING in his ears was drowned out only by the shocked inhale of his Shadow. That, more than anything else, told him this was really happening. That he hadn't imagined it.

He'd known Luna's Chosen would be a wild card. The man had been impossible to predict from the jump, but no one could have expected this. The absurdity of it . . . the sheer impossibility . . . it was inconceivable.

No one was that stupid.

No one, it would seem, but *him*.

The absolute nerve of this mewling pathetic *mortal*. He had to give it to the man—he had a set of bollocks that would rival any god's. But celestial-sized testicles or not, Ronan was no divine being. He was nothing more than a man. An insect, really.

And he'd just picked the wrong god to fuck with.

"You dare walk into my palace and demand my royal assassin as your trophy?" With each word his voice swelled until the walls fairly shook with the force of it.

"You misunderstand me. I don't mean forever. I only want to borrow her for the night."

It took everything in him not to snort. As if that made it any better. If not for all the eyes on them, Erebos would have ended this contemptible charade here and now. Instead, he was forced to grit his next words out through clenched teeth.

"A *person* is not a *prize*."

"Aren't they?"

In their shocked state, the crowd had remained quiet until now, but their stunned silence was quickly fading. Replaced by murmurs that, when combined, rivaled his own furious roar.

"Did you know about this?" Erebos snapped, finally addressing Shadow directly.

Eyes wide, she quickly shook her head. "No, my lord."

He released a tight breath, thankful to learn her betrayal hadn't gone that far, at least. But then the bastard spoke again, and any momentary relief he'd felt vanished.

"I don't see what the problem is. Women are gifted all the time. I'm not even asking for her hand in marriage, but I would like the chance to exchange trade secrets as it were. I mean, the woman had me at her mercy today. I feel that as your Champion, High Lord, it only seems prudent to ask her to *teach me her ways*."

Ronan won the crowd over with every new, poorly constructed innuendo that fell from his lips. He made it sound as though he intended to do nothing more salacious than pass the time chatting up a colleague, but only a complete twat would actually believe Ronan intended to do anything other than fuck her.

Defile her.

Ruin her.

It could not stand.

Shadow was *his* prize. Not just the final piece to a very elaborate puzzle, but the key to *everything*. Unlocking his full power. Restoring his legacy. Attaining redemption. Glory.

Revenge.

She. Was. His.

"Absolutely not."

Ronan quirked a brow. "You'd go back on your word?"

"My word?" he scoffed. "I made you no promises."

"That's funny. I clearly recall how only a few hours ago you promised to award me anything of my choosing. Was that a lie?"

Anger boiled in his veins, though he feigned disinterest as he shrugged. "I said anything within my power to give."

Ronan laughed, a loud booming guffaw meant to entice the crowd. "You act as though I mean to harm her. I told you I want to learn from her so that I may better serve you." He held out his arms, appealing to those standing on either side of him. "How is that anything other than honorable?"

Erebos's jaw was clenched so tight he could hear his teeth as they ground together. "Be that as it may, I cannot gift you another person. Shadow is not a slave." He didn't even realize he'd stepped into a trap until Ronan's smile turned lazy and a new light entered his icy gaze.

"Then perhaps we should leave the choice up to the lady."

He should have sensed the trick from miles away, but he'd been so distracted by the sheer audacity of the request he hadn't maintained his usual cool head. The fact that a creature as insignificant as an ant had outmaneuvered him cut deep. It was a slight that would not go unpunished.

The crowd snickered, more than one person growing brazen enough to shout out suggestions of their own.

"Do it! Say yes, Lady Shadow!"

"Don't waste your time on that frigid bitch!"

"Take me for a ride instead!"

"We love you, Butcher!"

"Very well," Erebos snapped, desperate to regain control. "Lady

Shadow, what say you?" After their lesson in the dungeon, he had no doubt his little moonbeam would know what part she was to play in this.

"Yes."

His head snapped to the side so fast he nearly gave himself whiplash. "Pardon me?"

She cleared her throat and lifted her chin, raising her voice as she repeated, "I accept your Champion's terms. Tonight, I am his."

Tendrils of black smoke crept into his vision, and Erebos knew he needed to get out of this room before he snapped and accidentally killed everyone within it. He'd never had such a flimsy grasp on his control. If he didn't get himself together, he was liable to raze the entire fucking city to the ground.

That wouldn't do.

That wouldn't do at all.

From the shit-eating grin on the Butcher's face, it was obvious he thought he'd won, but all the arse had managed to do was force his hand. Clearly, he had no clue just how formidable Erebos could be when backed into a corner.

But he was about to learn.

There were still plenty of moves to be made. One in particular seemed quite promising. He'd held off on it until now because of the potential side effects, but if ever there was a time, surely it was this one.

Yes . . . that will do nicely. Thank you, Butcher, for providing me with this golden opportunity. Because of you, I can now make this unmitigated disaster work out to my benefit.

Careful to keep his expression neutral to avoid telegraphing his intentions, Erebos turned to his general, keeping his voice low so as not to be overheard. "No one leaves. The night's festivities will go on as planned."

"It will be as you say, High Lord."

To Dovina, who'd stealthily made her way over to them during the ruckus, he said, "Keep your eyes on him. He doesn't so much as scratch his arse without my knowing. Wherever he goes, whoever he talks to, I want to know about it."

"Yes, my liege."

"Whatever you have to do, word of this does not leave the palace until morning when we issue an official statement," he added, looking to Dmitri.

"Of course, my lord. Anything else you'd like me to take care of?"

"I think it is a prudent time to open a few more casks of wine. Details tend to grow fuzzy after a night of overindulgence."

"Quite right," Dmitri agreed.

Satisfied that this part of the plan was sorted, he returned his full attention to the assassin who'd gotten them into this mess. "You," he snarled dangerously, grabbing her none-too-gently by the elbow. There was a flash of pain in her jewel-bright eyes as he dug his fingers into her tender skin, but she knew better than to express it. She was, after all, still his devoted shadow.

"Come with me."

CHAPTER 4

EREBOS

There was an art to compulsion. A technique to implanting suggestions and thoughts in another person's psyche, making the unsuspecting mortal not only embrace them but believe the ideas are their own. The unsophisticated referred to it as brainwashing, but there was so much more to it. It wasn't a simple wipe and replace. There was precision involved in the real thing. Subtlety. Nuance. Who could possibly understand the artistry involved in getting someone to not simply do or say the opposite of what was fundamentally part of who they were, but to make them fully embrace the foreign ideals so completely it *overwrote* those foundational layers?

For one such as him, a master of the craft, it was a straightforward affair. Or it was supposed to be. Against other celestials, such as Luna, it was far trickier to make use of his gift.

And then there were those rare cases where a mortal's will was so strong, they were immune to his suggestions. In those instances, the thoughts would dissolve as easily as candy floss in water. It was such a rare occurrence, in fact, he'd only come across it once—when dealing with the woman standing before him now.

Despite his best efforts with Reyna, there'd been no way to make his compulsion stick except to start with a clean slate. Even then, after hollowing out her mind like a ripe melon, every few months those instincts so innately *her* would rear their head. The defiance. The doubt. The independent streak that made her a perfect queen and terrible prisoner.

IT HAPPENED FREQUENTLY in the early days, but the more he siphoned her power, the less often he'd had to intervene, until he'd go months without needing to drain her or reinforce his lies.

At least, it had been until recently.

He did not suffer any illusions about the reason for the sudden change. Everything had gone tits up with Ronan's reappearance. It was like the Shield had reawakened some long dormant part of the Forsaken queen. Erebos hadn't had to play around in her mind this much since he'd first captured her. Now it was practically a daily ritual.

The only way he would get her to obey his newest order without question was to drain her nearly dry. He hated to do it—well, not really, the high was incredible—but it *was* inconvenient given the task he had in store for her. While siphoning her power was necessary to strengthen his influence over her, it would also leave her severely weakened. Even weak, she was still a formidable foe. He could only hope the element of surprise would be on her side.

So it was a risk, but a calculated one. Because if she succeeded, they'd both be rid of the redheaded bastard for good.

As if she could sense what he had in store for her, Shadow tugged against his brutal hold. "My lord, I promise, I didn't know—"

"Hush."

"If you would just allow me to explain—"

"Silence!"

She inhaled sharply but pressed her lips together as he continued towing her behind him through the palace and up to her private suite.

Pausing only long enough to shove open the door, he pushed her into the room and then kicked it, sealing them inside.

She spun around, wisely not keeping her back to him, and there was no hiding the anger burning in her gaze. That was all right. He appreciated her fire, and what he was about to do meant he could get away with being a little more honest than usual. She wouldn't remember anything but her mission and devotion to her High Lord by the time he was through.

"I'd hoped our little chat earlier meant we wouldn't need to do this again quite so soon, but, as you've just proven, you simply cannot be trusted."

"Erebos, please, listen to me."

He canted his head, his long hair sliding against his back as he did. "Why would I listen to you when every word out of your mouth is a lie? When did you turn into such a filthy liar, Shadow mine? And not only a liar, but a whore."

"I-I'm not."

"No? Then why agree to that man's ridiculous request? Why give yourself to him willingly?"

"To shut him up. He was making a fool of you."

"You made a fool of me," he thundered.

"I . . . I'm sorry."

The words were hard for her. For as often as she did it these days, apologies were not her forte, and it showed. They lacked the requisite remorse.

He tsked. "I blame myself. I've been too lenient with you. You clearly need a firmer hand. That's my fault. I mistook your obedience for loyalty. But you were never tame, were you? You were simply biding your time."

"No. Erebos—"

He backhanded her. "We are not equals. You do not address me by my name. I am your lord and master."

"Of course, my lord." She straightened, his handprint blazing on her cheek, her eyes defiantly meeting his.

It made him hard. The woman was fearless. Even when she was so clearly outmatched, she did not shy away from the fight. He took great pride in it, attributing her core of steel to the magic that ran through her veins, even as he wanted to snuff it out.

But wasn't that always the way with beautiful things? Like a wild horse that must first be broken in order to become a valuable asset. Beauty's true worth lay in ownership—if one could master it, they also inherited its power.

"Come here."

She hesitated only a second before closing the distance between them, her hands loosely fisted at her side.

He gripped her chin. "I take no pleasure in hurting you."

"Yes, you do."

His lips twitched. "Yes, I do. But only because I love to watch you break. I live for the moment you come back to me. When you remember you are mine."

She gasped softly, her eyes locked onto his as he latched onto her mind. Running his fingertips along the side of her face, he called his magic to the surface, pouring it into her. She shivered, her eyes going hazy as those first few tendrils took root and flourished. Like seeds newly planted, they leeched the soil of its nutrients, drawing that which they needed into themselves and growing stronger in the process.

His compulsion was the seed, Shadow's mind the soil, and her magic the nourishment.

"Do you know who I am?" he whispered once she began to sway.

Voice dreamy, she replied, "The one I live to serve."

"And who does that make you?"

"Your most devoted servant."

There you are, my beautiful girl. How I so love these moments of surrender. Even if they are forced.

Another time, her words would have been enough, but tonight he needed everything. There could be no doubt as to what happened once she was allowed to leave this room. So he continued to weave his web, taking full control of her mind while robbing her of her birthright. Her knees buckled, her already battered body unable to hold itself up against the onslaught. Having expected it, Erebos caught her easily, sweeping her into his arms and carrying her to her bed.

She could have been a princess from one of the mortal's faerie stories, in her black gown with her starlight-colored hair strewn over the silk of her pillow. Her pale skin and fever-bright eyes only added to the illusion of a woman in desperate need of a rescue. She had the kind of ethereal, timeless beauty men would immortalize in poems.

A low chuckle slipped out at the thought. In the would-be poets' desperation to impress and woo her, they'd compare her eyes to exotic gems and her lips to dew-kissed petals. None of them would guess, seeing her this way, that they'd got it backward. She wasn't the one that needed to be rescued. *They* were.

Shadow wasn't the rose, she was the thorn . . . and her prick was lethal.

She gave him a sleepy blink, every inch the compliant little doll waiting for instruction. That's when he knew she was ready.

Skating his fingers along her forehead, he planted his compulsion deep. When there was no reaction, no sign of hesitation or disgust, he asked, "Do you understand what it is I need from you?"

"I do."

"Tell me."

"You need me to destroy the threat."

"What threat?"

Her expression twisted, no longer peaceful but filled with righteous fury. "The red-haired deceiver. The one who seeks to take what does not belong to him."

"And what's that?"

"Me."

He cupped her cheek, his voice turning tender as he asked, "Who do you belong to, Shadow?"

"You, my lord. Always."

The proof of her successful reconditioning had the last of the tension and anger fleeing. He didn't just feel relief, he felt . . . giddy. Expectant. He'd gone from being issued a blatant challenge to his rule to finding himself on the cusp of dealing a devastating blow to Luna and using her own warrior to do it.

Everything he'd worked so hard for was finally within reach.

All because of her. His secret weapon.

There was no containing his predatory smile as he asked his final question. "And how are you going to deal with the threat?"

Her eyes glittered. "I'm going to kill him."

CHAPTER 5

RONAN

"Do not leave this room. Your . . . *prize* will join you shortly." Dovina spared him little more than a disdainful glare before slamming the door shut and leaving him alone. The solid *snick* of the lock sliding into place a not-so-subtle 'fuck you very much' from the Raven. If she didn't work for the enemy, he might have liked the woman.

In the aftermath of what essentially constituted a verbal duel, Dovina had swooped in like a thunderstorm and ordered him to follow her. Ronan wasn't surprised they wanted to isolate him. He'd proven himself to be a threat, especially when he'd gotten the crowd on his side. They'd found his little display amusing, not well-versed enough to recognize or appreciate the violent subtext in the very public exchange. That was probably for the best. He was here to save his woman, not start a bloody revolution.

Ronan glanced around the elegant but plain guestroom, using the time alone to take note of his surroundings and identify potential weapons—candlestick, poker, and letter opener—as well as any exits —the locked door behind him or the balcony to his right. Some habits died hard.

When he'd come up with his somewhat harried scheme, he'd pictured Shadow leaving the party with him then and there. Taking him to some sort of secluded hideout of hers just out of town, a romantic and quiet place where they could plot their next steps together. The realist in him knew that would never happen, but he hadn't really considered the alternatives either. An escape from the palace was going to be tricky, especially with the High Lord and his minions on alert. Hopefully Shadow knew of a secret passage or something similar they might make use of.

The goal was both simple and impossibly complicated. Get her as far away from Erebos before anyone realized she was gone. Simple in theory, nearly impossible in execution. Because once the alarm was sounded, staying hidden would require all of their combined tricks. If not for her familiarity with the area and getting around undetected, he wouldn't have much faith in their chances. Her willing participation in her own rescue was crucial to the success of the mission.

Ronan grinned, feeling confident it wouldn't take much to persuade her to leave with him. Not after the way she fell apart in his arms in that alcove. He let out a low groan, his body reacting instantly to the memory. He couldn't wait for a repeat performance. To hear her shatter when she didn't have to swallow back her cries of pleasure. To taste her when they had nothing but time so he could truly savor the experience. To explore and memorize her body, revealing all its secrets until he'd mastered each and every way to make her come.

He'd lied when he said he only wanted one night. One night would never be enough. Not for them and everything he had planned. He wanted to slide into her slowly. He wanted to fuck her hard. He wanted to satisfy her so thoroughly she could do little more than whimper his name. In short, he wanted to brand himself so deeply on her soul nothing could ever make her forget him again.

So no, Ronan didn't want one night with Shadow. He intended to claim them all.

They may not be each other's first lovers, but he would be her last.

He blamed the distracting nature of his thoughts for not hearing the door open. It wasn't until her voice hit his ears and her breath tickled his neck that he even realized he was no longer alone.

"That was very bold of you."

His body was strung tight with anticipation of what came next. The adventure they were about to embark on. The life they'd lead. All of it. He allowed himself a moment to revel in the sensation of being suspended on the edge of a cliff, seconds away from taking a life-changing leap. It should have been terrifying, and it was, in a way, but it was also exhilarating.

This was their turning point. The precise moment their future truly began. After everything it took them to get here, he almost couldn't believe it was finally happening.

Excitement and something that felt a hell of a lot like joy exploded in his chest. There was no hiding his smile as he turned to face her. "I wasn't the only one making bold choices today."

It only took a single look into those multihued irises to realize something was very fucking wrong. This was not a woman in love on the verge of getting everything she wanted. This was the High Lord's assassin.

Cold.

Calculated.

Murderous.

But there was something else too. Something that frightened him far more than the blade coming straight at him.

It was the empty, detached way she went about it. Where was the woman from earlier? The one who could barely stand to look at him as she held her dagger to his throat. What had changed in a manner of hours? Fuck, not even hours, minutes?

He'd seen her reaction to his request. The flush of her cheeks at the prospect of their night together. She hadn't been contemplating murder in that moment. He'd bet his life on it.

So why the one-eighty?

The answer was so obvious it was almost laughable.

Erebos.

The High Lord had gotten to her. Used his brainwashing magic to ensure his puppet finished the job she'd failed to do that afternoon.

It was only years of finely honed battle instincts that had him ducking away in time. "You don't want to do this, killer," he said, hands up as he tried to appeal to the woman trapped within an evil man's prison of lies.

She raised a brow. "Don't I? Funny, sure feels like it." She took another swipe and he another large step back.

"Trust me, kitten. You really don't."

"Well, only one way to find out. Let's test the theory." Faster than he could even track, she had a second blade in her hand and was throwing it.

Mother's tits, where had that one come from?

A well-timed blast of his Air knocked the blade off its course, saving him from a haircut he couldn't afford.

"I, for one, am certain the sight of you bleeding out on this dreadful rug will help me sleep like a babe."

He spared a glance at the offending item. It really was dreadful, a ghastly mix of olive green and piss yellow. He could see why she thought an exsanguinated corpse would be an improvement. Blood had a way of hiding all manner of sins. As did death, for that matter.

"If you're that set on redecorating, perhaps we can find someone—"

He grunted and lunged to the side as she made another series of attacks, the rush of air beside his face telling him he almost hadn't been quick enough that time. He didn't get the impression she was toying with him, not like their battle earlier. It was truly luck and years of practice keeping him a mere half-step ahead of her.

The realization sat like lead in his gut.

She was striking to kill. She honestly meant to end him.

"Will I never catch a fucking break?" he growled, hating that while he'd been locked in here daydreaming like a lovesick fool, she'd been plotting his murder. Perhaps not the real her, but a version of her. What a kick to the balls that was. He should have known better.

Clearly, he was destined to be miserable and alone. Or locked in a never-ending death match with the love of his life.

"You can catch this," Shadow crooned, delivering a series of blows so wickedly fast he didn't manage to escape them all.

He let out a hiss of pain as a thin strip of blood streaked across his chest. "Hey! That's my best shirt," he snarled, genuinely more offended about the ruined garment than his injury. Scars were a testament to battles waged and won. Warriors earned their scars. It was only right to wear them with pride. Shirts his size, however, were few and far between. And they cost a damned arm and leg in the rare instance he could find one.

"That so? Well then, I'll be sure to bury you in it," she returned sweetly.

He'd heard of star-crossed lovers, but this was fucking next level. Somewhere out there, fate had to be howling with laughter at him. He didn't know what he'd done to earn such devoted and relentless attention, but he would gladly relinquish the honor.

They'd gone nearly the length of the room in his retreat, and it was time to put an end to this. She had no intention of letting him walk out of here alive, and he had no intention of dying. Or leaving without her. Only one of them was going to get their way, and he was beyond tired of it not being him.

Recalling his earlier inventory and the placement of possible weapons throughout the room, as well as the two possible exits, he crafted a plan. It wasn't a very good plan, mind you, but what was the point in worrying about it when all his best, most well-thought-out strategies seemed to turn to shit anyway? Perhaps winging it was the answer.

Luckily for him, Shadow was so single-minded in her attempt to gut him that she didn't realize he was guiding her movements. For each lunge or flèche she made, he would time his next steps, essentially leading them in a violent dance to the balcony. Once the first brush of wind hit his battle-warmed skin, he knew the dance was at its end.

"Nowhere left for you to run, Butcher. Unless you rather topple over the ledge and save me the cleanup."

"Or perhaps we could call a ceasefire and do a little stargazing instead?"

Shadow rolled her eyes, but her lips twitched. He knew she was enjoying the fight, that it was rare she ever had to work overly hard for a kill. He knew it, because were their positions reversed, he'd be thinking the same. Facing off against a true equal made your blood sing in your veins.

This time when she came at him, he was ready. Spinning to the side, he threw out his hand, simultaneously calling on his Air magic to aid him once more. The candlestick he'd spotted earlier sailed across the room and straight into his outstretched palm. As he'd hoped, the decoration was thick and heavy, made of some expensive metal, he was sure. Wasting no time, he parried Shadow's next strike, slapping her dagger from her hand and swinging the candlestick down with all his considerable might.

She clattered to the ground at the same time as her blade.

"It actually worked," he said stupidly, breathing hard as he stared down at her unconscious form. With the way everything else had been going, he really hadn't been sure it would. "Well, genius, what's next?"

Knowing time was one luxury he didn't have, Ronan glanced around the room once more, seeking inspiration. The only way out of here with a nearly lifeless body was over the balcony. Getting down wouldn't be a problem. They were high up, but he was an experienced climber, and he distinctly remembered the palace's walls being textured. There would be hand and footholds aplenty. The bigger issue would be keeping Shadow's body secure for the descent.

"Think . . . think," he grumbled, his heart rate spiking with every second they remained still. The thick curtains hanging around the four-poster bed caught his eye. He took a quick peek at her slumbering form and then back to the strips of cloth.

"That'll do."

Tugging the fabric down, he fashioned himself a sort of over-the-shoulder harness, using his earth magic to reinforce the material so that it would easily withstand the dead weight. Once that was done, he carefully scooped Shadow off the floor and gently laid her inside the carrier. It was just a titch small, and her limbs hung out at awkward angles. She would be in a world of discomfort when she eventually awoke.

Realizing there was no help for it, Ronan sighed and shook his head. "You're going to forgive me for this once whatever hold he has on you fades." He wasn't sure if that was a promise or wishful thinking, but regardless, Ronan picked up the makeshift sling and maneuvered it—and her—onto his body. Her head was near his shoulder, her legs near his other hip, meaning the climb would be awkward with her between him and the wall, but since any other positioning would throw his balance off, this was their only option.

"You know . . . I really pictured tonight going differently," he murmured, keeping up his one-sided conversation. It was a much-needed distraction and helped him from thinking of everything that could go wrong.

Swinging his legs over the side of the ledge, he spent a final moment gazing out over the ocean and the distorted reflection of the stars above. If not for the thick swash of blood across her temple, Shadow looked as though she could be merely sleeping. He leaned his head down, running his nose along hers. "I'm sorry about this, kitten, but it was the only way. Perhaps, one day, we can laugh about it." Then he kissed her softly, his stomach clenching and souring when she didn't return it.

He pulled back with a frown, wondering if he'd ever get another willing kiss from her again.

It doesn't matter, Ronan. Just stick to the mission. Get her as far away from here as you can. Nothing else matters right now.

Beginning his careful shift from the balcony to the red patterned bricks that lined the tower, Ronan made sure he had a firm hold and then risked a glance over his shoulder to see just how far down they had to go.

He didn't have a fear of heights as a rule, but they were so far up he could only *just* make out the rooftops below them. It would be a damned miracle if they reached the ground in one piece or without one or both of them falling.

Releasing a heavy breath, Ronan swept one foot down, searching for his next toehold and muttering, "The things I do for love."

CHAPTER 6

RONAN

By the time his boot finally scraped against the ground, sweat poured into his eyes and his muscles shook from exertion. Not even his Earth-enhanced strength had been enough to offset the momentous effort required to scale down the palace tower with the cumbersome weight of another body strapped to him. There had been a couple of close calls where the wind had kicked up or his grasp slipped, and he hadn't been too sure they were going to make it.

It was through sheer force of will he was standing—okay, leaning —here now.

"Took you long enough."

Ronan snapped upright, one arm protectively curling around Shadow's unconscious form while the other groped for a weapon at his side.

"Peace, Butcher. I mean you no harm." Camille stepped into the soft moonlight, her hands outstretched to show she was unarmed.

He was too exhausted to do more than stare at her, his breaths labored and lungs burning. Though she'd done nothing but help him, he couldn't ignore the impulse to scan the darkness from whence she came, ensuring she was alone before finally mustering up the breath to speak.

"Are you waiting for me?" he rasped, voice threaded with fatigue.

"Yes."

"How'd you know I'd be here?"

"You aren't exactly invisible."

He vibrated with all the tension of a fully drawn bow. Who else might have spotted them? The urge to flee sent a spike of adrenaline barreling through him, suffusing him with renewed energy.

"Do not fear, Ronan. I have no reason to believe anyone else saw you."

"And you know that how, exactly?"

"No alarms were raised, for starters."

"So why are you here, then?"

"I have my own reasons for being outside tonight."

He raised a brow. "Do not think me discourteous, but I'm going to need you to do better than that."

She crossed her arms with a little smirk. "So untrusting . . . good. It's about time you remembered not everyone in this court is what they seem."

"Are you saying I shouldn't trust you?"

"Shouldn't is a matter of perspective, I suppose. But you certainly *can* . . . at least for the time being. I wasn't lying when I said I didn't mean you any harm."

"So, for the third time, what are you doing out here, Camille?"

"I was praying."

That brought him up short.

She laughed softly, the bell-like peals floating out into the night. "There is a temple on the bluff. A perfect place to view the stars and worship the darkness's sacred gifts."

Ronan continued to stare at her.

"What? Were you under the impression a whore can only worship on her back?"

"No, of course not—"

Camille laughed again. "I'm teasing you. Come, it's best not to linger. I know of someone who can aid you."

"I'm not sure . . ."

She reached out and placed a warm palm on his slick forearm, the overworked muscles jumping at the light contact. "She is a mutual friend of ours. You can trust her. She will help you get away from here. But we must hurry."

"Why?"

Camille tilted her head, a serene smile tugging her lips and making her appear positively angelic in the moonlight. Instead of answering, she asked a question of her own. "Did you know we refer to the moon as the Mother?"

Ronan went utterly still, his breath seizing in his chest. The Mother . . . surely the mention of his goddess at this exact moment was no coincidence. Clearing his throat, almost afraid of the answer, he haltingly asked, "Was she . . . the one you were worshipping tonight?"

"Yes."

He could have dropped to his knees in relief. She hadn't forsaken him. The Mother was still here, still watching, guiding him on what had started to feel like a doomed journey. "Is that normal for you?"

"It's not a daily occurrence, if that's what you're getting at. But I felt a strong pull to be here tonight." A strangled sound escaped his throat, and she waved a hand, the loose sleeves of her gown fluttering in the breeze. With her long curls and white dress, she could have been a young priestess in the midst of a sermon rather than an unexpected ally in an impromptu kidnapping. "Why does that surprise you, Butcher? I am a servant of the goddess, as are we all. When I hear her, I answer. Only a fool ignores the Mother's call."

Wasn't that the fucking truth. He'd never communed with the Chosen's creator directly, not like Helena and Effie, but he'd seen the reality of her power far too many times to discount it. There was nothing in all existence quite like a mother's wrath.

Except, perhaps, a father's.

The unwarranted thought made every hair on his body stand on end.

"So, are you coming with me, or are you some kind of masochist hoping to get caught?"

He blinked, mind emptying as he snapped back to the present. "Sorry?"

Camille gestured to him and Shadow. "Are you a glutton for punishment, Ronan? Or do you actually mean to get away with your prize?"

His grip on his would-be murderess tightened, and her head pressed more firmly against his shoulder. "I mean to take her to the ends of the earth if I have to. I won't stop running. Not until I'm sure he can never lay another finger on her."

Camille beamed. "Then come with me. Your ship sets sail before the dawn."

"My ship?"

Ignoring the question, she glanced at the horizon. "Hurry. We don't have much time."

Ronan tracked her gaze, but the sky seemed just as dark to him now as it had since he'd set foot on the balcony, so it was hard to know what she was using to track the time. "I'll take your word for it."

Camille tilted her head toward a path he could only just make out in the moonlight but didn't say anything further as she picked up her skirts and started to run.

With no option but to give chase, Ronan adjusted his hold on Shadow and did just that, his abused muscles screaming in protest as he pushed himself to the very limit keeping up with her. He wasn't out of shape by any means, but after the weeks of trials, back-to-back battles, and then scaling a damn tower—not to mention the emotional toll all of the above had taken—he was down to the very last dregs of what his body could physically handle.

It was hard to tell where she was taking him. There was no wall on this side of the palace because the cliffs and sea made a natural boundary, which also meant there was nothing to run toward. But then the path curved around a hill, and understanding dawned as he spotted the ships bobbing in the distance. This was a shortcut to the harbor.

Thankfully it wasn't long before a voice shouted out from the night. "'Bout fuckin' time. You think I enjoy standing out here with my tits flapping in the breeze?"

Ronan would recognize the foul-mouthed fishwife anywhere.

Glinta recognized him the same moment he did her. Her eyes widened, and she flashed him a familiar teasing grin. "Oi, if I'd known it was your sweet arse I was waiting on, I wouldn't have bothered putting my neck on the line."

"Glinta," Camille chided softly as they came to a stop between a large trawler and a sloop.

"Wot? The lad was feather-headed enough to go piss on someone else's pole. Ain't my problem he landed in a world of shit in the process."

"Glinta . . . we already discussed this. The passage has been paid. Stop teasing him."

"Passage?" Ronan asked.

"Aye. A one-way trip for two down to the Sea of Souls." Glinta's voice dropped as though telling a campfire tale. "Not exactly a honeymoon, issit? But then, I doubt ye'll make it that far. What with the Dweller and all."

"Dweller?" Ronan repeated.

Glinta squinted at him. "Something wrong with your tongue, boy? I remember you knowing a fair amount of right pretty words last we talked."

"It's been a long night."

She nodded slowly. "So it has. Well, it's a mite taboo to speak on it afore setting off on a voyage, but then I'm staying safe on land, aren't I?"

Ronan barely resisted rolling his eyes. He'd manned enough ships to be familiar with seafolk's superstitious ways. Though, he'd yet to see any of their silly practices make a damned bit of difference. "What dweller, Glinta?" he asked, impatience slipping into his tone.

"Of the deep, o'course. Most foul monster you ever did see. Or didn't see, until it's too late." She cackled gleefully. "You'll know when he's near. Nothing but a floating graveyard for miles around and the whispers of the dead drifting through a sea of mist."

"I'll make sure to keep an eye out."

She scowled at the derision in his tone. "Fine, don't believe me.

What's it to old Glinta? I've got my starlings. You're the one who'll find himself a watery grave soon enough." With that happy thought she spun on her heel and stormed up the gangway to the left, boarding the sloop.

"You sure we can trust her?" Ronan asked Camille.

"Don't let the old dame's bark fool you. She's one of your biggest supporters, has been since day one. She wouldn't risk her name buying you passage otherwise. The crew of the *Revenge* makes this trek often, following the eastern coast down and back as they make their ... trades."

The careful way she uttered the word told him everything he needed to know. This wasn't the kind of trading that included a detailed ship manifest. These were smugglers, if not out-and-out pirates. Not that he was complaining. Who better to help him make a grand escape than a bunch of thieves and scallywags?

Ah, Glinta, you cantankerous old bird. What other secrets do you have?

Knowing he may never learn the answer to that question, Ronan shook his head as he started after her, already anticipating the steady rock of the ship to lull him into a deep and dreamless sleep. He didn't care if his bed was a pile of wooden crates; he'd give anything to be off his feet for a while.

He didn't realize Camille hadn't moved until her voice called out after him. "Bon voyage, Ronan. This is where I leave you."

The thought of saying goodbye to another unexpected friend so soon after Bast was bittersweet. He never would have made it this far without Camille's help. "Thank you," he said, knowing it was nowhere near enough after all she'd risked for him, but meaning it down to the very depths of his soul.

She gestured toward the moon. "Never forget who watches over you. She will see you safely home. Wherever that might be."

Before he could say anything else, Camille disappeared into the night. Ronan took a deep breath of the brine-tinged air, already turning around when Glinta whisper-shouted down to him.

"Well, you festering boil, hurry up, or I'll push you overboard myself."

"That seems rather counterproductive after all you did to get me onboard."

"Not to me. Way I see it, it's the least ye deserve for making me wait on you all blasted night."

Ronan joined her on the deck. "Next time, you scale the castle wall, and I'll wait by the ship."

She glanced down at Shadow, still cradled against his chest, and grinned, true affection shining in her gaze, reminding him once more that despite her prickly demeanor, the woman was on his side. Voice gentler than he'd ever heard, she patted his cheek and said, "You did good, lad. Now, let's introduce you to the crew."

CHAPTER 7

SHADOW

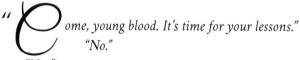*ome, young blood. It's time for your lessons."*

"*No.*"

"*No?*"

"*Ry doesn't have to go to special lessons.*"

"*Ryder isn't going to be queen one day. You are.*"

"*I don't want to be queen, mama. I want to be the wind.*"

Surprised laughter met the words. "The wind?"

"*Like you, mama. When you step off the nest and poof to the ground.*"

"*Oh, you mean when I call on the mist." There was a soft hum. "Well, I suppose you're old enough. Would you like me to show you how it's done?"*

"*You mean I can do it too?*"

"*Oh, yes, young blood. That is the very least of what you are capable of. Come. It's time for you to learn about who you truly are.*"

Shadow shifted restlessly, cheeks damp with tears she couldn't yet feel. Rolling to her side, the dream—which was nothing more than disembodied voices—changed. The voices were different this time. Distinctly male, but disorientating and hard to follow. Two halves of an unrelated conversation, like actors given scripts from two conflicting plays and instructed to perform anyway.

"Shall I make you purr, kitten?"

"Do not forget who you belong to, Shadow mine."

"I'll make you feel so fucking good."

"Why do you always make me hurt you?"

"I'll give you everything you want. Just say the word."

"Say it. Do not make me ask again."

"Say you're mine."

"You're mine."

"I'll never let you go."

"You'll never be free of me."

Shadow jerked upright, heart racing, a film of sweat coating her body and making her clothes cling to her. Her head ached, and the sudden shift in position made her stomach roll.

Or was that the ground? Why was everything . . . rocking?

A quick glance through slitted eyes confirmed she was not in bed . . . nor her bedroom . . . nor the palace. She groaned, pressing the heels of her palms to her eye sockets, trying to alleviate some of the relentless throbbing.

What happened last night?

Try as she might, she could find no answer to the question. Not for last night, or any concrete day prior. The last thing she remembered was standing on a balcony looking up at the stars, and who knew how long ago that was.

Okay then, don't panic, Shadow. Let's go over what you do *know.*

"One," she murmured, her voice rusty with disuse, "you remember your name. Yay." It was about as unenthusiastic a cheer as she could manage, but remembering anything right now felt like a victory worthy of celebration.

"Two, you work as an assassin for the High Lord of Empyria, annnd three . . . you're on a boat." Dropping her hands, Shadow forced her eyes open and scanned her surroundings once more. "How the hell did I get on a boat?"

As far as clues went, there weren't many to go by. Nothing to tell her whose ship she was on or what she was doing here. The cabin appeared to be as bare bones as it could get. No personal details. No chests filled with clothes or supplies. Just a single bed with rough but clean linens, a small pockmarked table, and a lone chair.

Realizing the only way she was going to get any answers was to leave her quarters, she stood on shaky legs, the subtle dip and sway of the floorboards sending her toppling off-balance. She threw a hand out, slamming it against the wall to keep from falling on her ass. Taking a second to find her balance, she stayed put, using the respite to perform a quick mental inspection. Her body was one never-ending ache. It felt as though she'd been bashed in the head and then flung off a cliff. Or repeatedly slammed into a wall of rocks. She peeled up her shirt, wincing at the purple and green splotches covering her stomach.

The rock theory was looking more likely by the second.

Once she felt steady, Shadow moved toward the door. Her steps were hesitant at first, but the fact that she was neither bound nor under guard gave her confidence. Surely if she was a prisoner, or even here against her will, someone would want her to stay put.

You're on a boat who knows how far offshore . . . where would you go? For a swim?

"Good point," she muttered, fully aware she was carrying on a conversation with herself and not remotely embarrassed by it. She'd spent countless days and nights on her own. Speaking aloud was a good way to stay focused and sane, even if it might outwardly appear to be proof of the opposite.

Reaching the door, she tested the knob, her breath escaping in a relieved whoosh to find it unlocked.

The ticks in the 'not a prisoner' box were adding up. Still, she moved carefully through the narrow hallway, ears and eyes seeking out any sign of life. She reached the end of the hall, ignoring the doors she passed on her way for now, and came across a staircase leading to the upper deck.

A staircase with a young boy, perhaps only ten or eleven. His eyes widened when they landed on her, his surprised inhale sounding like a soft whistle.

"Where's your captain, boy?"

He pointed a shaking hand behind him.

Either he knew who she was, or he was terrified of strangers in general. Not one to torment children—unless the pesky buggers asked for it—she gave him a nod of thanks, softening her voice as she asked, "Do you or your captain have a name, boy?"

"N-no Beard," he stuttered softly.

Shadow breathed out a laugh. "Your name is No Beard?"

"Not m-mine. Cap'n."

"And you?"

"Willie," he whispered.

"My thanks, Willie. Best be on your way. I didn't mean to interrupt your chores."

With a relieved nod, he scampered the rest of the stairs past her, darting down the hallway she'd just vacated.

Shaking her head slightly and then immediately stopping when it made her eyes swim, Shadow clung to the handrail and slowly climbed the stairs. She felt better as soon as the sea breeze hit her face, bringing with it a smattering of tiny droplets that both cooled and refreshed her.

Bracing herself for shouts or an attack, she took the final step onto the deck. She held her breath for several heartbeats, finally releasing it when no one immediately rushed her. In fact, no one really looked her way at all. There were six people in view, and all but one of them seemed to be in an intense conversation with a man that had to be the captain.

Thankfully the clouds were thick in the sky, keeping the change in light from being blinding, so she was able to get her bearings quickly. With the sun's position hidden, it was hard to know for sure, but her best guess was that it was around midday, give or take a few hours in either direction. She had no clue which way they were going, as there was no discernible landmark for her to see. Nothing save an endless expanse of rippling blue water and foamy white sea spray.

Since she seemed safe for the moment, Shadow took the extra time to gather as much intel about her fellow passengers as she could. She started with the man she assumed was the captain. He spoke with the easy authority of one used to giving orders, and the men around him hung on every word. He was tall, his torso heavy with muscle—a testament, she'd guess, to years spent working a ship. His face was sun-kissed and smooth, nose just a hint crooked as if it had been broken one too many times, and tousled honey blond hair threaded with white-gold highlights. As he spoke, his lips curled into an easy smile. He seemed more charming boy next door than bloodthirsty pirate, but perhaps that was his secret.

Two of the men stood with their backs to her, so she couldn't garner many details, besides their size. One was a hulking brute of a man, nearly twice as wide as the one standing beside him and at least a head taller. His glossy black hair was pulled back into a neat tail at his nape, and his clothing was notably finer than the others, including a velvet navy blue doublet and pristine cream-colored pants. Shadow was sure, were she close enough, she'd be able to spot her reflection in the toe of his polished black boots.

The man beside him was bald, still sizable compared to the others, but not quite meeting the height of the well-dressed fellow. She also caught the hint of a curly black beard and colorful tattoos peppering his sunburnt arms.

As for the last two, one stood in a straight line across the deck from her, and the other was completely obscured by the mountain of a man. Where the captain was all sunny smiles, the final sailor she could make out was the personification of a storm cloud. His lips were twisted down in a severe frown, a deep crease between his thick brows. He was as built as the captain, and what she could see of his skin was sun dark and scarred. But the features that most stood out were the dirt-stained cloth tied around his eyes and the metallic quality of his deep blue hair. It was a unique shade too dark to be turquoise and too green to be navy . . . Prussian, perhaps? Whatever the name, it called to mind gemstones and the secrets of the sea and made her fingers twitch with the need to touch it.

A tiny bird the color of sunset she hadn't noticed until that moment chirped on his shoulder, and the man's head snapped from the captain to her. As if he could see her through the band woven around his eyes.

Shadow swallowed when his lips moved, knowing her time was up. Rather than wait for the sailors to approach her, she strode toward them, calling out. "Captain No Beard, a word?"

Instead of meeting her polite greeting with one of his own, the captain tossed his head back and laughed. Deep, booming belly laughs that bounced around the expansive deck. And he wasn't alone; the rest of them joined in . . . except for the grumpy one, though his bird chittered enough to make up for it.

Cheeks burning, she realized her error before the smooth-faced one turned to her. "Forgive us, Shadow. But that never gets old. Journey with us long enough, you'll see what I mean."

"You know who I am?"

"We make it a habit to know the names of those who voyage with us."

"Then you have me at a disadvantage, for you know who I am, but I cannot say the same of you. I take it you aren't the captain?"

Laughter danced in his warm brown gaze. "Not the captain, no."

"Can you tell me who *is*? Or shall we start with something easier, like who *you* are?"

She was aware of all five men's gazes boring into her, but she kept her eyes locked on the one whose identity she'd mistaken. At least she did until he began introducing the others.

"Shadow, allow me to introduce you to a few of the high-ranking members of our crew. This is Bowie." He pointed to the man she hadn't been able to make out. Compared to the others, he was fairly nondescript, but there wasn't time to note more than that because he continued. "And this gloomy gus is Jagger the Unseeing—and before you ask, no, that band is not a bold fashion choice. His faithful companion Buttercup helps him get around." The frowning man didn't acknowledge her, but his bird gave a little flutter that Shadow would have mistaken as a curtsy were it human.

"This is, Cookie, our . . . well, cook. But he was named for his favorite treat, not his position." The bald man nodded, his burly build at odds with the announcement. She had trouble picturing someone with hands the size of dinner plates rolling out any kind of sweet treat. But unless the striped apron around his waist was a mere accessory, it seemed to be the truth.

"And this dapper gentleman is Tiny."

Shadow nearly choked on her tongue as she tried to keep her face schooled into a neutral expression. The man she'd clocked for his clothes was no man at all. She noted the curved horns and his bull-like nose with its ring and almost childishly small gold-framed spectacles that rested atop it. When her eyes finished their progress down his form, she realized her earlier assessment was both accurate and false at once. While they were polished and black, the split hooves could never be mistaken for boots.

Minotaur, her brain supplied.

A minotaur . . . on a boat . . . named Tiny.

"You're too kind, Bronn," Tiny murmured, executing a smooth bow that rivaled the very best she'd seen at court. His voice was deep and cultured and so unexpected coming from such a massive creature. "Welcome aboard the *Revenge*, lady Shadow."

"T-tiny?" she asked, her voice coming out a touch shrill as she struggled to marry the living, breathing embodiment of a creature she'd heretofore only read about in children's tales.

"My birth name is Mani, but I was the runt of the litter, which these rapscallions love to remind me of every chance they get." He shrugged, his lips quirking in laughter.

"Mani the mini, I-I mean Tiny the Minotaur . . . "

More laughter met her slipup, the men fairly dissolving into fits over it.

"Mani the mini minotaur, how did we miss that?" the blond—Bronn—asked.

"A gross oversight," Cookie said, the deep bass of his voice warm and rich. He reminded her of a bard who'd once visited the palace boasting of having the lowest singing voice on the continent. Cookie would have the performer beat, no contest. Assuming he could sing, that was.

Blaming the persistent throb in her temples for her numerous gaffes, Shadow offered Bronn a tight smile. "The captain, if you please. I seem to be missing key details regarding my voyage. I'd like to remedy that as soon as possible."

The laughter died down, she assumed in response to her obvious discomfort.

"Of course. You'll find Cal and your companion on the bow." He tipped his head toward the large white sail to indicate he meant the front of the ship.

My companion?

"Would you like one of us to escort you?"

"Thank you, but no," she said, distracted by everything she didn't know. "This isn't my first ship."

Bronn gave her a sunny smile. "I like that in a woman."

She quirked a brow but didn't say anything further. Instead, she simply walked away. More laughter followed what the others must have considered a hasty retreat. It occurred to her that it probably wasn't the smartest idea to offend potential allies, but she was hardly in any condition to flirt. Stars, she barely tolerated flirting on her best day. In this state, she was liable to cut someone's balls off for looking at her too long. Best for all involved if she just moved along.

She passed a few other sailors on her way to the bow, but no one tried to stop her. Other than a few polite nods, no one acknowledged her at all. It wasn't until she heard the murmur of voices that she slowed and finally located her quarry.

It didn't take more than a second to realize why her earlier error had been so amusing. Captain No Beard wasn't a man. She was a woman. A beautiful one. She leaned against the railing, her elbows resting on the smooth wood and one booted foot propped up behind her. The position showcased her lithe body and ripe curves. As did the wide V of her shirt and the embroidered black vest that pushed her breasts up and out of it. She was clearly enjoying herself, her head tipped back, rose gold hair flying behind her on the breeze. The series of beaded twists and braids were both elaborate and functional. Not even the velvet eyepatch over her left eye diminished her striking beauty. This was a woman born for the sea. One who reveled in adventure and the freedom of living a life solely for herself.

Envy burned a hole in Shadow's gut. This was a woman who possessed everything *she* wanted.

Eyes trailing to the redheaded man she was speaking with, Shadow froze.

Ronan.

Whispered bits of conversation floated through her mind.

'Don't cry, kitten.'

'My heart, my life, they're yours. They've always been yours . . .'

'Did you miss me?'

She didn't quite remember him saying any of those things to her, but there was a familiarity about the words she couldn't deny. She'd experienced this odd duality before—foundationless memories that simultaneously did and did not belong to her—so it didn't faze her as much as annoy her. Especially as she watched him with the captain. The strawberry-blonde leaned forward and rested her hand on the swell of Ronan's arm, playfully squeezing the muscle before smiling up at him.

He didn't stop her. Didn't pull away. Just laughed before continuing their conversation.

How dare you offer such words to me and then gift your smiles so freely to another?

Jealousy was a foreign sensation. It didn't sit well. It crawled up her neck like shame, burned through her veins like anger, slid down into her belly where it curdled like illness, only to finally come to rest between her ribs, where it smothered her beneath its weight like grief.

If you were just going to abandon me at the first sign of another, why bring me with you . . .

She was well aware the thought was hardly fair, but something in the question niggled in the back of her brain. Swirling around and around until she confronted it.

Bring me with you.

With. You.

He was the reason she was on this ship. Why her body ached and her memory was lost. Hands balling into fists, Shadow realized what she was feeling wasn't jealousy.

It was betrayal.

CHAPTER 8

RONAN

*T*here was no shift in the breeze or heavy footsteps to alert him to her presence behind him. None was required. The very air grew charged with her proximity, beckoning him on a cellular level he couldn't ignore if he wanted to. There was no way to fully quantify what her presence did to him. It was as if his skin grew tighter, his breathing both labored and measured, senses sharpened to the point he'd notice the barest change in her position from the twitch of an eyelash to the flick of a finger.

Everything in him was primed to react. To her whims. Her needs. Just . . . her.

Which made their current predicament a special form of torture.

It took little more than her sharp inhalation and subsequently terse, "Captain," for Ronan to get his answer to the question that had plagued him from the moment he knocked her out.

Would she still view him as her enemy when she woke?

As he turned to face her fully, the blank, almost bored expression on her face confirmed that yes, she did. It took everything in him not to let the weight of defeat send him crashing to his knees.

He could practically hear Effie's voice trying to comfort him. *Cheer up, Ro. It could be worse. She could have tried to kill you straight away. The lack of a dagger embedded in your chest has to be a good sign . . .*

Aye, because when it comes to Shadow, anything less than outright murder must be a declaration of love, he thought with a mental eye roll.

The only thing her inaction meant was what little she recalled of the other night was foggy at best.

What else was new?

It would almost be laughable if it wasn't so fucking tragic. They'd made progress, real progress, finding their way back to one another, only to end up back where they started because of whatever mental magic Erebos had spun.

And it *had* to be magic—there was no other explanation for the level of brainwashing the bastard achieved in such a short amount of time. Compulsion like that . . . Ronan had never seen its like. Though come to think of it, there had been tales passed down of Kiris who lacked Helena's benevolence and used their gifts to force truths from reluctant civilians or to influence political allies.

The Mother's chosen Vessel may not always be kind or just, but one thing each and every one had in common was access to the rare and powerful Spirit branch. Similar to the other magic branches with their ties to the elements, the Spirit branch was linked to the soul— the very flicker of life within all living beings. It was also known as the Mother's branch because only the creation goddess herself and those few women she'd hand selected to be her earthly representatives had access to it.

If Ronan didn't know better, he would have said Erebos was a Spirit weaver. Which was ridiculous because not only was he male— when no male in history had *ever* wielded the Mother's magic—but it would mean Luna had selected *him* over every other person in existence.

Ronan nearly laughed at the absurdity of it; he couldn't think of someone more undeserving of the honor. There simply wasn't a person alive he'd trust less with the power of the gods.

An uncomfortable prickling crept up his neck, and it took a heartbeat for him to identify what about that thought set off a discordant note in his mind.

He'd said *gods*. Plural.

A memory stirred at his unconscious word choice. Something about the nameless ancients. But try as he might, Ronan couldn't bring it into focus. Which wasn't surprising, really. Schooling had never been his thing, religion and history least of all, so the likelihood of him recalling such a detail was hopeless at best. He'd been half feral as a child, running around and going off on the sort of adventures only a young boy could appreciate. Getting him to sit still and not only attend lessons but actually pay attention to them was a fruitless endeavor.

Still . . . he'd bet Reyna's prized dagger there was something important about that distinction. If only he could remember what it was.

"Ronan?"

The captain's use of his name, combined with her amused tone, pulled him from his thoughts. Heat crawled up his neck and into his face when he realized he'd been standing there like a mute halfwit staring off into space while the two women had delved into conversation.

Mother's tits, man. You are never going to win her back like this. Get your fucking act together before you lose her for good this time.

"Apologies, my mind wandered."

"I can see that." Calypso's disconcerting gaze roamed over his face, likely reading far more in his expression than he was comfortable with if the laughter quirking her lips was any indication.

He could only meet one of her eyes due to the patch concealing her left one, but the orb had already changed colors twice since they'd started speaking. What started off a gleaming silver had bled to sky blue before settling into bright sapphire. Ronan was too familiar with Helena's magical quirks not to recognize them in another, but Glinta had warned him not to go around asking too many questions about the captain or her crew.

"They's private folk. Don't go poking your nose 'round where it ain't

belong. People have a habit of disappearing when they get too curious. You hear me?"

Warning in mind, Ronan opted not to ask what else she could see —because with an eye such as that, there was no way she was limited to that which was right in front of her. Instead, he opted for the far more neutral, "It would seem the two of you got on just fine without me." He kept his attention trained on Calypso, waiting for Shadow to acknowledge him in some way. Generally he wasn't one to walk on eggshells, but since he wasn't sure where her head was at or what she remembered, giving her space to set the tone seemed safest for all involved.

"When do women ever *need* a man to insert themselves into a conversation?" the captain challenged with a raised brow.

"Precisely my point. I was minding my manners," Ronan said, recognizing the trap and wisely retreating. He'd been Helena's right hand for far too long to wade into that verbal quicksand.

"Manners? Oh, that's pretty," Calypso said with a husky laugh. "What good are those on the sea?"

"They've served me well thus far."

"Hmmm . . . I do love a man that knows how to serve." A subtle gleam entered the woman's eye as she let her gaze roam down his torso.

As attuned to her as he was, Ronan didn't miss the way Shadow's body tensed at the captain's blatant appraisal.

Say something, please. Make your claim, kitten. Unsheathe your dagger and tell her in no uncertain terms that it's your name burned on my soul.

But she didn't. Of course she didn't.

Ronan was ready to walk headlong into the sail's rigging. A head wound would be less traumatic than this constant uncertainty. How many times would he be forced to lose her before she'd be his to keep?

When he couldn't take it any longer, he turned to Shadow, bracing himself for her anger but wholly unprepared for the indifference staring back at him. He would have preferred it if she'd kneed him in the balls. Physical pain he could handle, and anger was at least a twin to passion. But indifference? It was as if he meant nothing to her at all.

64

He couldn't go backward. Not again.

He wouldn't survive losing her another time.

"How are you feeling?" he asked, voice lowered as if they were alone.

"Like I was left for dead."

Ronan winced, but he couldn't exactly argue with her. She must have had one hell of a headache when she came to. And after the awkward way she'd been tucked into that sling, her muscles must be screaming at her in protest. It's no wonder she assumed the worst, especially when physical altercations were commonplace for her.

"Letting you sleep seemed kinder than waking you."

"Yes, I'm sure you would think so, considering you're the one who plucked me from my home and brought me aboard this vessel. Perhaps you'd care to fill in the blanks on *that* little development."

Not exactly what happened, but not entirely far off.

He'd waffled between sticking around below deck so he'd be there when she woke to explain and going off to familiarize himself with their new accommodations and the crew. In the end he'd taken the coward's way out, claiming hunger as an excuse to go exploring. In truth, he simply wasn't ready to face her.

But out here, there was no escape.

No escape . . . and an audience.

Calypso smirked as her gaze darted back and forth between them.

"Perhaps it's best if we have this conversation in our room."

"Oh, don't let me stop you. This is the most entertained I've been in weeks."

Neither of them spared the captain a glance. Instead, Shadow cocked a brow. "What's wrong, Ronan? Afraid of admitting you've added kidnapping to your list of crimes?"

She was fishing for information, and he didn't blame her. It had to be beyond disconcerting to wake in a foreign place with no recollection of how you got there. The grace with which she handled her situation spoke to a familiarity he didn't want to investigate too closely. It would only piss him off, and the last thing any of them needed was him getting into it with a bunch of pirates when he tried to commandeer their ship so he could go back to Glimmermere and murder Erebos.

He really should have taken care of that when he'd had the chance, but then he'd have ended up spending the rest of his life rotting away in a hole somewhere instead of . . . Instead of what? Sailing off into the sunset with a woman who could barely tolerate him most days?

Ronan resisted the urge to squeeze the bridge of his nose. This was hardly the best-case scenario, but at least they were together.

"I did not *kidnap* you, Shadow. I rescued you. My quick thinking last night saved both our lives."

My quick thinking . . . and the help of a couple of unlikely allies.

She scoffed. "And I'm what, just supposed to take your word for it? Please. I've never needed rescuing a day in my life."

"Here, here," Calypso muttered.

"How would you know? You can't remember any of it." Exasperation made his voice sharper than he'd intended, and he regretted the words immediately.

Her eyes narrowed. "I wonder whose fault that is."

He had to swallow back his bellow of frustration. He wanted to scream at her that it was Erebos's fault, but he had no actual proof, and she had no reason to believe him. And there was also the part where he *had* been the one to bash her upside the head with a candle-stick. So although his intentions had been noble, he didn't exactly have the moral high ground here.

Releasing a heavy exhale, he said, "Trust me, kitten, it was the only way."

That caused a reaction. She visibly flinched at the endearment, her jaw tensing. "Why should I trust you?"

"I've never lied to you."

"But you don't exactly tell the truth either."

He should have been ashamed they were having it out on the deck, but he was just too relieved that she was finally showing some emotion—or as much as one could expect from the assassin.

"You want the truth? I'll tell you anything you want to know." He crossed his arms and held her stare. "Try me."

"I should have asked Cookie to make me some of his popped corn," Calypso murmured.

"You can go," Shadow snapped, eyes flashing with green fire.

"Darling, it's my ship. I'll stand where I damn well please. No one gives orders here except me." The captain's voice was cold thunder, and Ronan would have sworn the gentle dips of the hull cutting through the waves grew more pronounced.

"I find it hard to believe the personal affairs of two passengers ranks all that highly on the list of things that you should give a single fuck about."

Mother's tits. If he didn't come up with a way to defuse this, they were likely to come to blows. That wouldn't be good for anyone. Least of all Calypso. The captain was clearly a woman familiar with getting her hands dirty, but Shadow was without equal. She'd kill the woman and not think twice about it.

"I wouldn't be much of a captain if I didn't make the affairs of my passengers my business. How else can I ensure the safety of me and my crew?"

"Be that as it may, perhaps you could try to do so without crawling quite so far up our asses?"

Ronan shifted, preparing to grab Shadow about the waist and haul her to their room before Calypso shoved her overboard. As much as he appreciated her fire, he was genuinely worried about her safety if she continued to goad the other woman. But the captain surprised him by laughing, her eye—which had deepened until it was nearly onyx—returning to sapphire.

"I think I like you, assassin."

"You know who I am?"

"Darling, you haven't been paying attention. I already told you, I consider it my business to know everything about the people aboard the *Revenge.*"

Shadow's lips twitched, and she tilted her head in his direction. "And you still let this asshole aboard? I'm surprised."

"Well, he is pretty."

Shadow cut her gaze back to him, running it from the top of his head down to his booted toes and then back. "Eh, I've had better."

You filthy liar.

Now he wanted to haul her over his shoulder and down to their room for another reason entirely. His palm tingled in anticipation of swatting her impertinent arse. He wanted to call her on her shit then and there. Remind her that not that long ago, he had her reduced to little more than wanton moans and breathy sighs as she begged him to fuck her. He'd walk away here and now if she could honestly name a single person who'd ever managed to do the same.

"What's wrong, Ronan?" she purred. "You look like you swallowed your shirt."

You want to play games, little one? We can play. But we'll play them in my bed. Naked. Don't start something you're not prepared to finish.

That's what he wanted to say.

What he actually said was, "I'm just trying to figure out why it is that *you*, the infamous assassin, believe that *I'm* the one she needs to be worried about?"

"Oh, I'm sorry. I forgot how empty that brain of yours is. But in my defense, with as fat as your skull is, it's an honest mistake."

"At least it's proportional to the rest of him . . ."

"I know where you're going with that, but I should warn you, you're in for a world of disappointment if you think that's the case for the rest of him."

"Pity."

What the actual fuck?

He growled while Calypso cackled and Shadow smirked. *Mother have mercy. They were ganging up on him.* He should have seen it coming. Wasn't that always the way when two forces of nature collided? A lot of noise to herald the storm before they ultimately blended into one terrifying entity? Just his luck to be caught between them. He was certain weaker men wouldn't survive.

To be fair, he still wasn't entirely sure he would, either. He didn't know much of Calypso's past, but he could guess it. One didn't become captain of a pirate ship by handing out cookies to her enemies. And as for Shadow . . . he'd seen firsthand just how deadly she could be.

"Here, allow me to explain. The difference is I only kill for money" —she patted the top of his head like he was a child half her size instead of a man fully grown—"but you are *always* an insufferable prick."

Before he could muster a worthy retort, Shadow spun on her heel. But not without delivering a final parting shot. "It was nice meeting you, captain. I'd love to continue our chat, but I find I simply cannot stomach the smell of all that horseshit." Her eyes narrowed as they shot to his, her voice decidedly less friendly. "Do. Not. Follow." Lips curling up in a wicked smile, she added, "Not unless you want to lose several inches."

"I could do with a haircut," he called after her once he picked his jaw up off the deck.

She paused, turned to face him fully, and shot him a grin that was somehow both sensual and filled with malice. "I never said which inches I'd be taking."

Fuuuck. He knew she didn't mean that in a sexual sense, quite the opposite, in fact. But damned if he could get his cock to understand the distinction. It jerked to attention at her words, swelling further as his mind filled with the various ways he'd happily help Shadow take *all* of his inches.

Beside him, Calypso chuckled. Finally she reached out, pressing the tip of her finger to his chin and pushing it firmly up. "So that was your lady Shadow."

"Aye."

"Is she always that feisty?"

"Since the day we first met."

"I can see why you're so taken with her."

There was a thoughtful, admiring quality to her voice that had Ronan turning his full attention back to her. "Don't go getting any ideas, No Beard. You may collect lovers like other people do jewels, but she's spoken for, and unlike you pirates, I don't share."

"That's too bad for you, Ronan. Sharing can be such fun. But far be it from me to try to convince you. If you're happy with your one true love, then my best wishes to you both. Though I have to say, I've seen men on shore leave who received a warmer welcome than you just did. Are you sure she's yours, Butcher?"

He knew she was teasing him, but his answer was dead serious. "I've never been more certain of anything in my damned life."

"Well then, does *she* know it?"

The question was an emotional gut punch because, no, she didn't. And wasn't that the crux of it all? Still, he refused to lose hope. Because even now, even without the benefit of her memories, Shadow was still drawn to him. On some primal level, part of her recognized they belonged together. Why else would she have gotten jealous at the attention Calypso had shown him?

Bolstered by the realization, Ronan steeled himself for the fight ahead. And it would be a fight because that woman was as stubborn as she was deadly. But he'd broken through her walls once before. He could do it again.

He *had* to.

Because she was it for him. There was no one else.

After a lifetime spent searching, Shadow was his happily ever after, and he damn well intended to claim it. If he had to spend the rest of his days making her fall in love with him over and over again, he would. And he'd consider himself blessed for the privilege. What better ending could there be for a man such as him? He'd been little more than a hopeless wanderer, going where he was needed, never putting down roots, never belonging anywhere. And he'd been happy with that path. Until her. Until he'd found the person who made him feel like he'd finally found a place to rest.

So even if it hurt. Even if it shredded him to the very marrow every time she looked at him and didn't remember, he would keep fighting. With his dying breath, he would fight for her. Because she deserved it. Because she was his.

Because she was home.

CHAPTER 9

EREBOS

The Lord of Death was not amused. In fact, he was feeling particularly murderous this morning.

Three of the palace staff had found themselves on the receiving end of his black mood before Dominic discovered their corpses and wisely kept everyone else at bay. But not even giving into the need to cull a spirit from its body had been enough to blunt the edge of his temper.

Even now, hours later, fury coiled in his belly like a serpent prepared to strike. All around him the darkness closed in, created by the little wisps of black floating off his fingers. Daylight might reign outside, but within these walls, the oppressive weight of night was so thick not even candles could fully penetrate the gloom.

She was gone. Taken. There was no doubt in his mind it was not by choice. He'd been thorough in his ministrations. Her loyalty was absolute. Which meant the blackguard had been planning on taking her. There was no other explanation for how he'd disappeared without a trace. One did not simply vanish without preparation.

Or help.

And Luna have mercy on their souls when he uncovered the identity of the traitorous letches—because he would not.

The door to his personal chamber opened with a soft click, and his body tensed. He didn't turn around to face his visitor; he didn't trust himself to keep up the pretense of mortality. His true self was too close to the surface, his control precarious at best due to his seething anger. The last thing he wanted was to accidentally kill one of his most loyal followers simply because they were the bearer of bad news.

Not while he still had need of them, anyway.

"Yes?" he snapped.

"No sign of either of them, High Lord," Dominic said, regret in every word.

"Any word from your sister?"

"I'm here, my lord, and no. The answer is the same everywhere. No one has seen Shadow or your Ch—"

Erebos hissed, stopping her before Dovina could grant the title to the unworthy swine.

"—the Butcher," she amended.

The need to rip and tear and destroy pulsed through him. In his mind, he'd already whirled around and upended every piece of furniture in the room. Instead, he sucked in a breath and gritted out, "That is not what I hoped to hear."

"Apologies, High Lord. We will continue our search," Dominic promised.

"You'd better. I expect more from you both. If you cannot do your jobs, I will replace you with those who will."

"They cannot stay hidden indefinitely," Dovina added. "We will find them, my liege. You have my word."

"Your word is useless to me. Bring me the girl. She is all that matters."

There was a beat of silence and then a rustle of fabric he knew would be Dovina fidgeting. His Raven was unflappable, but he didn't need to use his power to determine exactly which thoughts floated through her mind in that moment. The woman was as calculating as she was ambitious. She wanted to rule at his side. If she was the one he'd needed, the one he'd asked to be his lady, there would have been no hesitation. Not a single second of doubt. The fact that he hadn't even considered her for the position was a chink in her otherwise impenetrable armor.

"What of the man?" Dominic asked.

"I want him too."

"Alive?"

"Yes. His death belongs to me."

"I will have Dmitri make it known."

"See that you do. And Dominic?"

"Yes, High Lord?"

"I've had my fill of disappointment. Do not bother me again unless you have what I want. You do not want to find out what happens if you disappoint me further, I promise. Now, leave me."

The twins did so without another word, leaving him to stew with only his thoughts for company. Usually at least one of them would ask if he wanted them to stay. It was a testament to the violence rolling off him that neither so much as attempted to make such an offer. Smart of them, really. He made no promises about their safety if they stuck around.

Erebos continued to stare out the window, not seeing anything of the land or people that belonged to him. He knew their efforts would be fruitless. If there was anything to discover, they would have by now. Which meant it was time for him to stop relying on mortals and take matters into his own more than capable hands.

There was one surefire way for him to find his sweet Shadow. A realm where no matter how far they ran, none could remain hidden from him.

It was how he'd claimed his vessel, after all.

Closing his eyes, Erebos delved deep into the abyss where his power and godly essence rose, eager to do his bidding. Searching for the unique frequency of a mind at rest was not so much a science as a fine art. All around him, voices swelled, smoky, soft whispers of thought ripe to pluck and mold as he willed. The echoes were not as clear as if he'd been in his true form, but they were clear enough for this. All he had to do was focus on one, and the bubble of thought expanded for him, a portal ready for him to walk through.

It was really just a matter of finding the dreamscape he sought. Luckily, he was intimately familiar with the notes that comprised Shadow's psyche. Time and space were no obstacle. He would recognize her mind anywhere. Patience, that was all he needed.

Patience, and one very specific dreamer.

From there, all he had to do was step into her dream and pluck the information he needed from her mind. He would find her; it was only a matter of time. There was nowhere to hide from the Father of Dreams.

Taking a centering breath, Erebos settled in, ready to begin his vigil.

She had to sleep sometime, and when she did, he would be there. Lying in wait. The proverbial monster under her bed. The nightmare crooning in her ear, dragging her deeper into the void where he'd prey and feed on the very darkest of her fears until she shattered.

There would be no escape. Not this time.

Not from him.

The land of dreams was his domain, and he was a merciless and vengeful god.

"Sleep, Shadow. I'm coming for you."

CHAPTER 10

SHADOW

The problem with ships was that hiding, or rather, staying hidden, was impossible. It was only a matter of time before someone stumbled across you. Thankfully, the pirates were content to let her hide, and she'd managed to avoid Ronan for the better part of the afternoon while fighting to get her emotions under control.

This restless, unsettled feeling was uncommon for her. And it certainly didn't help matters that she didn't understand where her anger stemmed from, only that it was there. Much like she didn't understand the constant pull she felt to Ronan but could no more deny it than cease breathing.

She was no closer to puzzling out how she'd ended up on the *Revenge* or why. Nor had she come any closer to recalling the details about what happened during the trials. Everything was a blur of time passing. She obviously knew Ronan but couldn't recall when or where they met. Nor could she remember any relevant conversation they might have shared. It was like she'd woken up in the middle of somebody else's life, but that somebody was her. Or like being presented with an alphabet to a foreign language, but none of the words. She knew only enough not to be completely lost, but nothing that gave her any sense of true understanding.

That was the only thing that kept her from descending into a full-blown meltdown. She knew who she was. *What* she was. There was no doubt she could handle whatever was thrown her way. She simply needed to bide her time and let those around her fill in the blanks. Someone would slip up soon, and then she could put together a plan to get back to the High Lord.

You could always take Ronan up on his offer . . .

That pesky little voice in her mind had been unhelpfully offering advice all day. Shadow knew Ronan held all the answers, but she couldn't bring herself to go to him. Not even to ask the relevant questions. She told herself it was because she didn't trust him to tell her the truth.

Or maybe you're the one you don't trust . . .

Shadow let out a little growl, kicking at a bit of coiled chain. There was something patently unfair about being called out in your own head. Surely if there was someone she should be able to count on to have her back, it should be her own damned self.

You've never been a liar, Shadow. Why lie to yourself now? You want him . . . why else did you react that way to what barely even counted as flirting?

"Stop. It," she gritted out, kicking the chain a second time. This time with enough force, she felt the blow reverberate up her leg.

"Yikes. What did poor Archie do to deserve such punishment?"

Shadow spun around, finding herself face-to-face with the blond man she'd met earlier. *Bronn*, that perky little bitch of a voice supplied.

"Archie?"

He gestured to the length of chain. "The anchor."

She snorted. "You named your anchor *Archie*?"

"What else were we supposed to name him?"

"Uh, nothing?"

"Well, that seems rude."

Shadow couldn't help but laugh. The man was so damned earnest; there was nothing for it but to warm to him.

"There, that's better," he said, giving her a full-blown smile. "I hate seeing a beautiful woman frown." He glanced back to her feet, adding, "And commit unwarranted acts of violence on undeserving objects."

Were her mind not already filled with thoughts of another charming rogue, she might not have found herself immune to his beauty. As it was, she couldn't help but note the flecks of gold ringing his pupils or how they made her think of sunlight rippling along the surface of the cool water. Or the flex of muscle beneath the white cotton of his shirt. Another time, another place, she might have allowed herself to succumb. If only to collect the experience.

"Is there such a thing as a deserving object?"

"Aye. Plenty."

"Such as . . ."

"An empty cask of grog, for starters."

"Ah . . . of course. The bane of many a pirate."

"Just so."

They lapsed into a comfortable silence before she quirked a brow and asked. "I know you didn't simply happen upon me and intervene on poor Archie's behalf. What is it you truly wanted?"

"I was tasked with bringing you down to dinner."

"Down to dinner?" she repeated. "You mean with the crew?"

He nodded. "Aye, 'twas the captain's request. You made quite an impression on her, it would seem."

Shadow could feel the beginnings of a blush working its way up the back of her neck. Her barbed exchange with Ronan on the deck this morning was arguably not her finest moment. She wasn't one to engage in such public disputes. Her preference was to deal with disagreements by more intimate and *permanent* means.

"I . . . uh . . . that is—"

"If you're trying to find a way out of it, there isn't one. Her ship, her rules. We have a long way to go yet, so you best get used to it."

"Fine," she said with an inward sigh. "Lead the way."

They walked side by side for a few beats, Shadow feeling much steadier despite the gentle roll and dip beneath her feet. "So, where are we going?"

"To the captain's quarters," Bronn said, giving her an odd look.

Stars. She'd envisioned some sort of mess hall, but private quarters made more sense. A smugglers' vessel such as this would want to use any extra space to store precious cargo. Still, that wasn't what she was asking.

"No, I meant . . . you said we have a long way to go. I was asking after our destination."

He raised a brow. "You sought passage on our ship without knowing where it was heading?"

"To be fair, I didn't have much say in the matter."

Bronn, darkness bless him, went stiff. The gentle sea breeze began to gust, making the ends of her hair lift and snap across her face. "Are you here against your will, lady?"

Well, that was a question now, wasn't it? She had little doubt, were she to say that yes, she was, Bronn would do everything in his power to free her. Despite his lifestyle and the reputation that came with it, he struck her as a good, honest man. And while she could definitely argue she'd been taken against her will, the truth was she didn't *feel* like she was in danger. Confused? Certainly. Out of her depth? Without question. But not at risk.

"It's complicated," she eventually said as they started down the stairs. "But it's not what you're thinking."

"Well, we have ways of uncomplicating things if you have need." His grin was a little more pirate and a little less gallant gentleman. It suited him. As did the glint of a gold hoop in his ear.

"I'll keep that in mind."

He steered her to the left, and she had to file behind him as they moved down the hallway.

"For what it's worth," he called over his shoulder, "not one of us questioned his intentions with you. If we had, we never would have left you alone with him—or allowed him passage at all. But the way he held you when he came aboard . . . the man looked as though he'd take on Nereus himself to keep you safe."

"Nereus?"

"The god of the sea."

Shadow didn't know why hearing that made her heart race, but she blamed Bronn and the mental picture he'd provided for the organ's uneven tempo and resulting hitch in her breath. Yes, those were Bronn's fault . . . not the man whose icy blue gaze met hers the second she crossed the threshold into the captain's private rooms.

"Shadow," he greeted, the deep rumble of his voice sending pleasant chills up and down her limbs.

"Prick," she returned with a tight smile, much to the amusement of the others.

"Lady Shadow, I trust you remember these scallywags," Bronn said, gesturing toward the round table in the corner of the room where Ronan, Tiny, Calypso, and Jagger, along with his pretty bird, were already seated. She was surprised to see the minotaur, but only because he practically dwarfed everyone else. There was no way he fit into the same chairs they did. They must have had something custom designed for his bulk.

There were only two remaining chairs, which she assumed were for her and Bronn. As they neared the table, everyone, including the captain, stood. Ronan reached for her seat at the same time Bronn did. There was an uncomfortably tense moment as they glared at each other, each silently demanding the other to let go of the seatback.

"Oh, for fuck's sake," she muttered, plunking herself down and roughly scooting the chair forward out of their grasps.

The other guests chuckled again, making Shadow feel like she'd somehow become the evening's entertainment as they reclaimed their seats at the ornately set table. She couldn't help but wonder if this was a common occurrence or if Calypso was going out of her way for this evening's meal.

"There's no need for such fuss on my account," she said, glad that it was the captain seated across from her, so she could at least pretend she was unaware of the man to her left. There was no reason for anyone else to know she could feel Ronan's attention on her like a caress. Or that she wanted to lean into it and beg for more.

"Nonsense. You're my guest," Calypso said, "and dare I say the fanciest one we've had in quite some time. Allow us our indulgences. It's good for these mongrels to air out their manners from time to time. Never know when they'll come in handy."

Tiny gave an affronted sniff.

"You know I wasn't referring to you, Tiny. Your manners are impeccable. You're the pride of the crew. We would all do well to be more like you."

"Thank you, Captain. You're too kind." The minotaur beamed, his smile terrifying but somehow still endearing. *It must be the glasses,* Shadow decided, fighting against a smile as he plucked the elaborately folded napkin off his plate and gently set what looked like a pocket square between his thick fingers across his lap.

The others followed suit, though Shadow's eyes were drawn to Jagger, who, despite the band across his eyes, unerringly found his own napkin and tucked it into the collar of his shirt. His bird gave him an affectionate nibble on his ear, and she wondered just how deep their connection ran.

There was a gentle knock on the door.

"Enter," Calypso called. The door swung open, revealing Cookie with a large tureen held between his hands. "Ah, Cookie. Right on time. Please, come in."

Before Shadow could wonder how the cook had managed to hold the dish while simultaneously opening the door, she caught a peek of sandy hair and recognized her young friend from earlier. He was peeking around the doorway, his eyes locked on her. When he realized she'd caught him, his cheeks blazed pink and he ducked back out of sight.

"It seems you've been collecting admirers," Ronan murmured.

"One could say the same for you."

Shadow immediately wanted to kick herself. *Why? Why admit that you noticed or care about his interaction with the captain? For darkness's sake, Shadow. Get it together.*

Ronan's brows lifted, his lips slowly curling in a smile as Cookie started ladling a delicious-smelling chowder into the various bowls. "I'm surprised you noticed."

"Hard not to notice a grown man making an ass of himself," she whispered, accepting her serving with what she hoped was a convincing smile. "Thank you."

"I hope you enjoy it, lady. It's a crew favorite."

"I'm sure I will," she assured the cook.

Ronan sat back in his seat, arms crossed as he picked up their conversation once the cook moved on. "Is that what I was doing?"

"Not sure what else I'd call that pathetic display of male preening I witnessed."

"I don't preen."

"Are you sure about that?"

"Unequivocally."

"Ohh, fancy word, Butcher. Did Tiny teach it to you?"

The crew laughed again, not having missed their exchange despite their hushed voices.

Shadow's eyes shot to the minotaur's, an apology on the tip of her tongue in case she accidentally offended him. But he was chuckling along with the others, his spectacles in his hand as he carefully cleaned the lenses.

Ronan glowered at her, leaning forward until he was practically speaking into her ear. "I know lots of words, kitten. I made a point to memorize the ones that made your eyes cross and your knees weaken. Do you require a demonstration?"

Too flustered to manage a response, Shadow took a large bite of her chowder. Flavor exploded on her tongue. Having expected the fare to be flavorless or over-salted at best, she was stunned to discover it was among some of the best food she'd ever eaten. "Cookie, this is incredible," she breathed.

The big man blushed, bashfully twisting his apron in his hands. "I'm glad you enjoy it, lady."

"Wait until you try his biscuits," Bronn said. "They're the size of his fist, but damned if they aren't flakey, buttery bites of heaven."

"I'll make you a batch in the morning," Cookie promised. "Along with my gravy."

"You spoil us, Cookie," Calypso said, earning another blush from her cook.

"It's no trouble, Captain." The bald man expectantly turned to Jagger, who'd yet to say anything but was happily spooning bite after bite into his mouth.

Bronn must have kicked him under the table because his head shot up and he scowled over at him.

"What?" he snapped, surprising Shadow with the harsh rasp of his voice. It was obvious he rarely, if ever, spoke. Bronn jerked his head toward the cook. Jagger's expression cleared, Buttercup fluttering on his shoulder. "It's good," he grunted before returning to his meal.

Cookie's face relaxed back into a happy grin. Shadow thought it sweet that he cared so much what the others thought about his meal and that they indulged him. With as much time as they spent at sea, having someone with his skill onboard was a blessing, and it was clear they recognized and celebrated it. Shadow couldn't help but like them. The care the crew showed one another spoke to the kind of people they were.

He started to turn, and she thought he was leaving, but instead Cookie looked expectantly at Ronan, the only one who'd yet to take a bite.

Shadow readied her foot, more than prepared to send a swift kick to the shin his way if necessary, but he needed no prompting. Taking a big bite, Ronan's expression flickered. She wasn't sure anyone else would catch it, but there was a momentary flash of panic in his blue eyes.

Worried he might be about to hurt the big man's feelings, Shadow held her breath, but Ronan forced a smile and asked, "Clam?"

"Aye."

"Delicious."

Shadow wondered if anyone else caught the strangled note in his voice.

Cookie clearly didn't, because he let out a big breath. "Good. Good. Well, I'll be back in a bit with dessert."

As soon as he left, she leaned over and whispered, "Are you all right?"

He subtly pushed his bowl away. "Allergic."

Her eyes went wide. "Ronan—"

She broke off, her mind running wild until he held up the balled-up napkin in his fist. He must have managed to spit the bite out without anyone being the wiser. Shadow felt some of the ice around her heart crack. He could have made a big thing out of it, but instead he'd recognized the vulnerable nature of the cook and protected the man's pride in front of his captain and crew. That told her more about Ronan than anything he could have told her himself.

He was kind when he didn't have to be.

Whatever else he might be, Ronan was *good*. She may not know why he'd brought her here, but Shadow had no doubt she was safe with him.

"Do you need me to find you something else—"

"No," he said softly. "Don't worry about me. Enjoy your meal."

She held his gaze, feeling both conflicted and relieved. It was as though she was of two minds. One half determined to paint him as the villain, the other desperate not to.

In this moment, desperation won.

Without looking at him, she slid him her dinner roll. "Eat up. You need your strength."

"For what? More verbal sparring with you?"

"Exactly. It's no fun swabbing the deck with you when you're not at your best."

He chuckled softly, the sound washing over her and making her belly knot in a way that had her pressing her thighs together. She watched from the corner of her eye until he bit into the roll.

"Thank you," he said after a beat.

Her heart tumbled at the sincerity she found there, and she almost choked on her wine from the shock of it. Or maybe that was due to the strength of her own as she whispered, "You're welcome."

Silence stretched between them, neither one sure what to say when they weren't actively taking shots at one another. She took another bite of her soup, scrambling for something to talk about that wouldn't ruin the moment and coming up short.

Thankfully, salvation came in the form of the sailor on her right.

"So, Shadow," Bronn said, breaking the silence and drawing groans from the rest of the table in the process. "Are you familiar with the story of how our captain acquired the *Revenge?*"

CHAPTER 11

SHADOW

*D*inner was long over, and as the candles burned low, the conversation turned to old seafarer tales about the kinds of monsters who lurked in the inky depths.

"Piss off. Everyone knows the Lusca is the true terror of the deep."

Calypso's comment had Bronn snapping his mouth shut and Tiny politely hiding his laughter behind his napkin. The ever-stoic Jagger didn't react, but Buttercup let out a soft tweet that sounded like agreement. Meanwhile, Ronan had abandoned all pretense of paying attention and was currently snatching another of Cookie's frosted cakes off the platter that had inched its way closer to him over the course of the last half hour. The man might have had to skip the main course, but he'd more than made up for it with the petite desserts. That was the seventh she'd seen him take, and she wouldn't have been surprised if he'd managed to sneak others. Who would have predicted the merciless Butcher had a sweet tooth?

"Lusca?" Shadow asked, curious to hear more about the monster that had several grown men squirming in their seats.

"Aye, a fearsome creature it is," the captain said, her eye appearing almost violet as she leaned in with all the zeal of a storyteller knowing she had a captive audience. "Two hundred feet at least, with massive tentacles that can crush a galleon as easy as this here butter. Those who don't drown from the wreck are sucked into the Dweller's mighty maw and swallowed whole. Dead before they even realize they was caught."

"Dweller? I thought you called it—"

"The Lusca, aye. Though there are many that refer to it as the Dweller of the Deep since there's power in a name and they believe to utter it is to summon it."

"But not you?" Shadow asked as goosebumps prickled the length of her skin.

Calypso shrugged. "I have more realistic fears."

"That's because you know it's a myth," Bronn scoffed, balling up his napkin and tossing it on his plate. "Besides, what's so scary about a toothless squid? What Meg lacks in size, she more than makes up for with all those teeth. A creature that can tear you to shreds *and* ensure you feel every miserable second leading up to your death? *That's* a monster worthy of fear."

Ronan snickered, and Shadow gave him a curious glance.

"What?" he asked with a shrug. "The man makes a valid point."

Shadow shook her head, thinking she wasn't keen on meeting either the Lusca or the Megalodon—Meg as Bronn called her. It was a good thing these were all just tales sailors made up to frighten their swabbies . . . weren't they?

"No," Jagger rasped, with a slight shake of his head.

It was only the second time he'd spoken all night, and everyone turned his way in surprise when he joined the conversation.

"You disagree?" Bronn asked. Jagger dipped his chin in a jerky nod that Buttercup echoed with a soft chirp. "By all means, enlighten us."

Tension radiated from the bosun, a muscle fluttering wildly in his jaw. After an affectionate nuzzle from his bird, his throat bobbed and he said, "It's worse not to know." For a second Shadow thought that might be *all* he intended to say, but then Jagger cleared his throat and continued. "Pain is forgotten. True fear is not . . . the mind . . . it can . . . it is . . ." He huffed out a frustrated breath as he trailed off, jaw clenching tight as he struggled to find his words. When he did, he nearly shocked her with their eloquence. "There's nothing worse than what the mind conjures in the face of the unknown."

Jagger may not speak often, but it was clear to Shadow that was due to choice rather than circumstance. It made her itch to learn what secrets he was keeping . . . and why.

Bronn wasn't nearly as impressed with the answer as Shadow, perhaps because he was better acquainted with the mysterious bosun. Instead of agreeing with the assessment, he snorted. "How is being swallowed whole by a creature so vast you don't even know it's happening any different than being snuffed out in your sleep? It's a mercy if you ask me. One should be so lucky."

The question was rhetorical, so Shadow didn't think she was alone in her surprise when Jagger spoke up once more. This time, she almost wished he hadn't.

"The difference lies in the darkness. Terrible, never-ending dark-ness with only your thoughts for company. A mind splinters under the weight of it . . . becomes twisted in its desperation. Unrecogniz-able . . . until it inevitably shatters."

Delivered in his hoarse rumble, the words held a sinister edge that had a shiver of foreboding skittering down her spine. It was as if they were torn from deep inside him without his consent, filled with the agony of a festering wound. Her heart twisted in the confines of its bony cage, his remembered pain summoning hers, forcing her to share in the horror of it.

It wasn't until Ronan's hand snaked out, covering hers, that she realized she'd been holding her breath. She sucked in air with a stran-gled gasp, forcing herself to shake off his touch and instantly mourning its loss when he allowed it.

The jovial atmosphere from dinner was officially gone, their easy banter replaced by the guttering of the candles. Everyone seemed caught in the spell Jagger's words had woven until Calypso reached out, resting her hand on his knee with a concerned frown. The moment of tender comfort between the captain and her bosun was unexpected and hinted at a relationship far more complex than simple crew dynamics. Not for the first time, Shadow wondered about the people that manned the *Revenge*. Specifically about the kind of lives they'd led and how such an unlikely bunch found themselves together.

"Annnd on that joyful note, I think it's time we turn in for the evening."

Bronn's proclamation had everyone up and moving. It was almost comical the way they all jumped into action at once. As if time had slowed to a crawl and they were now forced to act in triple time to make up for the delay. But she knew the truth was far less fanciful. It was simply relief. The quartermaster had provided them with an excuse to run away from the bleak despondency Jagger's words left them trapped within, and they all gratefully latched onto it. Only the forced smiles of the crew hinted that it would take more than a speedy exit to reclaim their equilibrium.

Hoping to help them along, Shadow followed Bronn's lead and offered a gentle tease of her own. "Perhaps next time we could opt for sea shanties as the after-dinner entertainment."

"I didn't realize you were such a fan of music," Ronan murmured, his eyes crinkling with amusement as he helped her from her chair.

She shot him a wary glance. Why did she get the feeling the man was privy to far too many of her secrets? The possibility of it made her feel defensive, so she snapped back, "Since when is it a crime to appreciate culture?"

"It isn't," Tiny assured her.

"Shanties we can do," Bronn added, "but I'm going to have to insist you join in."

"Oh no, I don't sing," she protested with a laugh. "Not unless you want tales to spread over both land and sea of how the crew of the *Revenge* murders cats."

"She's not joking. I had the rare honor of hearing her in the shower once. I damn near beat the door down thinking she was under attack, only to realize she was alone. Tone-deaf as they come and butchering a poor helpless song as if she intended to have it for supper."

Everyone laughed, though it was Ronan's deep chuckle that made her cheeks warm and her lips pull into a frown. *When had he caught her in the shower . . . and what had he seen?*

Bronn patted her shoulder, and there was no missing Ronan's scowl when the quartermaster didn't immediately remove his hand. "Nonsense. Everyone can carry a shanty. It's part of the charm. You'll see."

"Aye, we'll make a night of it," Calypso agreed.

"I'll let Cookie know," Tiny said, holding out the captain's chair as she stood.

"Cookie?"

"Cooking is his passion, but music is his true gift," Calypso explained. "He has siren blood in him, that one. I'm sure of it."

"Many say the same of you," Bronn murmured, his eyes warming as they fell to—and lingered on—his captain.

Calypso ducked her head and tucked some hair behind her ear in a rare display of shyness. "Aye, well. Most people are ignorant fools, aren't they?"

"Ready?" Ronan asked.

"Hmm? Oh, yes."

He moved to stand beside her, resting his large palm on the base of her spine. Heat shot through her at the contact, causing her to suck in a sharp breath. Laughter danced in his eyes, but his voice revealed none of it as he turned toward the captain. "Thank you for the meal, and the company," he added with a polite nod.

Calypso waved a hand. "Please, you did us the honor."

Shadow opened her mouth to protest, but Tiny interjected before she could. "It's easy to grow weary of the same old stories when we've got only each other to tell them to. You've breathed new life into our tired tales, and onto our ship. You have our deepest thanks for that." He dipped into a courtly bow only a touch less formal than the one he'd given her that morning.

"I'm familiar with the phenomenon," Ronan said dryly, steering her toward the door. "There were many a night my *cil'virga* and I experienced the same. Though we were more liable to punch each other in the throat rather than suffer through a story we'd heard countless times before."

While the others snickered in understanding, Shadow's body tensed and her smile turned wooden. She'd never heard the term before, she'd swear to it, but as soon as it left Ronan's lips, her mind was filled with the image of a group of elite soldiers. How could she know *that* when she remembered next to nothing else?

Ronan shot her a questioning glance, and she shook her head. Even if she was of a mind to explain, how could she? Her frequent loss of memory was her burden to bear, not to mention a weakness she had no intention of allowing anyone—let alone virtual strangers—to exploit. She'd made it this far on her own, without someone becoming the wiser. She wasn't about to change tactics now, especially not when she was so far out of her depth.

They left the captain's quarters to a chorus of well wishes for a night filled with restful sleep, but Shadow knew that wasn't in the cards for her. Between Jagger's haunting warning and her own agitated thoughts, rest would be a long way off.

That, along with the near-constant buzz of awareness coursing through her due to the man currently prowling down the hallway on her heels, had her walking a razor's edge.

"A ship this size, and you couldn't manage to find your own accommodations? I'm sure there are a couple of rats that would welcome you into their hidey hole," she snapped when he moved to follow her inside the small cabin.

"What's the matter, kitten? You afraid of a snuggle?" He dropped his voice and leaned in closer, crowding her with his body and the scent of campfire and leather she'd come to associate with him. "Or are you afraid of how much you'd enjoy it?"

She threw him what she hoped was a believable glare, hoping he would misread the flutter of her pulse at her throat as anger instead of interest. "Not remotely, because if you're going to insist on sharing a room—"

"How else can I keep you safe?"

"—then *you* are sleeping on the floor."

"The hell I am."

Her jaw dropped. "Excuse me?"

He pushed past her into the room and sat down on the bed, wasting no time before leaning down to remove his boots. "The way I see it, there's nothing remotely fair about me being the one to take the floor. You got a problem sharing a bed with me, you're welcome to sleep somewhere else. But I'm the one that got us passage, meaning I'm the one that acquired these lodgings. As such," he said, tossing his boots on the other side of the narrow cabin and leveling her with his smoldering gaze, "the bed and everything else in this room is mine."

When she didn't immediately respond, he stood and removed his shirt. Holding her stare in a blatant challenge, he grasped the dark fabric from the back of his collar and pulled it slowly up and over his head.

Her stomach clenched as slab after tantalizing slab of defined, rock-hard muscle revealed itself, though her eyes seemed caught on the dusting of dark hair running down the center until disappearing beneath the waistband of his pants. If she'd been in a position to form a coherent thought, she would have been furious at herself for becoming so distracted by a few measly muscles.

The perky bitch was back in her head again, her peals of laughter practically deafening.

Measly? Oh, sweetheart, you're not even fooling yourself with that load of horseshit you're shoveling. Everything about this man is perfection. Your mouth is literally watering. Careful now, you might actually be drooling.

Shadow belatedly turned away and wiped at her mouth, face on fire and heart racing.

That stupid voice continued its tirade, though this time it was accompanied by Ronan's knowing chuckle. *He's luring you in faster than a fisherman with a net. What are you waiting for? Just give in already. You know you want to.*

She knew it was a study in madness to argue with herself, but she felt compelled to do it anyway. *He's my kidnapper.*

No, he isn't. If you really believed that, you would have gutted him and fed him to the sharks by now. Stop lying to yourself. Whatever reason he had for bringing you on this journey, harming you was never part of it.

Mouth dry, Shadow licked her lips and willed her breathing to even out. That inner voice might be annoying, but it had a point. Not once since waking and seeing he was onboard with her had she believed she was in any kind of danger. She may not know his motives, but she trusted him. Without knowing anything else, she knew that.

"A gentleman would sleep on the floor," she grumbled.

"I never claimed to be a gentleman."

A low throb pulsed between her legs. *Stars, but he made that sound like a good thing.*

"You're serious about sharing the bed?"

"Sweetheart, I'm already under the covers."

She spun around, finding him reclining on the feather mattress with a blanket draped over his lower body. "You better not be naked under there."

"Or what?" He quirked a brow, sitting up a little and making all those muscles . . . *activate.*

Who needs that many abs?

"Shadow?" he pressed, the hint of a laugh in his voice.

She was caught out, and she knew it. "Ugh, fine. We can share, but there are rules." Stomping over to the bed, she pulled the pillow out from beneath his head along with two others and lined them up in the middle.

"Do you really think a pillow is going to stop me if I had a mind to hold you?" he asked, his voice low and teasing.

The throb between her legs became more insistent, and she had to fight hard to keep from returning his playful smile. "It will if you know what's good for you. Any part of you touches any part of me in the night, I'm breaking it off." She eyed his crotch meaningfully. "So I'd recommend you keep to your side of the bed."

His smirk turned to a baleful glower as he protectively cupped his lap. "What happens when you get cold and end up being the one reaching out to cuddle me?"

"Never going to happen, Butcher."

"You sure about that, kitten?" His voice dropped in a delicious taunt. "I've made a liar of you before."

Her heart gave a little flutter. She may not remember the occasion in question, but she had no trouble believing it was true. Still, this was one battle she refused to lose. Leaning down until their noses all but touched, she matched his soft croon, "There's only one way that scenario is ever going to play out, Ronan."

"Mmm . . . what's that? I'm all ears."

His eyes dipped down to her lips as she whispered, "In. Your. Dreams." She pulled back, not bothering to hide her laugh when he had to blink a few times to refocus on her face. "I'd rather die of frostbite than turn to you for warmth."

"You say that now. Wait until you're in danger of your tits falling off. What a tragedy that would be. There's a shortage of perfect breasts, you know. Would be a shame to lose yours."

"I'll take my chances," she said with a huff of genuine laughter. Grumpy Ronan was fun to poke, and sexy, swoony Ronan made her decidedly hot, but playful Ronan? He was damn near irresistible. She couldn't let him realize it, or he'd use it to his advantage and wear her down . . . more than he already had.

Adopting her usual waspish tone, she snapped, "Close your eyes. I don't want you playing Peeping Tom while I undress."

He groaned. "You're no fun."

She made her eyes as big as she could before batting them at him, her voice dripping with sarcasm as she pressed her palm to her chest. "Whatever gave you the idea that I would be? My talent for killing people or my love of a good knock-knock joke?"

Ronan snickered but surprised her with the intensity of his answer. "It's the way you come alive when you take shots at me. All fiery eyes, fierce words, and heaving breaths." He gave an excited little shiver, matching her own exaggerated pantomime. "Reeks of a good time."

She swallowed, scrambling to regain her unaffected posturing. "Ah, so the killing people, then. Figures you'd be a masochist. Now, cover your eyes so I can get these pants off." He waggled his brows. "I didn't mean it like—" She sighed heavily. "Will you just close your damn eyes?"

With a pout, he pressed a hand to his eyes only to immediately spread his fingers, his ice-blue gaze unrepentantly meeting hers.

"Ronan, darkness help me, I will blindfold you if I have to." The threat would have sounded better if it lacked the undercurrent of laughter.

"Now you're just being cruel. Don't make promises you aren't going to keep, kitten."

Thankfully he covered his gaze as he said it, so he missed the way her knees wobbled and her whole body flushed. Why did he have this effect on her? No one else had ever turned her insides liquid with a few well-aimed comments. But he did it without even trying.

Quickly pulling off her boots and wiggling out of her leather pants, Shadow eyed her shirt and decided it was best to leave it on. It fell to about her thigh, covered the majority of her bruises, and would give her a little protection in case someone got handsy in the middle of the night. She was going to have to figure out what to do about clothing come the morning, though. There was only so long a single pair of pants and a tunic were going to last at sea.

Crawling beneath the blankets on her side of the bed, she softly called, "Okay, I'm decent."

He peeked over at her from his side of the pillow wall she'd erected. "Hmm, I don't know about that. I'd say you're practically indecent."

She reached out and grabbed a pillow, thwacking him in the face with it before returning it to the lineup and rolling onto her side. "Goodnight, Ronan," she singsonged, lifting the protective glass casing and blowing out the candle beside her bed.

"Goodnight, killer."

His disgruntled tone had her shoulders shaking with quiet laughter. If he wasn't so aggravating, he might have made a great friend. Sometimes, when she forgot she hated him, she quite enjoyed his company.

You don't hate him, Shadow. And you don't want to be his friend.

Tucking her hand under her ear, she frowned into the darkness. It was rare for her instincts to be so divided. Her gut told her Ronan was safe, and there was no denying she was attracted to him, but she couldn't ignore the instinct to keep him at arm's length either.

Just once, she wished her heart, mind, and body would align. Things would be so much easier if she could just decide whether she wanted to fuck him or kill him.

Fuck him, the perky bitch chirped in the back of her mind. *You definitely want to fuck him.*

Despite her earlier concerns about not falling asleep, she drifted off almost immediately. The still awake part of her brain distantly realized all the back and forth with Ronan had calmed the restlessness that had been hounding her since dinner. She wondered if that had been his intention. If he'd allowed himself to be a sort of punching bag while she worked through her unease.

She wanted to ask him why he bothered. There didn't seem to be anything in it for him, but his steady presence and the sound of his even breaths lured her deeper into sleep.

Everything was peaceful until a familiar seductive voice called out from the void.

"Ah . . . there you are."

Erebos's voice in her mind should have frightened her, but she wasn't capable of drumming up more than a ripple of confusion. *"High Lord?"*

"Oh, yes. Now that I can definitely use."

"What . . . what do you mean?" She looked around, but there was nothing to see. As always, her dreams were nothing more than a hazy mist.

"You've been a naughty girl, Shadow mine. But that's okay. I've got you now."

Sleep no longer felt safe. She wanted to wake up. She wanted . . . Ronan.

"Tell him . . ."

Fear skated along her veins, filling her with icy dread. *"Tell who, what? What am I to say?"* A slight whimper slipped into the question. *"I-I don't understand."*

Silence stretched between them, heavy and thick, the unsettling hush underscored by the erratic beats of her heart until finally he answered.

"Tell him that Death is coming . . . and there'll be no escape."

CHAPTER 12

RONAN

*T*onight had been unexpected for all manner of reasons. Chief among them, the woman lying in bed beside him. Correction—beside the Great Pillow Barricade.

His lips twitched with laughter as he readjusted his position, folding one arm back behind his head and bringing the hand of the other up to rest lightly on his chest. Big Bad Shadow thought she needed protection from him, which she'd created in the form of downy bricks stacked along the middle of the bed. Considering all the other options available to her, it wasn't exactly a bold choice. And given their rather tumultuous relationship, that was a massive win in his book.

Actually, in many ways, the night as a whole felt like a resounding success. Which was as startling a realization as it was welcome. Since she'd avoided him all afternoon, he hadn't known what to expect when she'd walked into the captain's quarters. But even if he had, it wouldn't have prepared him for when—at least for a moment during dinner—it felt as though he'd had her back.

The *real* her.

Her mask of indifference had begun to crack as their hosts impressed and charmed them with stories of their nautical exploits. It fell away entirely not long after when she'd slid him her bread. There was no mistaking it. He'd seen the spark of concern in those beautiful irises blossom into empathy as she studied him. The emotions themselves wouldn't have even registered if not for the fact that the woman had been coming for his throat less than twenty-four hours prior and still couldn't stand the sight of him as recently as this morning.

Finding Shadow after all these years had been one mindfuck after the other. For every step forward, there were at least seven back. But tonight, despite every odd, it started to feel like those backward steps didn't matter. The lost years. Their forgotten history. Erebos's interference. None of it.

Regardless of the obstacles between them, his soul called to hers, coaxing it out from its hiding place and setting it free from its prison.

He'd witnessed the truth of it with his own eyes. Proved his theory to be correct. Their playful bickering over the bed only verified it. The more time they spent together away from the High Lord's influence, the more frequent those flickers of *her* came and the longer they lasted.

One day, hopefully soon, they'd break through the last of the bonds holding her captive, and it wouldn't just be a flicker he'd see but a full-on blaze.

His heart ached with longing at the thought. He missed her, maybe more now than before he set foot on Empyrean soil. Before she was just a memory, her edges softened by time and fanciful remembering. But now she was real. A living, breathing representation of everything he wanted, and it killed him to lie next to her and not touch her. Especially with the taste of her fresh in his mind.

He swallowed a groan, his body reacting instantly to the reminder of his fingers sheathed in her slick heat while his mouth devoured her cries.

Fuck. Me.

He might have continued torturing himself with his reminiscence, but he didn't much enjoy the thought of silently fucking his fist, and that was the only way he'd find any semblance of relief from his pent-up need. Even then, it would be a poor substitute for the friction his body craved, and there was no chance of pretending any differently when Shadow was right there reminding him of everything he was missing.

Like the masochist she'd claimed he was, he turned his head to steal another look at her. She was alluring, even in sleep. Her hair shimmered like strands of starlight across the pillow, the sweet curves of her body begging for his touch. If not for the hitch in her breathing followed by a nearly inaudible whimper, he might not have realized something was amiss.

"Shadow?" he called softly. She didn't respond, unless the slight jerk of her body counted. He rolled fully to his side, pushing up onto his arm to get a better look at her. "You awake?"

All he got this time was a distressed moan.

Who would have thought the realm's deadliest blade had trouble sleeping? It was almost sweet, humanizing her in a way he would have thought impossible, but there was something about the deep line etched between her brows that gave him pause.

She looked tormented.

He reached out, intent on waking her, but then her words floated through his mind, and he hesitated, hand hovering just over her shoulder. *'Any part of you touches any part of me in the night, I'm breaking it off.'*

"Is this a test? Are you tricking me into touching you, so you'll have an excuse to break my fingers?"

He wouldn't put it past her. It seemed like just the sort of trick she'd play on him. But then she cried out, and her terror sliced through his heart. There was no faking that sound. He'd only heard its like on battlefields and in sickrooms.

"Shadow? Shadow, love, wake up." He grasped her shoulder, giving her a quick shake. She didn't react beyond another low moan. "Sweetheart, you're dreaming. Wake up."

"Ronan," she sobbed, limbs thrashing as she rolled onto her back. "It's coming."

There was no time to process the fact she was dreaming about him, or that she was trying to deliver a warning. He was too focused on pulling her from her nightmare.

Knocking the pillows to the floor, he moved until Shadow's body was cradled in his lap, his arms banding around her and holding fast. Dropping his lips to her ear, he began murmuring reassurances, "Concentrate on my voice, kitten. I'm right here. You're safe. Nothing will happen to you, I promise. I won't let anything hurt you."

As she settled into his hold, he started to believe it was working. But then she screamed, jackknifing up and cracking her forehead against his jaw.

"Motherf—" he cursed as pain exploded up the side of his face. Tears blurred in his eyes, but he blinked them away, stubbornly pushing past the throb to focus on the woman in his arms. "Shadow, are you all right?"

"Ow!" she gasped, collapsing in on herself.

He couldn't see her face, but he didn't need any help processing the splash of water on his skin. She was crying, and he knew it wasn't from the pain. Whatever had plagued her sleep had been terrifying enough to reduce one of the strongest women he'd ever met to tears. He couldn't begin to imagine what it would take to send her over the edge.

He shifted, pulling her up with him until her face was tucked into his neck, her legs draped across his lap. "Shh, it's all right, sweetheart. I've got you. You're safe."

"R-Ronan," she hiccupped, her fingers digging into his skin as she clung to him.

That alone would have told him everything he needed to know. Shadow wasn't the kind of woman to seek comfort in another. Doing so now only emphasized how deeply distressed she was.

He lifted a hand, cupping her cheek as his fingers tangled in her hair. He brushed a kiss against her forehead, whispering, "I'm here. I'm right here. I'm not going anywhere."

"He . . . he told me—" She broke off, struggling to catch her breath.

"It's all right. Just breathe with me. In . . ." He sucked in a breath and held it, beyond grateful when she matched his rhythm. "And out . . . .Good. That's good, kitten. And again." He continued breathing with her until she seemed to have gotten herself mostly under control. "Now, start at the beginning. Who was talking to you?"

She pulled away to blink up at him. "I . . . I don't remember."

"Do you remember what he said?"

Her tongue darted out to wet her lips, and she gave him a stilted nod. "I do. He . . . he said it's coming." A shudder racked her body. "For you."

He stiffened, his body bracing for attack. It took considerable effort to keep his voice even as he asked, "What's coming?"

"Death."

Whatever he'd been expecting her to say, it certainly wasn't that. Now was hardly the time to launch a full-scale investigation, no matter how badly he wanted to pump her for answers. She was in no state for it. Instead, he reeled in the instinctive need to negate the threat and focused on comforting the woman still trembling in his arms.

"Well . . . that's hardly a surprise."

"W-what?" she sniffled, pulling back to look up at him.

He forced a shrug. "Death comes for us all eventually. I accepted that long ago." She opened and closed her mouth, finally huffing out a disbelieving laugh. Taking that as a good sign, he let instinct guide him as he added, "You know, if you changed your mind about wanting a cuddle, you could have just asked. This all seems a rather extreme way of going about it."

"I . . . that's not what . . . you—" she sputtered, body squirming against his.

He had to fight a moan at the delicious friction that created, so close to what he'd been fantasizing about only minutes prior. Tightening his arms, he leaned back, pulling her with him until they were both lying down. "I know. Only teasing. But I got you to stop crying."

She went still, her body stiff against his for a full heartbeat before she melted into him, holding onto him a little tighter and making no move to pull away. "I don't know what came over me. It felt so real." Her voice was soft and tinged with embarrassment.

The last thing he wanted was for her to feel a second's shame. He only wanted her to know with absolute certainty that he would protect her against any foe. "I will *always* have your back, Shadow. Against monsters real or imaginary."

A puff of damp air washed over his chest. "Thank you, Ronan."

"You don't need to thank me, kitten."

"But I do. I . . ." She hesitated, and he held his breath, silently begging her to finish the thought while he gently ran his palm up and down her spine. "I've never had someone look out for me before. It feels . . . nice."

Nice was a far cry from all the things he wanted her to say, but he'd take it. He'd take it and fucking run with it. "You do now."

She was quiet for so long, he didn't think she was going to say anything else until a whispered, "So do you," reached his ears.

Throat tight, he squeezed his eyes shut and forced out a shuddering breath.

There it was. More proof. Another glimmer.

Hope.

CHAPTER 13

RONAN

*S*hadow's warning still echoed through his mind hours later. The haunted, hollow cast of her voice only added to the menacing nature of her message.

Death was coming—for him.

Well, it wouldn't be the first time. He'd been courting it for years.

That wasn't what had him standing out here staring at the horizon while his thoughts chased each other like a dog after its tail. It was her forewarning. Messages like that, sent through dreams . . . it reeked of the divine.

But why would the Mother send Camille to save him, only to turn around and place him on the path of certain death? It didn't make any sense.

Nothing did these days.

He rubbed at the back of his neck, the skin there warm and stinging. He'd been standing in the sun too long, watching the waves break as the ship cut through them. It was another calm day at sea, the breeze steady, only a few clouds in sight. The water was jewel-bright, and it was easy to make out the silvery glint of fish darting beneath its surface. He squinted, peering a little harder at an inky stain that seemed to be unfurling from the depths.

"Many a man's gone mad, chasing after the horizon."

The voice startled him, making his heart lurch and pulse race. He spun around, finding both the ship's quarter and sailing masters standing there, staring at him with amused expressions. Bronn tossed him a canteen, his smile holding an edge of mischief. "Didn't mean to frighten you. Here, it looks like you need this more than I do."

Ronan caught it, taking off the cap and drinking greedily. "Thank you." Once he slaked his thirst, he recapped it and threw it back.

"You seem troubled, Ronan," Tiny said, the minotaur's dark eyes glinting brightly behind the spectacles resting atop the bridge of his nose.

Not wanting to get into the messy tangle of his thoughts, he opted for a safer and far less revealing answer. "Thought I saw something." He gestured back out to sea, where his attention had been caught by the oily-looking shadow slithering in the water. He frowned, realizing it was still there, but closer than before. A blot of darkness marring the otherwise pristine pool of blue.

Bronn clapped him on the shoulder. "Classic side effect."

"Side effect?" he parroted, struggling to tear his gaze away from the anomaly he'd found. "What do you mean?"

"This always happens after a night spent listening to stories such as ours. Someone inevitably starts spotting monsters lurking in the deep the next day."

Tiny chuckled alongside him. "It's true, I'm afraid. We should have warned you last night."

Ronan frowned, finding it hard to dismiss what he'd seen with his own eyes. He didn't consider himself particularly suggestible; then again, he'd never traveled these seas before. He had no way of knowing what was usual or, conversely, unusual. For all he knew, the darkness was an illusion caused by the undertow.

He cast a final wary glance over his shoulder, the dark patch so close it almost looked like they were sailing over it. Which should be impossible since it was coming from the opposite direction.

Before Ronan could mention it, Bronn started speaking again. "There's no end to the dangers that roam in these waters, Ronan.

There's a reason most don't travel this far south. The Sea of Souls has more than earned its name from the thousands it has claimed. But you and your assassin could not be in finer hands. Tiny here knows these waters like he was born in them. Never come across a finer chart reader in all my days.

"And the captain isn't just some bonny figurehead. She's a skilled navigator. Easily the best Empyria has ever seen. We wouldn't follow her otherwise. It's no easy feat being the captain of the *Revenge*. The only way to claim the honor is to earn it—by blood and deed.

"So trust me when I tell you, even if we were to run afoul of some bloodthirsty creature, Calypso and her men know what to do. We will see you safe to your destination. You have my word."

It was a hell of a speech. One he had no doubt Bronn wholeheartedly believed. But it did nothing to ease the prickles of foreboding racing down his nape.

And when it came right down to it, believing something didn't actually make it true.

SHADOW

SHADOW PLUCKED at her borrowed clothes, eyeing the colored fabrics and feeling like an impostor. As she walked out of Calypso's room, she couldn't recall ever wearing anything other than black, gray, and the occasional white.

I guess there really is a first time for everything . . .

She could have borrowed something from one of the men onboard, but no one besides the captain was close to her size. So when the much more adventurous dresser laid out some options, it was either step out of her comfort zone or put back on the same stained garments she'd been wearing—and sweating in—for the last few days. Desperation beat out personal aesthetics, which was how she found herself returning to the deck clad in a vibrantly embroidered cream silk shirt, plum-colored breeches, and thigh-high heeled boots in the same shade.

Shadow was still looking down, readjusting the buckle of her belt, which is why she didn't see the towering wall of brooding male heading her way until she bounced off it.

Please don't be him. Please don't be him. Please, if anyone out there is listening, don't be him.

The moment she and Ronan shared last night ranked among the most important and meaningful in her life. It was the first and only time she could remember letting her guard down with anyone since Erebos found her. But vulnerable Shadow had made a full and hasty retreat with the dawn. In the dark it had been easy to lean on Ronan, to admit things aloud she'd barely even acknowledged in her own mind. However, in the soft light of the early morning, what felt safe became all too real and overwhelming.

So she'd run.

As far and fast as she could on a boat. Which was how she'd ended up outside the captain's door before the sun had fully risen, begging for something to wear. Much to the other woman's amusement.

Emotions now safely locked away where they belonged, Shadow lifted her chin and braced for a confrontation she'd hoped to avoid. Not forever . . . just another eighty years or so.

She'd only just managed to lift her eyes to a muscular chest when a shrill chirp answered her prayers. Her breath left her in a gusty exhale as her head shot the rest of the way up, Buttercup's inquisitive squawk as much a relief as it was a surprise.

"Jagger!"

The boson reached out, steadying her as he let out a grunt she translated to mean, "You all right?"

"Sorry," she blurted, giving him an embarrassed shake of her head. "I should have been watching where I was going. I'm usually much more graceful, not to mention aware of my surroundings, but it's taking me a while to find my sea legs with the rocking, and . . ."

His lips twitched, and she realized she was babbling.

"Sorry," she repeated lamely.

He gave her shoulder a squeeze and tilted his head toward the stairs behind him. This time she guessed he was asking whether she was going up on deck.

Shadow nodded. "Thought I might see if there's something I can do to help. I'm not used to being idle."

Buttercup trilled in what Shadow hoped was approval and not the avian version of derision.

Jagger dipped his chin and then swept out a hand for her to go around him, so she did. But his enormous frame made that difficult in the cramped quarters, and she couldn't help but laugh, feeling as though they were in the midst of some sort of partner dance but neither of them knew the steps.

Once she'd squeezed past, she lifted her hand in farewell, only for him to frown and gesture for her to start walking.

"But you just came from this way," she said, her brow furrowing.

He nodded again, his expression seeming to indicate that she was stupid for stating the obvious.

"I know I was a little clumsy, but I promise I don't need an esco—oh!"

Before she could even finish saying the word escort, the entire ship jerked sharply, sending her flying into the wall. Jagger remained upright, arms out on either side, knees slightly bent, but she was sure it was only experience with rogue waves that kept him from crashing into her.

Heart hammering beneath her ribs, she pushed herself upright. "Is that norm—ahhh!"

Another shudder beneath her feet knocked her back. Jagger's lightning-fast reaction was the only thing that kept her standing. He reached out, fisting her shirt and tugging her forward. She was going to ignore the fact that his fingertips ran nearly the full length of her cleavage because his intention had been to help, not grope. Still, she was relieved as soon as he let her go.

Before she could ask what in the darkness was going on, shouts from above reached them.

"Sound the alarm!"

Jagger jumped into action. He flung an arm out, opening a door and shoving her toward it with his other hand.

"If you're thinking I'm going to stay down here and hide instead of fight, you've got me seriously confused with someone else."

One side of his mouth curled up. Instead of wasting time debating the point, he pulled free one of the twin cutlasses from the scabbard that sat low on his hips. "Here," he rasped.

She returned his grin and pulled out two of the daggers she'd tucked into a special belt that hid them along her lower back. "I'm all set."

His laugh was a breathy rumble. "Suit yourself."

Buttercup flew ahead, likely scouting so Jagger's steps would be sure as they made their way up the stairs. With each one, the panicked cries of the crew only grew louder and more frequent. It didn't take more than a single glance to see why.

A gasp was ripped from her as she tried to make sense of the chaos on deck. Two thick black snakes . . . no, not snakes. Though they slithered and moved with the overly articulated grace of a serpent, they were the size of fallen oak trees.

Then the rest of the creature rose from beneath the sea, cresting up over the side of the ship, and her brain emptied of all coherent thought. Suddenly her daggers were feeling woefully inadequate.

Shadow didn't have the word for the monster before her . . . but Jagger did.

"Lusca."

"Wait, that was real?"

He didn't acknowledge the question. Why bother when the answer was literally in front of her?

Faster than should have been possible given its size, one of the massive tentacles lifted and slammed down on the deck, causing the *Revenge* to groan under the impact. Wood splintered and cracked, the ship shaking as crew members were flung off the sides. Now the shudders and jerks that sent her toppling made a lot more sense.

"Man the cannons!" Calypso shouted, her voice steady amidst the fray. Shadow could just make out the fierce cast of her face. She didn't look scared; she looked pissed. There was something comforting about the captain's lack of fear, and Shadow immediately began breathing easier.

"Aye, captain," Bronn and several others called back once they were in place.

"Fire at will!"

Shadow scanned the line of cannons, searching for someone that might need her assistance. She was no expert, but she could follow orders. When her eyes landed on a familiar redhead loading the cannon closest to the creature's amorphous head, her heart tripped over itself. Her sudden terror was so potent and all-consuming, she could hardly draw breath around it. Especially when two more tentacles drew up from the water. One by him, the other right beside her.

"Ronan, look out!" she yelled, trying to alert him to the danger. But her cry had the opposite effect. Instead of spotting the glistening black arm lined with horrific maroon suckers, he turned to her.

All the color drained from his face.

"Behind you!" she screamed, but he was frantically pointing behind *her*.

"Get down!" he shouted back.

But there was nowhere for her to run. As one, both tentacles snapped forward, reminding her of a striking serpent as they went for their targets.

One curled around Ronan's waist, tugging him up and back straight off the ship right as the first of the cannons fired.

"No!"

Her heart lodged in her throat as she watched the cannonballs sail through the air, narrowly missing Ronan and the tentacle as it whipped past.

She was so focused on him that she wasn't paying any attention to the very real danger heading for her.

"Fucking move!" Jagger snapped, his voice holding more power than she'd heard from him as he bowled into her, knocking her to the sea-sprayed boards.

Buttercup let out an ear-piercing shriek as the tentacle meant for her collected their master instead.

What transpired next happened so quickly, Shadow wouldn't have believed it possible if she hadn't witnessed it with her own eyes. The tentacle holding Jagger curled back, preparing to reel him into the watery depths. As it arced up, Buttercup flew straight for it, their tiny body transforming in a kaleidoscope of sparks. The sparks twisted and spun, creating a massive fireball in the sky. The ball of light and flame collapsed on itself before rapidly expanding back out.

In the wake of the explosion, a huge firebird remained.

But that wasn't Buttercup's only trick. The cocoon of flame that allowed their metamorphosis wasn't just a pretty light show. It was a weapon in its own right. Everywhere the sparks landed caught fire. The ship, its sail, the deck, and . . . the monster.

The enormous beast let out a bellow that made the ship quake, sending mighty waves hurling up and crashing onto the deck. The benefit of that was that the waves put out the flames. The downside was even more men were pulled into the unforgiving sea.

Opening their beak, Buttercup spewed out a jet of molten flame aimed directly at the tentacle still holding their master captive. The flame seared the flailing limb, cleaving it in two, triggering another wail from the Lusca and sending both halves down to the sea.

The phoenix swooped, wings spread wide and ready to catch the man they'd fought so beautifully to protect.

Shadow pushed to shaky feet, relieved that saving her hadn't spelled death for the boson. Unfortunately, the same couldn't be said for Ronan.

As she spun, searching for the tentacle that had captured him. Neither could be seen.

Her stomach clenched, dread settling between her ribs like a fist-shaped stone.

Just like so many others, Ronan had been lost to the sea.

CHAPTER 14

SHADOW

There was no time for hesitation. No time to second guess or worry about what came next. Instinct was in charge, and it screamed at her to act. Now. While there was still a chance.

The possibility it was already too late wasn't even a consideration.

Shadow sprinted across the deck, stumbling a bit as the ground rocked beneath her, but her panic must have given her wings because it felt as though she flew across to the other side. She scrambled up, ignoring the hand on her arm and Bronn's voice at her ear.

"Shadow, don't! It's a death sentence!"

Hair whipping past her face, she raised to standing, arms lifting above her head as she prepared to jump. "Death and I are old friends. If it's time for the Father to reap my soul, so be it."

She wasn't sure where the words came from. She wasn't sure of much of anything as she dove off the ship, a sudden tilt of the starboard side launching her up and ruining what might have otherwise been a flawless swan dive.

Teeth clenched, she opened her eyes as soon as she broke through the surface. The sting of salt was nearly unbearable, and she worried the resulting tears might hinder her sight. As it was, the tears didn't make a difference because there was barely any light to see by. The sun should have penetrated at least a little, but the Lusca appeared to have been crafted from the very heart of darkness. Its inky body consumed the feeble rays, casting everything around it in gloomy shadow.

But that wasn't the only abnormality. The water was far cooler than she expected given the time of year, and it pricked at her skin like thousands of tiny knives as it pulled her under. Because there was no mistaking it, the sea *was* tugging her down. She wasn't swimming as much as going in the direction it insisted.

The anomalies on their own wouldn't have troubled her, but taken together, along with the presence of the gigantic sea monster, and there was no ignoring the overwhelming sense of *otherness*. This didn't feel like a normal attack. It was too convenient for one—what were the odds a Lusca would strike the morning after she first learned of their existence? Though she supposed she could explain that away as coincidence since the stories had to come from somewhere.

What could not be explained was the sensation of being watched. The creature's eyes were on either side of its bulbous head . . . which was still above the surface. Yet as she moved deeper into the abyss, an electric tingle ran along the back of her neck and spine. And it only grew worse the farther into the depths she was pulled.

How could that be when the Lusca could no longer see her? Unless it wasn't the Lusca watching her, but something else.

Perhaps the very thing surrounding her and drawing her in.

The darkness.

Shadow wasn't used to defending herself against something without a face—without a shape—but as soon as the thought took root, she recognized the truth of it. The dark was not only sentient, it was the true threat, making the Lusca a distraction. A monstrously effective one, but a distraction nonetheless.

She needed to find Ronan and get them both as far away from here as possible. Even if all she found was a corpse, she felt obligated not to leave him in a watery grave.

Why she felt obligated was a question for another day.

When her lungs started to burn, she knew she was running out of time. Thankfully her eyes had begun to adjust to the dim waters, and it was no longer impossible to differentiate the Lusca's individual tentacles.

The writhing black limbs were all empty.

He wasn't here.

She craned her neck side to side, becoming desperate in her search. *Why* wasn't he here? Her throat flexed convulsively, her lungs compulsively seeking the oxygen she was denying them. But she couldn't leave. Not without him.

Little lights started to explode at her periphery, a signal from her body that time was up. A scream of denial tore up her throat, but it never left her lips. She flipped, trying to reverse her direction, but no matter how hard she kicked, she sank deeper.

Is this really how it ends? Alone . . . in the dark?

Only it wasn't dark. Not anymore. A ball of light streaked through the water, lighting up the nearly black water like the night sky on solstice. The closer it came, the brighter and larger it grew. Her brain suffered from the lack of air, and it was hard to think, let alone force her limbs to continue functioning. But there were enough synapses firing to identify the creature shooting through the water toward her.

Buttercup.

The phoenix wasn't done with rescues, it would seem.

Water slipped into Shadow's nose, and she coughed, which only drew more of the salty liquid into her mouth, but then the firebird was there, reaching for her. Shadow blamed her oxygen-starved brain for the hallucinations she was so clearly seeing because Buttercup was no longer a bird at all, but a person.

Protector, her brain supplied. She could think of no other word to attribute to the magical shapeshifter as the androgynous figure took her face in their hands, dozens of tiny bubbles flowing from their lips as they sealed their mouth over hers.

Shadow was helpless to do anything but clutch onto Buttercup. She took in their long strands of flame-colored hair, piercing blue eyes, and the way their luminous skin seemed to be lit from within as her lungs gratefully accepted the life-restoring air they passed to her.

"He needs you, Forsaken. Go to him. Save the one whose soul calls to yours before it's too late."

"I don't know where he is." She wasn't aware of sending the thought. It just floated through her mind, and she could only assume the protector heard her because they took her shoulders in their palms and spun her around before giving a little shove. *"There."*

And he was. The man she'd come after, the one she'd been so intent on saving, was right there. Floating face down. Still. Lifeless.

Her heart stuttered.

No.

No!

I can't be too late.

She kicked hard, swimming to his limp body as fast as she could. The lure of the darkness aided her, still eager to draw her down. As soon as she reached the warrior, she wrapped her arms around his muscular torso and did her best to pull up. They didn't move much at all until Buttercup grasped him on the other side.

"Kick, Forsaken. Do not stop until you reach the shore. I will not let you drown."

Shadow could do nothing but obey. She scissored her legs as if her life depended on it, or, she supposed, Ronan's.

Even with Buttercup's aid, it was slow going moving through the dark. Her body was weighed down, and it soon felt like she was attempting to swim through sludge rather than the sea. Her lungs screamed in protest, barely healed from their first bout of deprivation, but she couldn't allow herself to doubt they'd make it.

Just as her lungs began to seize a second time, they broke free of the surface. Clinging to Ronan's limp form, she gasped for air. "Th-thank you," she panted, the words nearly impossible to form around her heaving breaths.

It was impossible to look at Buttercup straight on, their luminosity blinding without the suppressive effect of the darkness. Instead of answering, the protector shifted once more, returning to their phoenix form and letting off a series of soft trills Shadow interpreted as an invitation to climb on. She couldn't help but wonder why the protector would abandon their means of direct communication, and her confusion must have been on her face because the protector spoke in her mind once more.

"Using my power in this realm is a far greater drain, so I am selective in its use."

That made sense. Looking from Buttercup to Ronan's floating form, she shook her head, still blinking salt water from her eyes. "I don't . . . I can't leave him."

"No one asked you to. Just grasp onto me, Forsaken. I will take care of the rest."

Swallowing, she simply nodded her agreement. She was in no position to question the offer of aid. Perhaps once she was safe, she could afford to be more discerning, but for now, the only order of business was getting Ronan on dry land . . . and maybe napping for a dozen years or so.

Buttercup twisted in the air, shaking their tail feathers in invitation. *"Hold on tight. I will tow you to shore."*

"But that will take—"

"No time at all. Do not let go—of me or your mate."

The title sent shockwaves through her very core. "Mate?" Shadow rasped, her throat burning from the excess of air it attempted to pull into her lungs.

She would have sworn she heard soft snickers float through her head. But that would mean all of this was real, and she wasn't fully convinced she wasn't still aboard the *Revenge* having the dream of a lifetime.

"Just take hold."

Lifting one arm out of the water, she grabbed a fistful of Buttercup's surprisingly sturdy feathers, keeping her other arm banded around Ronan's thick chest. He hadn't so much as twitched since they'd come up to the surface, but she couldn't think about that right now. The only way to keep the fear at bay was to focus on getting out of the ocean. She'd worry about him after.

As soon as her hand was secured, Buttercup took off, the tips of their fiery wings causing steam to rise whenever they made contact with the water. Behind them the Lusca was still engaged with the *Revenge*, though the pirate ship had split in two, both bow and stern sinking quickly into the depths below.

There wasn't time to mourn for the vessel or its crew, but her heart ached regardless. She prayed Calypso and her men would survive.

"Why me?" The thought left her of its own volition.

"You as opposed to . . ."

"The rest of the crew."

She couldn't seem to do more than hold on as Buttercup towed her and Ronan, the conversation taking place in her mind both surreal and a wonderful way to ignore how Ronan didn't seem to be breathing.

"What makes you think it's either or?"

"The part where they're going down with the ship and you're choosing to save me."

The rocky shore finally came into view, and a shiver of relief worked itself over her.

"Destiny has marked you, Forsaken. It is not your time."

Shadow's grip fell slack at the unexpected words, and she almost fell, but a harsh squawk had her readjusting her hold. They were so close now, and she didn't want to swim the rest of the way.

"W-what do you mean?"

"Worry not about the path, Forsaken. The stars will lead you where you need to go. Trust yourself to recognize the way and the man in your arms to guide you."

"But—"

There was no way to finish the question bubbling up because the tips of her toes were scraping against the sand and Buttercup was no longer towing them as much as flying ahead. Shadow collected Ronan's waterlogged form, using everything she had left to half carry, half drag him to the sandy beach. She was tripping over her feet, the crashing waves more than she could handle once they reached her thighs.

"Come on. Almost there," she grunted to herself.

But her poor body had reached its limits. Between the fire in her lungs, the burn in her limbs, and the lingering ill effects of the abuse she'd already sustained, the best she could do was drop to her knees. Even so, she refused to give up. Rolling onto her butt, she took a fistful of Ronan's shirt in each hand and dug her heels into the sand. A scream tore from her throat, her body trembling as she inched them both to safety.

Ronan still hadn't reacted in any way.

Once they were a safe distance from the lapping waves, she let go of him, chest heaving and limbs quaking from exhaustion. Now that they were out of the water—and away from the darkness—there was no ignoring the panic that had taken up residence within her. Ronan had been in that water far longer than her without the benefit of Buttercup's resuscitating air.

Her eyelids fluttered, threatening to close. She could no longer see or hear Buttercup and had no way of knowing if the phoenix was still trailing her or if the protector had gone back to rescue others from the ship.

"Ronan." She cupped his face, turning it toward her. "Please. Wake up." There was so much more she should do, that she should say, but she was so damned tired. It took more than she had to keep her head up, her eyes open. "Ro . . . nan . . ."

His name was barely more than a rasped plea as her eyes rolled back in her head and she lost consciousness.

EREBOS

THE FATHER of Dreams sat back on his throne, lips twisted in a cruel smile. Many might see today as a loss, but for him, it was an undisputed success. He'd found her, just as he planned. And now he had her trapped in one place. It was almost too easy. He'd forgotten how much fun could be had in the chase.

So why make it quick? Why not draw it out and play with his pet a while, make it an experience to savor? Why not let her believe she'd won? There was nothing as delicious as destroying the last flicker of hope within a soul. He intended to be there when it happened, to revel in the moment when darkness utterly obliterates the light.

Sinking into the familiar dreamscape, he crooned, "Come out, come out, wherever you are."

As it had been ever since he warped it, there was nothing to see in this dreamscape but a dense shroud of mist. But that was no matter. He didn't need to see her to know she was there. To taste her fear and deliver his message.

"Do not think you've bested me, Shadow mine. You live because I will it. So run. Hide and lick your wounds. Believe the danger is past. It will only make it sweeter when I catch you. If I'm going to hunt, I want to ensure the experience is worthy of my effort.

"You know better than any other that I'm just getting started."

CHAPTER 15

RONAN

*T*he gulls registered first, their soft caws the perfect accompaniment to the crash of the waves. Next was the gentle breeze, carrying the scent of sea, sun, and the barest hint of burning wood. Before he could question it, the extreme difference in temperature hit him. His back was chilled and damp, but his front side was warm to the point sweat trickled from his temples. Or was that salt water?

Blinking open his eyes, Ronan slowly sat up. A low moan fell from his lips, the vibration from the sounds making him wince. His throat and lungs burned as if someone had reached inside him and clawed them both to ribbons. Almost worse was the sand. He was covered in it, the gritty black motes itchy and unbearable.

What in the Mother's name?

Slapping it off his arms and chest, he tried to piece together how he'd ended up here. The answer arrived in a series of terrifying images.

Cannon fire.

Tentacles.

Lusca.

He looked immediately to the horizon, searching for the *Revenge,* but it was empty save a few pillowy clouds and one hungry gull. Next he turned to the obsidian sands of the beach. Interested only in Shadow's motionless figure no more than an arm's length away from him, his frantic gaze barely took in anything of the turquoise waters, tropical trees, or distant cliffs. The long strands of her pale hair were strewn across her face, her hand outstretched as if reaching for him.

Nothing about her sleep seemed natural or peaceful. He couldn't even determine whether she was breathing—which should have been easy given the way her still damp clothes molded to her body.

Ronan scrambled to her side, sand flying as he clawed his way across the short distance. Grasping her shoulders, he shook her and cried out her name in a panicked rush. "Shadow. Come on, sweetheart, you have to wake up for me. Shadow . . . Shadow, please!"

He continued to shake her, drawing up one of her hands and pressing his fingertips to the inside of her wrist, barely breathing until he detected the faintest tattoo against his fingers. Instead of relief, all he tasted was fear.

If she was truly well, she'd be alert, wouldn't she? What if she hit her head? What if she'd inhaled too much sea water? Or maybe it was poison . . . who knew what that creature was capable of?

Only one of those scenarios involved a solution he could actually provide. If water remained in her lungs, he could help flush it out. Driven only by the need to do something, he didn't stop to think it through. Instead, he moved them both into position, tipping back her chin, linking his fingers together and pressing the heel of his palm against her sternum.

"One, two, three, four," he counted under his breath as he began a series of compressions.

There was a very strong possibility he was overreacting, but Ronan couldn't get the sight of that monstrous tentacle swooping toward her out of his mind. Until her gaze was on his and one of her silky insults had been aimed his way, he wouldn't be satisfied she was out of harm's reach. So if there was anything he could do to ensure it, even if there was only a slim chance it would work, he had to try.

Finished with the compressions, he plugged her nose with one hand and leaned down to expel the air from his lungs into hers. At first there was no reaction, not that he'd expected one. He'd seen this method used before, and oftentimes it took several rounds before the person reacted. But before Ronan could resume compressions, the body beneath him shifted, stiffening and then almost immediately relaxing. Her lips beneath his were no longer lax but trembling slightly before firmly applying their own pressure. Then her fingers threaded through his hair, not pushing him away but pulling him closer, as she let out the sweetest sigh of surrender.

He was so stunned by the change he didn't even register Shadow was kissing him—until she wasn't.

She jerked her face away, chest rising and falling in shallow pants. "What the hell do you think you're doing?"

"Uhh . . ." Mind still filled with the taste of her, it took him a moment to process the question. "Saving you."

Her voice was hoarser than usual as she shoved him off her and sat up. "There you go again, insisting I require saving."

"But . . . you were unconscious."

Her green eyes flicked to his, their combination of jade, amber, and moss so brilliant he nearly lost himself in them. "I hate to break it to you, Ronan. But you didn't save me. I saved you."

"No, you didn't."

"Well, what else would you call me diving in to find your sinking body and dragging it back to shore with my last breath? Having a bit of fun?" She scoffed, shaking her head in disgust. "I don't know why I bothered. I must have suffered from a momentary lapse of sanity. Glad to see I'm now fully recovered."

He was still hung up on the part where she'd just admitted to coming after him. *Willingly.*

"You really did that? For me?"

She wouldn't meet his gaze. "Buttercup helped."

"Buttercup?"

"Jagger's bird. If not for his protector, we would have still been trapped in the ocean."

He had trouble picturing the little finch being at all useful with a sea rescue, let alone offering assistance, but Shadow distracted him when she pressed a hand to her head and grimaced.

Before he could ask if she was all right, she muttered, "There was something off about it."

"The bird?"

"No, the darkness."

"Besides the giant sea monster trying to eat us, you mean?"

"It didn't want to eat you."

"How do you know? Are you a Lusca expert now?"

She glared at him. "No, but I have a brain and two eyes. It's called critical thinking. Maybe you should try it."

He snorted, crossing his arms over his chest as he demanded, "All right, genius. What did you see with these eyes of yours that convinced you I wasn't about to become the creature's next meal?"

"It let you go."

"Let me go?"

She nodded emphatically. "You were just drifting down deeper into the darkness. If the Lusca wanted to eat you, it would have plopped that fat head of yours straight into its mouth."

The proof that she was not only alive but very much well had him feeling giddy. He couldn't help but goad her further, enjoying this exchange far more than he probably should, given that they were shipwrecked, without supplies, and potentially all alone in unfamiliar territory.

Ronan made to stand, holding out a hand to help her up. She accepted it warily as he said, "Perhaps it merely hunts for sport."

"Sport?"

"You know . . . catch and release?"

She shook her head, but her lips twitched with amusement. "You're impossible."

"That's hardly the worst thing you've called me."

They shared a smile, the breeze picking up and lifting the ends of their hair. For a full heartbeat, they weren't shipwrecked, stranded, or even enemies. They were just a man and woman savoring the undeniable chemistry between them.

"Shadow—" Before he could finish his sentence, a shout rang in the distance, drawing their attention to the far end of the beach.

"Ahoy!" A man shouted, waving his arms and sprinting in their direction. "Ahoy there!"

"Is that . . ."

"Bronn," he confirmed, recognizing the quartermaster.

"Oh, thank the darkness. Last I saw, the ship had split in two, and I worried there wouldn't be any other survivors."

The pirate looked rough for wear, skin smudged with all manner of dirt and grime, one shirt sleeve missing, and several holes peppering his trousers. It was a sharp contrast to how he'd last seen him. "Thank Nereus you're alive! I never thought we'd see you two again," he panted.

"We?" Ronan asked, locking onto the word. "Are there others here as well?"

He nodded, looking solemn. "Only three of us so far. The captain, Jagger, and I. Well, and Buttercup makes four, I suppose. Plus the two of you now."

"The others?" Shadow asked, hesitant.

The look Bronn leveled her with spoke volumes. "No way to know. But I wouldn't lose heart just yet. The crew of the *Revenge* has a way of surviving. I wouldn't be surprised if they were already launching a rescue mission to come find us. Well, Cal, at the very least. A crew needs a captain."

"Do you happen to know where we are?" Ronan asked.

"If Tiny were here, he could tell us. The man could identify an island as easily as a freckle on the back of his hand."

Ronan was fairly certain the minotaur had no freckles to speak of, but since that wasn't the point, he didn't bother.

"Though if I had to guess," Bronn continued, looking around, "I'd say we're on one of Darkhollow's many isles."

"That far south, really?"

"We may not have reached the official border of the territory, but its islands run all along the coast, and I don't know of any other beaches with sand this shade."

Ronan could hardly argue with the explanation. It was as good of one as any.

"Do you know anything about these islands?" Shadow asked.

"What do you mean?"

"Well, are we likely to find food and clean water? Shelter?"

Bronn scrubbed a hand over his chin, eyes taking on a faraway cast as he considered the question before eventually nodding. "It's likely. Smugglers have used these islands for years for their network of caves and relative lack of settlers. We should be able to scavenge easily enough until help arrives."

Ronan didn't love the absence of settlers—that spoke to either hostile terrain or a lack of essential supplies. Though there was something to be said for not accidentally trespassing on someone else's property.

"And if help doesn't arrive?" Shadow prompted.

"Then it looks like we'll be building a raft, doesn't it?" Bronn said with a smirk. Though Ronan couldn't help but note the exhaustion lining his features.

No one was building a raft today.

"Have you three found a place to make camp?" Ronan asked.

Bronn shook his head. "Jagger and Buttercup went scouting, though. We should head back, see what they've found. I don't much enjoy the idea of leaving Caly on her own for long either."

"I'm sure your captain can take care of herself," Shadow said with a smile.

"Without a doubt. Doesn't mean she has to."

When Bronn turned and started back the way he'd come, Ronan nudged her with his elbow. "See, he gets it."

Shadow didn't pretend to miss his meaning. Instead, she rolled her eyes and started jogging backward so she could hold his gaze. "The day I depend on a man to wipe my ass for me is the day I'd gladly die."

He snorted. "There's a fair bit of tasks between taking care of you and wiping your arse."

Shadow smirked, but there was no mistaking the edge to her voice when she shot back, "I'm no one's damsel, Butcher. Nor do I aspire to be. Best you get used to it." She started to turn around, then, thinking better of it, added, "If I invite a man into my bed, it's because I want him there. Not because I need him."

Is that an invitation? Because I gladly accept, kitten.

"There's nothing wrong with needing someone," he called, jogging after her. It was a fact he'd come to begrudgingly accept himself. Life wasn't worth living if you didn't have someone to share it with. He saw the truth of it day in and day out, first with Von and Helena, then with Lucian and Effie. His own lonely existence and resulting downward spiral was a perfect counterpoint to theirs. Needing someone didn't make you weak; it meant you had something worth living for.

"We're going to have to agree to disagree, because the only person I will ever count on is myself."

"That's a lonely way to live," he called as she raced away.

"At least I'll never be disappointed," she shot back.

Ronan ruefully shook his head. Mother, but she wasn't making this easy on him.

Good. She shouldn't.

That way, when he finally won her over, he'd know he earned it. Not just her body, but her heart. And he'd spend the rest of his life rejoicing in the fact that he'd accomplished what no other man could.

He'd earned her love.

CHAPTER 16

SHADOW

*C*alypso sat on a flat rock, head tipped toward the sky, hair spilling down her back, fanning her face with her tricorn.

"I'm surprised you managed to keep hold of that," Shadow murmured as she joined the other woman.

The captain opened one eye and offered a grin. "That's what we refer to as a priority. What's a pirate without her hat?"

Shadow chuckled, taking a seat beside her in the sand. "Forgive me for saying so, but you don't seem very upset, considering."

"Considering my ship has sunk and my crew is lost at sea?" She smiled at Shadow's stricken expression. "I'm not heartless, I simply know my crew, and I know these waters. Some might be truly lost, and I will mourn them deeply. But I have no doubt many, if not most, survived. As for the *Revenge*"—she shrugged prosaically—"it wasn't mine to begin with. Just a placeholder."

Before she could ask what the captain meant, Bronn and Ronan joined them.

"Any news?" Bronn asked.

Calypso shook her head, her brow furrowing slightly, hinting at far deeper emotions than she outwardly expressed. "Jagger and Buttercup haven't returned, but I expect they will soon."

"What makes you think so?" Shadow asked.

Pointing to the sun, Calypso said, "They've already been gone for a couple hours. They would have turned around by now to ensure they didn't get lost or cut off from us. Anything more than an hour's search without the full party in unfamiliar territory is asking for trouble. We'd rather take our chances walking blind than get separated."

Ronan nodded as if he understood exactly what the captain was getting at. Shadow might be more familiar with working alone, but even she appreciated the reasoning behind such protocol. What made less sense was what came after. Camping for one night, even two, was easy. But what would they do longer term?

"What's the plan?"

"What do you mean?" Calypso asked with a slight frown.

"They return, we find a place to make camp, then what? What will we do about food? Long-term shelter? Are we going to search the island in the hopes of seeking out help, or are we waiting for someone to come rescue us?"

Calypso pressed her lips together. "You're not used to taking it easy, are you? Islands are notorious for relaxation and downtime. Perhaps you should see this as an opportunity for a vacation."

"A vacation," Shadow repeated.

"You've never taken one, have you?" Ronan asked, amused.

"What gave me away?"

"How you said the word as if you'd never heard it before."

She crossed her arms, her cheeks and neck suddenly hot. She was aware of the term, obviously, but she hadn't actually participated in one. The idea of downtime with nothing to keep her busy sounded terrible. What was she supposed to *do*?

"And I bet you take them regularly?" she scoffed.

"No," Ronan said, to her surprise. "Never. I can't remember the last time I so much as took a day off."

"Me either," she murmured.

"Did we just find common ground?" Ronan asked with exaggerated shock.

Shadow took a fistful of sand and flung it in his direction, much to the captain and Bronn's amusement.

"Do they remind you of anyone?" Calypso asked beneath her breath.

"Are you referring to us, by chance?" he returned with a fond smile.

"Back when we first met. I could barely stand to breathe the same air as you."

"What changed?" Shadow asked, curious despite the fact that they were mocking her.

"He proved his worth," she said mildly.

"I wore her down," Bronn corrected.

Calypso rolled her eyes.

"Does that mean"—Shadow pointed a finger between them—"are you two . . . together?"

"Nereus, no!" Calypso shouted, her face turning crimson.

Bronn smirked. "Much to Caly's endless disappointment."

"Oh, get over yourself."

"I'd rather get under you."

"You were saying something changed?" Ronan drawled, breaking the tense moment and their narrow-eyed stares.

The pirates shared an embarrassed look and then let out small huffs of laughter. "I guess I was mistaken," Calypso said.

"I thought you never made mistakes," Bronn taunted.

"The occurrence is rare enough as to be negligible."

"Mmm . . . must be nice."

"It is," she shot back.

Shadow risked a glance at Ronan, who was already looking her way. "And I thought we were bad," she muttered.

"I'm almost disappointed in us," he agreed.

"Disappointed? Why?"

He lifted one shoulder in a shrug. "If we can't be the best, what's the point?"

"Is that your way of asking me to take even more shots at you? Because I should warn you to be careful what you ask for."

He waved a hand at Bronn and Caly. "It wouldn't hurt to feel like you were making an actual effort."

A bubble of laughter escaped, and then another. What an absolutely ridiculous thing to say. Especially in light of the day they'd had, but somehow that made it the *perfect* thing to say. All the worry and stress crowding her mind fell to the wayside, along with the weight that came with them. There wasn't room for them with the new emotions Ronan and his playful words evoked.

If *he* wasn't worried, perhaps it was too soon for her to be.

Perhaps she could take Calypso's advice and simply . . . enjoy this unexpected reprieve. The monster hadn't killed them. They hadn't killed each other. In fact, for as long as she could remember knowing him, Ronan had never done a single thing to purposely hurt her.

Eyeing the man in question, she couldn't help but wonder what it might be like if she just . . . stopped. Stopped fighting. Stopped resisting. Just *stopped*.

Maybe it was time to see what they could be when she didn't force herself to treat him like the enemy. Because while what she'd said to him earlier was absolutely true—she would never *need* a man—maybe it was time to allow herself to want one.

"JUST A BIT FURTHER," Jagger grunted, shoving a palm frond out of his way.

Not only had the boson and his bird found a place for the five of them to camp, they'd found the whole survivor's trifecta. Shelter, food, and clean water. They'd discovered one of the smuggler's caves still filled with crates of supplies. Better still, it was connected to a series of freshwater canals.

"Are you sure there aren't booby traps or something we should be on the lookout for?" Shadow asked. It wasn't that she was truly worried about the possibility; she just didn't much enjoy the idea of finding herself strung up by her ankle or caught in a net.

She wasn't sure what it was about this place, but as soon as they'd left the crash of waves behind to venture through the foliage, her mind was overcome with images of another forest filled with such traps. Traps . . . and entire towns crafted amongst the treetops.

Her eyes scanned the tree line, a small frown settling between her brows when she found nothing but dappled sunlight.

Where were these images coming from, and why were they making her chest ache?

"Booby traps?" Bronn asked, letting Caly walk ahead of him. "Why would smugglers set traps in their own hideout?"

"To ward off trespassers."

He flashed her a grin. "The island tends to do that on its own."

Tension crawled between her shoulder blades. "Why? Is it a secret volcano or something?"

"What?" he asked with a bark of laughter. "No. Of course not. Well . . . I don't think so. It's just that these isles aren't exactly easy to get to. Anyone who stumbled on one of them likely did so intentionally."

"Except for us."

"We do tend to be the exception rather than the rule," he said with a smirk.

Shadow didn't have as easy a time dismissing the possibility, which was why she continued to sweep her gaze across the ground, checking for tripwires or other potential hazards.

"You should look where you're going," Ronan murmured, shooting her an amused glance as he lifted a branch out of her way.

She blinked up at the thick limb she'd almost walked straight into. "Thanks."

He nodded, that small smile still playing about his lips.

"What?" she demanded, hesitating before walking on.

"It's almost like old times."

"We don't have old times."

His smile dimmed a bit at the edges, but he shrugged and kept his voice light. "It's not the first forest we've traipsed through together."

She couldn't exactly refute the point. With the gaps in her memory, it was certainly possible she'd forgotten such an occasion.

For the first time, the possibility of lost moments between them really bothered her.

"It's a jungle, not a forest," she snapped, her frustration with her own shortcomings leaking out in her voice and sounding like an attack.

He dropped his hand, letting the branch smack her in the face. "Call it what you will. We're hiking through trees and other green shrubbery, and not for the first time."

I . . . deserved that. She sighed, her shoulders slumping a little as she spat out what she hoped were only a couple of leaves and followed along after him. *Perhaps antagonizing the man you just decided to explore things with is not the wisest course of action, Shadow dear.*

She hadn't meant to. Really. She just wasn't used to being . . . nice. Not that she walked around making a point of verbally cutting people down, she just hadn't had much of a reason to make an effort to be friendly. The people she was surrounded by rarely spoke to her outside of issuing orders or asking for progress reports, and the townsfolk were terrified of her. Neither situation lent itself to developing any sort of meaningful relationship. Platonic or otherwise.

Shadow frowned. Did she really not have any friends? Did she want them?

Dovina and the rest of the flock hardly counted. They were more like coworkers or fellow soldiers. People that one spent time with due to proximity rather than intent. Besides, the Raven only saw value in others based on the information they could provide. One would have to be a fool to consider the spy a friend.

A feeling that could have been loneliness crept through her chest, weighing down her heart. Shadow blamed the day's near-death experience on her uncharacteristic melancholy. She was an assassin, for fuck's sake. What in the darkness was she supposed to do with a *friend*?

"That's a new expression for you."

Shadow snapped to attention a mere step away from walking face first into a tree. *Stars.* "What is?"

"Thoughtful," Ronan replied, his lips tugging up in a teasing grin.

"I think," she said, indignation giving the words bite.

Did I really just say that? Laughter made his eyes dance, and embarrassment crawled up her neck. *Stars, I did. It's no wonder you've never had a long-term lover, Shadow. With your scintillating conversational skills, why would any man want to keep you around for longer than a single night?*

It wasn't just that, though. This was Ronan. Talking with him had always felt natural. Granted, they were usually trading insults, but there had been an ease to it. As if they'd done the same countless times before and took comfort in the ritual. Why, then, did every interaction with him suddenly feel so complicated to navigate? Ever since he'd held her while she wept, every word felt as if it conveyed a dozen potential meanings. It likely didn't help that she'd come to with his lips pressed to hers and instinctively reacted by pulling him closer and kissing him back. That was sure to send some mixed messages.

Another soft sigh slipped out. She was woefully out of her depth. How was she supposed to do . . . *this?*

And yes, she was well aware not knowing what *this* was, was another issue entirely.

"We're going to be okay," he said softly, likely misinterpreting her anxiety as a response to being shipwrecked rather than over him. Which, for a normal person, would have been an appropriate assumption. Still, his reassurance was welcome.

Not ready to give herself away, she kept her eyes trained on her boots and nodded. "I know."

"Cave's just over there. Behind the rocks," Jagger called.

"See," he said, nudging her with his shoulder.

They picked up their pace, rushing to join the others at the cave's opening.

Calypso pointed out a series of symbols along the wall. "These tell fellow smugglers what to expect inside." She gestured first to a rudimentary sketch of a tree. "Firewood." Then to four wavy lines. "Drinking water." Some kind of bottle. "Rum."

"All the necessities," Bronn said with a wide grin, clapping his hands together and rubbing them eagerly. "Let's get settled, shall we?"

Time moved quickly after that, their small group splitting up tasks to ensure they were set for the evening. Ronan was in charge of the fire, which was cheating in her opinion because it required zero effort on his part. Calypso and Bronn were sorting through a stack of crates, looking for anything they could use. Already they'd found a couple of blankets, some salt pork and hardtack that seemed edible, and the rum Bronn had been so excited about. She'd been tasked with bottling up drinking water from the little stream trickling along the back of the cave while Jagger checked the nearby offshoots to make sure they wouldn't be happened upon by any cave-dwelling creatures in their sleep.

By the time Jagger and Buttercup returned, they were settled around the fire, food warm and rum flowing.

"Anything to worry about?" Calypso asked.

"Storm's coming," he grunted with a deep frown.

"Then it's a good thing we've got cover," Shadow said, just able to make out the soft trickle of rain over the crackle of the flames.

But Jagger shook his head. "Stream's already rising."

The way the pirates were exchanging looks had Shadow shifting uncomfortably on her makeshift driftwood seat. "You don't think the cave is going to flood, do you?"

"It's a possibility," Caly said, worrying her bottom lip. "It might be wise to head for higher ground. Just in case."

"Last thing we want is to be caught unaware in our sleep," Ronan agreed.

Exhausted from the day's event, Shadow rebelled against the idea of having to leave the warmth and safety of the cave. They'd been lucky enough to find everything they could need. What were the odds they'd be so lucky a second time?

"Quick, eat up and then pack whatever you can carry," Ronan said, taking charge. "If the cave does flood, it might be a few days before we can get back in here. And if we're going to go, we should do it before we lose all sunlight."

The relaxed atmosphere of moments before was gone. Their movements were hurried and fraught with tension.

The blankets were turned into knapsacks and loaded up with cans of food, the bottles of water, some flares, first aid supplies, and of course, rum. The men split the sacks between them, leaving Calypso and Shadow to hold pieces of driftwood they could use as torches as they headed back out into the twilight.

"Ready?" Caly asked, looking around.

"Lead the way, captain," Bronn said.

They left the cave single file, the rainfall far worse than it had been even minutes prior. Shadow was drenched in a matter of seconds, the trees doing little to act as a barrier to the sheets of rain falling from the sky. If not for Ronan's magic protecting the flames, their torches would have instantly died.

Jagger hadn't been exaggerating when he'd called for a storm. The rain came down at a diagonal, lashing them across the face and making it impossible to see more than an inch or two in front of their faces. If not for Ronan's hand firmly in hers, she might not have made it up the curving path from the jungle to the northern cliffs.

She was still wiping rain from her eyes as they finally crested the top of the path, teeth chattering from the combination of rain and wind.

"Looks like there's another cave ahead," Bronn called. "We should be able to make camp there for the night."

"Thank fuck," Ronan said, giving her hand a squeeze as he helped her climb up and over a waist-high boulder.

Shadow echoed his sentiments, more than ready to keel over. She'd pushed herself beyond her limits, and then kept going. Tired wasn't even close to what she was feeling right now.

Delirious. Half-dead, perhaps. But nothing as simple as *tired*.

As they neared the cave Bronn had indicated, a series of wooden structures came into view.

"What is that?" Ronan asked, squinting.

It was practically impossible to see past the torrent of rain to get a clear image of the three objects lined up outside the cave.

"They look like cages," Shadow murmured, not sure if she was seeing bars or simply imagining them.

"Suspended ones," Calypso confirmed. "There are some tribes known to imprison their quarry in such cages. It would make sense."

"Is there . . . someone in one of them?" Shadow asked, her eyes barely able to make anything out beyond the soft glow of her torch.

"What are the odds?" Ronan mumbled at the same time Bronn said, "I think you might be right."

Holding one of their two torches up, Calypso took a few tentative steps forward until the aura of light fell above the nearest of the cages. The poor creature suspended in the air made a pathetic moan and curled into themselves, their turquoise shirt nearly black from the rain.

"Ahoy!" Bronn called softly, trying to draw the poor letch's attention without alerting whomever their captor might be.

The figure's head shot up, eyes wide, face pale and etched with fear.

There was something familiar about the man, but Shadow couldn't quite place him. And then Ronan's bewildered call rang out into the night.

"Bast?"

CHAPTER 17

RONAN

"Oh, merciful darkness, Ronan. Is that really you?"

The absolute shock of finding Sebastian here held him rooted to the spot.

Bast shuffled forward on his knees, hands grasping the bars as he pressed his face through the space between them. "You're not just going to leave me like this, are you?"

Ronan blinked, then jerked forward as the words penetrated. If Bast wasn't doing anything to disguise his voice he must be alone, at least for the moment, which meant it should be safe enough to approach. Meanwhile, Calypso and her men were looking to him for answers.

"You know this man?" the captain asked.

"Aye. From Glimmermere."

"Well, don't downplay it, Ronan. Tell them the truth."

The pirates stared at him expectantly. Shadow seemed content to watch Bast as she slid one of her daggers free. He appreciated her distrust of the imprisoned man. It was nice to see her skepticism aimed someone else's way for once.

"That is the truth," he ground out.

It would seem that even when captured, Bast was a right pain in his arse. Good to know some things never changed.

Sebastian rolled his eyes. "You make it seem as though we're mere acquaintances." He shifted to look over Ronan's shoulder so he could address the others. "Ronan and I are best friends."

Bronn's bark of laughter was disguised as a cough. Calypso hid a smile behind her hand, while Shadow didn't bother. Jagger's expression remained unchanged, though Buttercup did a little dance on his shoulder, which Ronan could clearly picture as someone doubled over in laughter.

"You might want to reconsider annoying me until *after* I free you from the cage. I have no qualms leaving you locked up in the rain."

Sebastian gasped. "You lie. You would never leave me here to fend for myself against those monsters."

The mention of monsters had everyone's smiles fading.

"How *are* you here, Sebastian? What happened to Loren?"

"It's a long story. Just get me down before they get back."

"They?"

"The men with the dragons."

"Did you say *dragons*?"

"What else would you call giant winged lizards that breathe fire?"

"Drakes," Bronn said, his expression somber. "Dragons haven't roamed these skies in centuries, but drakes—their smaller but just as fierce cousins—are still spotted from time to time near The Crags. They and their riders have quite the reputation for preying on those stupid enough to venture into the Savage Pass."

"I guess it wasn't that long of a story after all," Bast muttered before adding in a much more indignant manner, "And those fuckers were the size of a house with scales the size of dinner plates. I'd hardly call them small."

"A dragon would be the size of a castle," Bronn returned.

Bast let out a derisive snort. "Well. Whatever they're called, I do not much enjoy the thought of being their next meal. As it is, I'm sure to be haunted by their glowing yellow eyes and tree trunk-sized fangs for the rest of my hopefully long life. So would you please. Get. Me.

Out." Each desperate word was punctuated with the rattle of the cage door.

"Your friend has quite the gift for embellishment," Caly murmured.

"You have no idea," Ronan said with a heartfelt sigh.

"He'd make an excellent bard."

"Don't encourage him."

Drawing on his Earth power, Ronan grasped the bars in his hand and pulled once, hard. The barricade snapped free as easily as twigs from a branch. Instead of jumping down to the ground, Sebastian threw himself at Ronan, grabbing onto him with all four of his limbs.

"I'm never leaving you again," he fervently cried.

Shadow's chuckles grew louder as she came to stand beside them. "Shall we leave you two alone?"

"Look, Shadow, I found a new target for your dagger," he answered dryly.

"My lady Shadow, what a pleasure to see you again," Sebastian said, all simpering charm despite the fact he still clung to Ronan like a damned monkey.

There was a flash of panic in Shadow's eyes Ronan was starting to recognize as the sign she didn't remember. Her memory loss had been an issue for her even before his reappearance in her life. How many times had she woken up unsure how she'd gotten there or run into someone claiming to know her with no idea as to the circumstances of their meeting? No wonder she greeted everyone with suspicion and kept most at arm's length. It had to be easier than the alternative.

"I don't believe you two have been formally introduced," he interjected, coming to her rescue in a way she seemed to appreciate, if the relief he read in her face was any indication. "Shadow, this is Sebastian Jean-Rene Villehardouin of Colvers—"

"Ronan," he gasped with delight, squeezing even harder. "You remembered!"

Ronan glowered at the top of the blond man's head, his voice cooling considerably, "—a consummate thorn in my side."

"That makes him my dearest friend and new idol."

Sebastian beamed at her. "I knew you were a woman whose taste would live up to her exquisite beauty. Please, call me Bast."

Ronan snarled softly and shoved Bast off, nearly sending him toppling onto his arse. Only some quick footwork and the flailing of his arms kept the bedraggled fop from losing his balance. "Not my best dismount, but I suppose under the circumstances it can be excused," he mumbled, much to the others' amusement. Then he let out a soft wail. "These breeches are ruined. Ruined!"

Continuing with the introductions, Ronan gestured to the three sailors. "Bast, allow me to introduce you to Captain Calypso No Beard, previously of the pirate ship *Revenge*, her quartermaster Bronn, and their boson Jagger." Buttercup gave an irritated chirp. "And his protector, Buttercup," Ronan added, using Shadow's term for the finch.

Sebastian, still sulky about his mud-splattered trousers, glared at Ronan over his shoulder before sweeping into his deepest bow. "*Enchanté, mes nouveaux amis.*"

Bronn and Jagger didn't seem to appreciate Sebastian's courtly charm any more than Ronan did. As one, they stepped in front of their captain. She let out a husky chuckle, then peered over the wall of their shoulders.

"It's always a pleasure to make the acquaintance of such a dashing courtier."

Sebastian preened under her regard while Bronn and Jagger glowered.

Casting a glance up at the sky, Ronan asked, "Looks like the storm isn't letting up anytime soon. Did we still want to make camp here and risk the return of the riders? Or shall we press on?"

Shadow whimpered softly, and he had to fight against the impulse to offer to carry her. He knew she must be exhausted, but she would be the last person to dare admit it. Shadow would never admit to anything she perceived as a weakness, nor would she allow him to offer his aid unless she was on the brink of collapse. Even then, it was more likely she'd keel over first.

"We should be safe enough here," Calypso said, following Ronan's line of sight. "The riders won't risk flying in this downpour. They'll have bunkered down for the night, so even if they are still on the island it'll be morning before we need to worry about them."

"Island?" Bast repeated. "This isn't an island, captain."

"How do you know?" Ronan asked.

"My captors flew along the mountain range to the coast, but never crossed over the water. I believe we're on a peninsula known as Twilight Cove."

"How do you know so much about this land?" Ronan asked.

"How do you not?"

"I'm not from around here."

"Neither am I, and yet I made time to do my research."

Ronan narrowed his eyes, wondering what would ever prompt the self-proclaimed playboy to do something as responsible as research.

Paying no attention to them, Bronn murmured to himself. "Twilight's Cove . . . that sounds familiar. Why do I—of course," he breathed, his eyes wide as they met his captain's. "Smuggler's Rock."

"That's not what I . . ." Bast deflated. "But then Smuggler's Rock has a nice ring to it. Not as atmospheric as its *actual* name, but who am I to judge?"

Bronn and the other pirates ignored Sebastian's rant. They were too busy exchanging loaded glances.

"Do you think—"

"Could it be—"

"It's possible," Calypso said, answering her crewmembers' half-voiced questions.

"Tiny would have recognized the markers."

The captain nodded, her excitement palpable. "The crew could already be on their way there."

"Where?" Ronan asked, tired of feeling like he was missing something.

"If we did land on Smuggler's Rock, there's a town of sorts along the northern beach."

"No, there isn't," Bast insisted.

"It's a well-kept secret, for a reason," Caly said with an indulgent smile. "Our kind doesn't exactly advertise its existence."

"Smugglers always need a safe place to fence ill-gotten gains and—"

"Find a cure for all manner of appetites," Bast interrupted Bronn, nodding along sagely. "Speak no more. When do we leave?"

"It could take days for us to get there. We should rest up tonight and make our way in the morning, assuming the storm has passed by then."

With a plan in place and the hope of a friendly port in the not so distant future, sleep sounded like a fantastic idea. Jagger and Buttercup moved to the entrance of the cave, though no one seemed inclined to head too deep into its depths.

Bast clapped a hand on Ronan's shoulder. "I don't know who I pleasured in a past life, but the stars must be shining on me now. I have never been so glad to see someone I had no intention of fucking in my life."

Ronan huffed out a laugh. "I missed you too, Bast."

"I mean it, Ronan. I thought I was dead for sure. Those men came out of the sky and . . ." He sighed and shook his head.

"Loren?"

"I don't know. They separated us, and I haven't seen him since."

"I'm sure he's fine. If anyone can single-handedly fend off their captors, it's the pride of Glimmermere." Loren's skills were legendary. The man had been a finalist in Erebos's trial for a reason.

"I'm sure you're right," Bast said, but his smile didn't quite reach his eyes. "Wherever he is, I'm sure Loren is already working on a rescue plan to come save me as we speak."

CHAPTER 18

EREBOS

"Ｈigh Lord, are you sure this is—"

"Leave me."

"But, sir . . ." His general trailed off, looking beyond uncomfortable.

Erebos raised a brow. "Yes?"

Dominic rolled his lips together, biting back whatever words of warning he desperately wanted to impart. He'd never seen a man so torn between his conscience and the desire to follow a direct order.

"Well, spit it out."

"It is only that we do not know these lands, and you did not allow me to bring a full contingent. How can I ensure your safety if you insist on being left out here alone?"

"Do you think me incapable of looking after myself?" His deceptively soft snarl was a warning to tread *very* carefully. A warning that did not go unnoticed.

Dominic gulped, a rare display of vulnerability from the man known throughout the realm as the Vulture. "Of course not."

"Is it your own skills you doubt?"

"Never."

"Then I don't see the problem."

"How can I protect you if you are sending me away?"

Erebos barely resisted the urge to roll his eyes. Loyalty in a follower was all well and good until it infringed on one's right to privacy. The goal was to find one who served without question. Dominic seemed to have missed that very vital part of the memo.

"I am going to go over there"—he pointed to the cliff jutting out over the sea no more than twenty feet away—"to meditate. What exactly do you think is going to happen to me?"

"You could fall, or—"

"Now you're insulting me. Go. Stand guard from over there if you must, but do not, under any circumstances, interrupt me until I am finished. Or you will be the one falling off the cliff. Do you understand?"

"Yes, High Lord."

Erebos spun away from the other man and walked over to the lookout. He hated the necessity of traveling with a caravan. But the High Lord of Empyria could hardly make a trip of this magnitude alone. He could, however, insist everyone fuck off when he needed quiet time to focus.

Eyes closed, he drew the sea and salt scent of the air deep into his lungs. The distant crash of the waves below was a perfect distraction to quiet his mind.

He was getting close now.

He could feel it.

Another day, perhaps two at most. Especially now that they were trapped, like little mice whose tails have been caught beneath a lion's paw. They were clueless about the danger of their situation, which was exactly where he wanted them.

His lips lifted in a slow, cruel smile as he transitioned into the realm of dreams.

"Well, well, well . . . what do you have for me this time, Shadow mine?"

CHAPTER 19

SHADOW

*T*he rain didn't let up until late the next afternoon, leaving them with little way to spend the morning besides taking turns standing guard. In a cave with only one entrance, guard duty translated into restless pacing broken up by a series of even more restless naps. With no way of knowing when it would be time to go, it was difficult to do more than exist in a constant state of mild panic. Unsurprisingly, it wasn't exactly the ideal atmosphere for fostering the sort of creativity or meaningful conversations necessary to help break up the monotony.

Though stars bless him, Sebastian certainly tried.

Jagger was the one who finally snapped, shocking them all by jumping up and poking Ronan in the chest. "If you do not put a stop to your dog's incessant barking, I will. And I will do so by stringing him up by his toes and shoving his dirty stockings down his throat."

"By all means, be my guest," Ronan replied without missing a beat. "You'd be doing us all a favor."

Bast gave an offended huff, peering up at his friend from his place at the campfire. "You would never let that happen. Tell them, Ronan." When the only response he got was a contradictory lift of his brow,

Sebastian turned bright pink and addressed the group at large. "He would never let that happen."

"If you really wanted to frighten him," Bronn chimed in mildly, "you should have threatened to use your stockings."

Calypso cuffed him upside the head but did a poor job hiding her amusement. It was the highlight of an otherwise dreary morning.

Finally, the sun broke through the clouds, signaling they were free to venture out and begin the journey north to the pirates' secret port town. They were up and out of that cave as if the promise of a vast fortune was on the line. No one was keen to be caught unaware by the mysterious drake riders. Despite his time as their prisoner—and rather ironically, given how he ran his mouth about everything else—Bast had been closed-lipped regarding the riders themselves. Other than to say their breath rivaled that of their foul beasts.

That had been hours ago. Now the sun was low on the horizon, and they could just make out the suggestion of buildings beyond the trees.

"Is that your town?" Sebastian asked, hope lending his voice an earnest edge that made Shadow think of the palace's litter of puppies.

"It wouldn't be very secret if it was out in the open, would it?" Caly answered with a soft laugh.

Shadow would have laughed at Bast's crestfallen expression too, except she shared his disappointment. It wasn't that she didn't appreciate a good adventure as much as the next person, or even the rare opportunity to explore an unknown and exotic territory, for that matter. But since waking, she hadn't been able to shake a creeping sense of doom. Between yesterday's Lusca attack and a second night of fitful sleep plagued with nightmares, she was on edge and likely looking for monsters where none existed. A safe haven would go a long way to quashing her mounting unease.

Ronan and Jagger took the lead, moving ahead to investigate what appeared to be a small settlement. Buttercup took to the sky, circling overhead before returning to Jagger's shoulder.

"All clear," Jagger confirmed.

"Do you know who might have lived here or why they left?" Ronan asked as he rejoined their small group.

"No, but that doesn't mean anything. I've never ventured this far inland before. As far as I know, this place could have been abandoned for days as easily as years."

"Years," Jagger grunted.

Shadow was inclined to agree with the boson's one-word assessment. The buzzing of insects and the hooting of birds were far more prevalent than they would have been if a large group of people was nearby. Despite the obvious development of the land, there was also a sense that the wilderness had reclaimed it. Anyone who once lived here moved on long ago.

"Well . . . their loss is our gain," Bronn said, his sunny smile a perfect match to his breezy tone.

Ronan nodded, his hand scraping over the days' worth of thick stubble along his jaw. "I think we just found our camp for the night, unless anyone objects."

"A place with four walls and a roof?" Caly shook her head. "You won't hear any complaints from me."

"Don't get too excited. We don't know what we're dealing with yet," Ronan warned.

"It was good enough someone wanted to put down roots here," Bronn pointed out.

And for them to up and leave.

"Plus, civilization usually means fresh water," he continued. "There should be a well or river nearby we can use to refill our flasks."

"A bath wouldn't go amiss either," Sebastian said, clearly still sulking as he gave the pirates a blatant side-eye.

Entirely unfazed, Bronn held up the two jugs of rum he'd faithfully carried all day. "What do you say, mateys? Shall we claim our bunks then meet up for a proper meal and celebratory swig?"

At the promise of alcohol, Bast perked right up. "I say, home sweet home," he crowed, rushing off to select his choice of lodgings.

With an aggrieved sigh, Jagger and Buttercup followed.

"Keep an eye on him, yeah?" Ronan called.

Jagger stopped only long enough to call over his shoulder. "Not my circus."

Ronan's expression clouded. "What the hell does that mean?"

Calypso and Bronn laughed. "He was saying Sebastian's your problem."

"Don't I know it," Ronan said darkly.

"We'll look out for him," Caly promised. "Come on, Bronn. Let's check out our fancy new digs."

Ronan fell quiet, then shook his head and let out a soft chuckle. "I still can't believe it."

"That he was captured and left to rot?"

"Ha! That I have no trouble believing. You've met the man. Who wouldn't want to lock him up and throw away the key? Can you imagine how much those riders regretted their decision the second Bast opened his mouth?" He huffed out a laugh. "No, I just meant that he's *here*."

"It is quite the coincidence," Shadow agreed.

"I don't believe in coincidence."

"So, what then? You think the stars brought him to you?"

His gaze turned considering. "Stranger things have happened. Especially recently."

"Well, enjoy your gift from fate." She gave his shoulder one heavy thump and made to move past him.

"Hey!" He grasped her belt loop and reeled her back. "Where do you think you're going?"

Jerking her thumb in the direction of the abandoned village, she said, "To claim my room and celebratory rum before they drink it all without me. After the last two days, I think I've more than earned it."

His eyes searched hers, genuine concern stamped on his handsome features.

"What?"

"Just wondering what else is going on in that head of yours. You've been quiet today."

"Who could get a word in edgewise?" she replied, her tone bland but lips curved.

"Welcome to life with Bast."

She laughed along with him.

"Now," he murmured, brushing a piece of her fallen hair behind her ear, "tell me the real reason you've been so in your head."

Tingles exploded across her skin as his knuckles idly stroked along her jaw. It was the first time he'd touched her since they woke up on the beach, and she was no more immune to him now than she had been then. How was it he could make even the most innocent caress feel intimate?

Then he rocked her further when he proved with a single question just how attuned to her he really was.

"Did you have another nightmare?"

She flinched.

Ronan took a step closer, his voice dropping until it seemed they were the only two people in all of existence. "Tell me."

"I-I can't."

"You can." Another step. "Come on. Let me share the burden."

Her palms were pressed against his stomach, her breath hostage in her throat. Mutely, she shook her head.

"Please, kitten. Let me in."

"It's not that I don't want to," she admitted, the confession pulled from her without conscious thought. "I don't remember specifics. Only that there was a voice."

"What did it sound like?"

"Cold . . ." She shuddered as the echo of those terrifying whispers skittered through her mind like so many insects. "And so angry."

"What else?"

"I . . . don't remember."

"Was it the same voice as last time?"

"Maybe? I'm sorry. It's all just a blur. The only thing I recall is how it made me feel."

He shifted until his hands were braced on her shoulders. "How did it make you feel?"

Her tongue darted out to wet her lips, dread curling in her stomach. "Scared."

His fingers spasmed as his grip on her tightened. "Anything that has the power to scare you terrifies me."

She didn't know how badly she needed those words until he uttered them. She'd been feeling off all day, internally tearing herself apart for being weak and skittish. But to have this man—this warrior—validate her feelings . . . it was everything.

"Ronan," she whispered, her hand lifting of its own accord to cup his cheek.

His breath stuttered out of him, surprise making his eyes flare wide before pleasure turned the icy blue a molten silver. His gaze dipped to her lips, his own parting as he leaned half an inch closer.

"Hey!" Bast shouted, making them jerk apart. "You two coming?"

Ronan's groan echoed in the very depths of her soul. "I'm going to murder that fool in his sleep."

"I'll help."

Wrapping an arm around her neck, he pulled her into his side. "Come on, kitten. Let's find you a bed and then get our hands on a good . . . stiff—" He let the word hang until heat crept into her cheeks. "Drink."

Her laugh wobbled at the edges. She knew that had been what he was going to say, but for a second there, her lower belly clenched and . . .

"Why Shadow, you look disappointed. Were you hoping I was going to offer you something else?"

"What? No, of course not. Don't flatter yourself."

His arm flexed around her, and he dropped his mouth to her ear. "You say the word, kitten, and that can be yours too."

Her stomach swooped, and she stumbled—to her never-ending shame. Empyria's assassin did *not* trip over her own damn feet. Shoving Ronan away, she snapped, "You wish, Butcher."

His laughter chased her as she stormed ahead of him. "Aye, that I do. But from the looks of it . . . so do you."

She had to bite the inside of her cheek to keep from saying anything else, because it would only be a lie, and they both knew it. The simple truth was, Ronan was right.

And she didn't know what in the darkness to do with that.

~

"COME ON, come on. Stop making googly eyes at the assassin and pay attention," Bast demanded.

In a move that surprised no one, Sebastian had taken over the celebration by insisting they get to know each other better through a game of feats.

"The rules are so simple, even Ronan can't fuck them up," he insisted.

"You have to fall asleep sometime, Sebastian. And when you do . . . you will pay for that," Ronan snarled softly.

He gulped, then laughed away his momentary panic. "You . . . always jesting, ha ha ha." But the laughter was uncomfortable and clearly forced. Poor Bast. The more time she spent with him, the more and more he reminded her of an overeager puppy. She couldn't help but feel protective.

"Be nice," she whispered to Ronan. "Can't you see you're wounding his feelings?"

"That would require him to possess some."

"Ronan. The boy clearly adores you. It wouldn't kill you to be a little nicer to him."

"This from the woman who founded the stab first and always school of etiquette."

She chuckled at the rather accurate assessment.

"And for the record, it likely *would* kill me, and that *boy* is a man who knows exactly what game he's playing. Do not fall for his tricks. It's a trap meant to lure in the unsuspecting. If you're not careful, you'll end up taking him under your wing, and then you'll never be rid of him. Trust me," he added with a baleful sigh.

"You're fonder of him than you let on."

"Of Bast? Mother's tits, how much of that have you had to drink?" he asked, reaching for her cup.

"You are," Shadow insisted, holding her rum out of reach. "I saw your face when you realized who was in that cage. There's no faking that kind of concern. I think you're rather attached to him."

"Only in the way one is attached to a fungus."

"Fine. Lie to yourself, Ronan. I see straight through you."

"You always have," he uttered so softly she almost thought she'd imagined it, until she glanced up and found herself caught in his intense stare.

"Okay, I'll go first," Bast called, once again unknowingly interrupting the charged moment. "I will name a feat I've accomplished. If you can claim the same, you drink. Alternatively, you can call my bluff, and if I'm lying, then I must drink."

"If you think for one second a single word out of his mouth isn't utter horse shit . . ." Ronan muttered, taking a drink from his dish. They'd salvaged drinkware from the houses, but of what little remained, most was shattered or badly cracked. In the end, Ronan and Jagger had both ended up with what appeared to be finger bowls instead of mugs. Shadow couldn't help but give in to the wave of snickers every time they lifted the tiny dishes in their meaty hands and sipped. It was almost reminiscent of a child's tea party. But with rum and pirates instead of imaginary friends and tea.

"Feel free to call my bluff, Ronan, but I assure you, you will only end up well in your cups."

"It'll take more than a few swigs of this to get me off my face," Ronan replied.

"Don't be too sure of that," Bronn said with a knowing smirk. "There's little more sacred to a pirate than his rum, so I can promise this here's quality product. It may taste sweet, but it's got a kick, and it will sneak up on you if you're not careful."

Shadow eyed the foggy liquid in her glass with new interest. Oblivion might be nice, but she wasn't sure it was wise to pickle herself out here in the middle of the jungle.

Or maybe taking the edge off will help you get out of your own way so you can finally have some fun . . . with a capital R.

Her eyes drifted back to Ronan, who was smiling and shaking his head at whatever Caly had just said.

Heat that had nothing to do with the lingering humidity swept through her. Instinctively, she took a large gulp from her glass, eyes immediately watering and throat burning from the pirate's brew.

Ronan clapped her on the back while the others laughed. "Take it easy, kitten. The idea's to sip it."

She leveled him with her most scathing look. "You don't say. Here I was thinking you were supposed to choke on it."

"I mean, if you're looking for something to choke on . . ." he crooned, words just for her as he hid his lips and wicked grin behind his makeshift cup.

"Ronan, Shadow, you aren't paying attention," Bast complained.

Ronan offered an apology, but Shadow was too busy mentally picking her jaw up off the floor to do more than gape at him. Somewhere between their kiss on the beach and earlier conversation, Ronan had decided the gloves were coming off. The man was on the hunt, and she was his prey.

With the way her thighs clenched and the juncture between them throbbed, she was ready to be caught. More than, if she was being honest with herself.

Come and get me, Ronan. I'm so tired of fighting against what I want.

Sebastian, however, was through being ignored. He lobbed a stick at Ronan's head. Without taking his eyes off hers, Ronan caught it in midair. The unexpected demonstration of skill only made the flutters in her belly stronger. What was it about a competent, capable man?

With a smirk that told her he knew exactly what he was doing to her, Ronan glanced in Bast's direction and snapped the twig in two.

Sebastian flinched but bravely held his gaze. "Pay attention, or next time it will be a rock."

"Behave, or next time it will be your neck."

"You'd have to catch me first."

"If the drake riders managed, I'm sure I'll do just fine."

Sebastian glared at him. "You owe me."

"Owe you? How do you figure?"

"After those lessons I gave you." He waved dramatically at Shadow. "Clearly, they're working. You're welcome, by the way."

"What's he talking about?" Shadow asked with a lift of her brow.

It was Ronan's turn to blush. "Nothing. He's full of shit. Just ignore him."

"Mmhmm."

"I, for one, think the game sounds like fun," Bronn said, earning himself a wide grin from Bast.

"You're interested in anything that involves the opportunity to drink vast amounts of rum," Caly teased.

"What's your point?"

The captain pressed her lips together and shook her head. "Jagger, will you join us?"

He turned his head in her direction. If he were anyone else, Shadow would have described the move as shooting her a disbelieving glance, but with his blindfold, she wasn't sure she could categorize it as such. Without a word, he stood and walked into the house he'd selected and shut the door.

"Suit yourself," she called after him. "Count the rest of us in, Bast."

Sebastian took that to heart, despite Ronan's protest. "Finally. Okay. I won my first sword fight at five years of age."

"Horse shit," Ronan coughed. "How can you even prove it?"

Sebastian pointed to a nearly invisible scar on his chin. "The only blow that landed."

"That doesn't prove anything."

"The truth is the truth. Now, drink up, Ronan."

"You heard the man," Shadow said. "Drink up."

He scowled at her. "I can't believe you're taking his side."

"I can't believe you called him out after only the first round. He warned you he'd make you drink."

Ronan begrudgingly took a sip of his rum. "This game is stupid."

"You're a sore loser."

"Anyone else win their first fight at the tender age of five? Nobody?" Sebastian looked entirely too pleased with himself.

"I'll go next," Bronn called out. "I stowed away on my first ship at the age of eleven."

Caly glared at him. "You're only saying that because you know I'll have to drink."

Bronn was all smiles as he drained his rum and refilled his glass. "So? I didn't hear anything in the rules against that."

"Quite so, quite so," Bast agreed.

"You're right, Ronan. This game is rigged." Sighing, Calypso took a swig of her rum. "All right, me next," she said, her eye twinkling as it landed on Bronn. "I didn't lose my virginity until I was twenty-three."

He leaned forward, elbows resting on his knees. "That only works, sweetheart, if someone doesn't happen to know for a fact it's a lie and call you on it."

Shadow smothered a grin. Caly had tried to out Bronn with one of his own secrets, only to fall victim to the rules of the game.

Realizing her mistake, Calypso groaned. "I thought you'd still have to drink."

"Nope. Not if I correctly called your bluff. Right, Sebastian?"

Bast nodded, grinning from ear to ear at the pirate's antics.

The game continued on in this manner for a few more rounds. Ronan always calling Bast out and having to drink. Bronn and Caly each trying to embarrass the other. Ronan's feats were less revealing, but every bit as impressive. Shadow was the only one who'd managed to avoid sharing any details about herself. Which worked out in her favor until Bast caught on.

"No, no, no, it's Shadow's turn. Dazzle us, my lady! Surely the things you've accomplished will set the rest of us to shame."

She grimaced, racking her brain for something that wasn't equal parts horrific and depressing. Somehow, mentioning the time she'd severed a man's spine while slitting his throat or that she'd once killed eight armed guards in less than five minutes didn't seem like it would match the jovial mood Sebastian had worked so hard for.

"Um . . ."

The only thing that came to mind was so embarrassing she wasn't sure she wanted to share it. Then again, maybe no one would believe her, and she could get everyone else to drink.

"We're waiting," Ronan prompted, his smirk knowing as he turned to face her.

"I mastered Salome," she blurted, her pulse pounding in her ears.

She waited for his reaction, but there wasn't one. Or at least not the one she expected. Ronan's brow wrinkled in confusion. "Salome? Is that some kind of martial art?"

Sebastian snorted. "You could say that."

"It's a dance," Calypso offered, her gaze lingering on Shadow. "A very sensual dance." Without looking at anyone else, she lifted her glass and drained it—indicating it was a feat she'd also accomplished. "One of my personal favorites."

"Really?" Bronn asked, his interest undeniable as his gaze swept over his captain. "Caly, you've been keeping secrets."

"If you think that's the only one, you haven't been paying attention."

"Perhaps you could dance for me sometime?"

Her lips curled playfully. "You wouldn't make it past the second veil, Bronn."

"Challenge accepted."

"Veils?" Ronan asked. "What am I missing?"

"The dancer removes them one at a time," Calypso supplied helpfully, eyes sparkling with laughter.

"Oh." Ronan's expression was priceless when it finally sunk in. "Ohhh." He cleared his throat. "That . . . erm . . ." He shifted in his seat, clearly flustered as he pictured what the dance entailed. A second round of throat clearing ensued before he gruffly managed, "Sounds like a very effective way to get close to your marks."

"It is."

That was the entire reason she'd learned it. No one ever suspected their evening's entertainment was actually their assassin.

"I'm with Bronn. I'd like to request Shadow give us all a demonstration," Bast said.

Shadow dipped her chin, allowing her hair to fall forward and conceal her expression. The thought of performing for the group held little appeal, but performing for Ronan . . . that was very appealing indeed. If for no other reason than to watch his face as the veils were removed until none remained. She thought Caly had the right of it. Ronan wouldn't make it past the second either.

"The hell she will," Ronan snarled.

From the way Sebastian doubled over in a fit of laughter, he'd been waiting for such a reaction.

Realizing he'd overreacted, Ronan blushed all the way to the tips of his ears. "I mean, unless she wants to."

He couldn't meet her gaze, which only endeared him to her more. She'd discovered a lot of sides to the mercenary in only a matter of days, but this was the most unexpected. She wasn't sure which was more attractive. The possessive instinct to keep her body to himself, or the admission that regardless of his personal feelings, it was her body to do with as she pleased.

The way this man constantly proved that he'd put her needs above his own, that he'd not only protect her physical well-being but her mental and emotional well-being as well . . . it was beyond anything she'd ever experienced before. And it made him far and away the most attractive man she'd ever known.

In the last twenty-four hours alone, he'd held her while she cried, asked her to share the burden of her nightmares so he could help carry their weight, and he'd tried to save her life. Even though her life hadn't been in any danger at the time.

Unlike Erebos, Ronan didn't want to control or use her. He just wanted to be hers. In any and every capacity she'd allow. And with him, for the first time, she wanted it all.

The revelation was startling. Not because of what it said about Ronan, but because of how acknowledging it lit her up from the inside out. The feeling was so foreign it took her a second to identify it.

This was happiness in its purest, rawest form.

It was joy.

No, this was *love*.

She was in love.

These strange feelings and impulses she'd tried—and failed—to deny weren't simply desire or attraction. This wasn't just chemistry. She. Loved. Him.

Instead of questioning how she could possibly fall for a man who was still a stranger in so many ways, Shadow gave herself permission to bask in the truth.

Empyria's most notorious blade had finally fallen in love.

Just as her heart took flight in her chest, an arrow called reality brought it crashing down.

The man who'd captured her heart happened to be the realm's greatest threat, and she was duty-bound to destroy him.

CHAPTER 20

RONAN

Something shifted in Shadow's expression. A softening of her gaze and lips, a flush of color along her cheeks. It was a stark contrast to her usual mask of indifference, and he couldn't help but apply meaning to it. Perhaps he was a fool of the highest order for doing so, but he didn't care. He'd fight entire armies barehanded if it meant she was coming back to him.

Time away from Erebos had done her a world of good. With every passing hour, Ronan caught more glimpses of his Reyna and less of the cold-hearted Shadow. Though, the better he got to know this version of her, the fewer differences between the two he could find. The woman at the core of her was the same. Fearless. Alluring. Independent. Brilliant. Maddening.

His.

She was his. And if the hope nearly bursting from his chest was any indication, she might have just come to the realization too.

Finally.

Before he could take advantage of the moment either by molding his lips to hers then and there, or doing something even more barbaric like hoist her over his shoulder and take her somewhere he could peel the clothes from her body and lose himself inside her, a rustling sounded in the trees.

"Did you hear that?" Sebastian asked, twisting around to stare up into the darkened treetops.

Everyone tilted their faces to the sky, but there was little to make out beyond the warm orange glow of their fire. Only the ring closest to them was illuminated, the firelight not strong enough to penetrate the dark any further.

That left them with little to go on beyond what they could hear. And feel.

From the second the rustling started, the hair on the back of Ronan's neck and arms stood on end, signaling approaching danger. Some might not trust their instinct, but he knew better. With the Mother's hand so firmly entrenched in his life, there was little doubt this was another extension of her.

A warning.

Something was coming.

"Get up," he said, his voice pitched low but no less of a command.

There wasn't time to say anything else, but the others picked up on his intensity. They might not sense what he did, but they weren't going to question him either. After the last couple of days, their small group had bonded in the way only survivors could. Their trust was innate and absolute.

Bronn was on his feet, body angled protectively in front of his captain. Bast moved so that he was in a similar position in front of Shadow. Recalling the last time they'd fought together, he appreciated the other man's willingness to defend her, even though Ronan had every intention of seeing to the job himself.

The assassin gave him an arch look, but Bast didn't budge. She may not require protection, but she'd found herself a new protector regardless.

While this silent showdown took place, the quartermaster let out a low whistle, and the door to Jagger's cabin silently cracked open. Buttercup flew out, orange feathers rippling and transforming into a muted gray hue, allowing the protector to blend seamlessly into the darkness. Jagger wasn't far behind, a bundle of weapons in his arms.

Ronan automatically reached for the short sword he'd discovered in the smuggler's cave and bit off a curse. He'd stupidly left it in the room. A quick glance around confirmed that the others were similarly unarmed. Rookie mistake. They might have found a new base camp, but they were still in a foreign land. They shouldn't have dropped their guard for even a second.

Thankfully, the boson had them all covered and quickly passed out the scavenged weapons.

"Any idea what it could be?" Bronn whispered, the question aimed at his crewmember. If Ronan hadn't already seen the connection between Jagger and Buttercup in action, the inquiry might have seemed strange. As it was, he was thankful for the finch's eyes in the sky and their ability to share what they saw with the blue-haired man.

Jagger cocked his head, listening to something no one else could hear. "Airborne. Coming fast." One of his brows arched in what must have been surprise. "Shadowmelded."

A similar look of disbelief drifted across Calypso's and Sebastian's faces.

"Shadowmelded?" Ronan repeated, the word unfamiliar but sending a trickle of unease along his spine.

"Camouflaged," the captain explained. "Moving through the air but appearing as nothing more than a dark smudge."

The explanation was so similar to what he'd seen in the ocean prior to the Lusca attack that Ronan went on high alert. This was no coincidence. They were being hunted.

Shadow seemed to reach the same conclusion. She elbowed Bast behind her, borrowed daggers in hand and eyes trained on the sky.

"Meaning we won't know what's coming until it's too late," Bast said grimly.

"Or unless you have true sight," Bronn added, eyes shifting to Buttercup as she returned to her perch on Jagger's shoulder.

Yet another term Ronan was unfamiliar with, though this one he could guess easily enough. As if confirming his suspicion about the boson, Jagger let out a soft grunt.

"Drake. But like none I've ever seen."

"How so?" Calypso asked, but the time for information gathering was over.

"Incoming," Jagger rasped.

Right on cue, a shadow slipped across the moon, leaving them with only the flickering flames to illuminate the night. It was impossible to have any sense of the creature's size, but with the way it seemed to blanket the visible portion of the sky, making the very stars themselves seem to blink out, he was going to assume it was significant. Then again, he'd dealt with creatures no larger than a marmot that caused no end of damage. There was no direct correlation between size and danger, but bigger was rarely better when dealing with monsters.

Ronan had faced off with all manner of beast, but when the creature dropped the magic keeping it hidden, there was no denying the wave of instinctive panic.

Mother have mercy.

It was crafted from the very worst nightmare. Horned. Skeletal. With milky eyes twice the size of his head and an elongated snout dripping with acidic saliva. The sinewy black fiber running the length of its wings and body stretched so tautly it may as well not have been there at all. But when the spiked tail came into view and plumes of ash-colored smoke curled from its nose, Ronan realized the true threat remained unseen.

Fire and acid? Mother's tits, how were they supposed to fight this thing when even getting close to it presented a problem?

"What's it waiting for?" Bast hissed.

"Some sort of cue, I'd wager," Ronan answered.

"From who? There's no rider," Bronn pointed out.

"I don't understand. I thought all drakes had riders," Sebastian said. "Is it wild?"

Jagger shook his head. "Whatever *that* is, it's not a drake. Not one hailing from The Crags, anyway."

"So what is it?" Ronan asked.

"A nightmare," Shadow whispered, face leached of color. "One of Erebos's special fiends." She swallowed, never taking her eyes off the creature hovering above them. "Have you ever wondered how the High Lord came to power? How he convinced all those people to follow him?"

Shock and disgust warred within him. He'd known the man must have schemed his way into power, but he'd never guessed the full extent of his depravity. "He sent these things after them?"

"Not exactly like this. The creatures are never the same."

"So, he what? Creates them, sends them in to wreak havoc, and then comes to the rescue of the poor people he terrorized?"

It was unspeakable. The worst sort of manipulation. And it was exactly the sort of thing Erebos would do, Ronan realized. Especially when one considered the way he treated Shadow. If he'd do *that* to someone he cherished, what was actually off the table?

Shadow nodded but still wouldn't look his way. He sensed the shame rolling off her, likely for the part she played in his machinations. Willingly or not.

Not for the first time, Bast revealed a surprising moral compass. "And you were okay with this?" he asked, his voice scathing.

"I didn't really get a say in the matter."

"But you serve him anyway."

Her eyes flashed dangerously at the accusation. "I didn't get a choice about that either. The man saved my life more than once. I owe him everything."

"Including blind loyalty? What about the people he killed? What do you owe them?"

Ronan was about to interject that this was hardly the time to throw stones, but Shadow's tortured reply beat his own.

"How can I condemn his actions when I am no better myself? My body count is easily as high, if not higher. I am an assassin, Sebastian. Vilify me if you must, but do not act as though I've been dishonest about who or what I am."

"The only one you're lying to is yourself," Bast said, disappointment heavy in his tone. "And the only person who gets to decide what side you fight on is you. Everyone is a villain in someone else's story, but at least be the hero of your own. You are better than this, Shadow. Your morals might be gray, but they exist. Do not make excuses for a man who doesn't deserve them—or you. Especially not when you have one right here who so clearly *does*."

Ronan stilled when Sebastian meaningfully looked his way. The impassioned speech was so unexpected, so out of character for playful, fun-loving Bast, that it took a moment to recover.

"As much as I appreciate the show of support, I don't think this is the time," he said, the creature hovering above them weaving its serpentine neck back and forth, as if seeking out its target.

"I don't understand why it's just hovering up there," Bronn whispered.

"It's waiting for permission," Shadow said, voice flat. Her expression was devoid of emotion, but he could tell she'd taken Bast's words to heart. He couldn't help but wonder if this was her first crisis of faith regarding Erebos.

Or what the outcome would be.

But regardless, the tingles racing beneath his skin told him this was a turning point.

"So what are we waiting for? Shouldn't we run, or I don't know, *do* something?" Calypso asked, gaze wary as plumes of smoke began to fill their little clearing.

"What would you suggest we do?" Ronan asked. "We can't reach it with normal weapons, and I doubt throwing them will be particularly effective. We certainly can't outrun it."

"What about your Fire?" Sebastian asked.

Ronan glanced at the very flammable trees and buildings all around them. "It's an option, but a dangerous one. Especially since the beast can send fire of its own right back. I can smother the flames, but who knows how much damage they'll cause in the meantime?"

"What if I can keep it distracted?" Shadow asked, her eyes narrowing as she scanned the trees.

"Distracted how?"

"Leave that to me."

"Shadow, wait—Fuck!"

She was already off and running, shimming up the nearest tree and climbing its branches with a skill that spoke of a lifetime living among them. She reminded him so much of the woman he'd first met in that moment that his breath stuttered. She wasn't just a child of the forest; she was a protector of the wild things that lived alongside her.

Their queen, first and always.

There was a split second of confusion when she grasped the topmost branch and lifted her leg, curling it up and over, then repeating the move with her other until she was seated on the bough. That's when he understood her intention and knew Bast was to blame for the heroic—albeit idiotic—act.

After her earlier confession and his well-meaning admonishment, Shadow now felt as though she had something to prove. And it just might be the death of her.

But even if Ronan wanted to intervene, it was too late. Everything happened so fast, he was helpless to do anything but react. When she stood on the branch and launched herself at the creature, her name was torn from his throat.

"Shadow!"

"What the fuck is she doing?" Jagger snapped.

"Nereus save us," Calypso breathed, hand pressed to her chest as she stared at the other woman.

Ronan had never known terror like he did in that suspended moment when Shadow's body arced through the air with nothing to catch her. When she finally hit the nightmare's back, his breath left him in a whoosh, only to lodge itself in his throat when she immediately began to slide off. The hitherto stealthy and silent predator let out a roar that shook the very earth, jerking its body to and fro in its attempt to rid itself of the unwanted rider.

"Mother fuck—"

"Ronan, do something," Bast cried.

What could he do? With all the gifts at his disposal, he was utterly useless in that moment, and it shredded him. He did not come this far, only to lose everything now.

But neither did she.

Shadow adjusted her grip, wrapping an arm around the drake's neck and using the leverage to better seat herself on its back. Then in a display of dexterity and speed that should have been impossible, she freed her daggers from the sheath hidden at her back and drove them into the creature's eyes, blinding it.

"Does the woman have a death wish?" Bronn shouted, face pale, when the beast bellowed in pain and released a jet of molten flame that came straight for them.

The five of them still on the ground scattered, each diving in an opposite direction as they tried to escape the torrent of fire. Ronan tucked, somersaulting and springing back to his feet a few yards away.

"Ronan, now!" she screamed.

Not requiring any further prompting, Ronan summoned his magic. Using a combination of Air and Fire, he took control of the wild flames, corralling them and sending them spiraling back toward the nightdrake, as he decided to call it. While impressive to look at, the ball of flame didn't do more than explode harmlessly across the beast's chest. He'd been afraid of that. The fire-breathing creature was immune to the element. So much for his magic being the answer.

He prayed Shadow knew what she was doing because he sure fucking didn't.

Then she pulled one of the blades free and twisted to the side so she could tear into the membranous flesh of the creature's wing, and he understood her plan. Her goal was to debilitate its wings so it fell to the ground where the rest of them could hopefully make short work of it.

It was a brilliant, if not short-sighted, plan. What the hell did she think was going to happen to her when it fell from the sky?

"Get ready," he called to the others. "We're only getting one shot at this once the beast falls."

Already the nightdrake was listing to the side, shooting off more jets of flame in various directions as it struggled to combat the pest seated between its shoulder blades. He was so caught up in banking the errant fire and keeping an eye on what Shadow was doing that he barely had time to warn Bast about the fireball heading his way.

Rather than leave it to fate, Ronan raced forward, bodily shoving the other man out of the way and helping him narrowly avoid the deadly spray. Unfortunately, he wasn't as lucky. Nor was he impervious to fire—despite his ability to wield it.

A strangled cry left him as the nightdrake's fiery breath ate through cloth and flesh, crawling along the left side of his body before he had a chance to drop and roll. It was already tearing through muscle before Ronan managed to fully suppress it.

But that didn't mean he was out of danger. Far from. For that was when he learned the agonizing truth regarding the monster's ability. The acid he'd seen drip from the fang-filled maw was woven into the flame. And what the fire couldn't burn, acid could.

Ronan had been able to nullify part of the threat, but not all of it. The Air magic he'd used to bank the flame was useless against its chemical counterpart.

Rolling to his back, it was all he could do to draw in a breath through the overwhelming pain exploding up the left side of his body. He knew better than to look over and assess the damage to his limbs mid-fight. It would only distract him, and he needed to focus. It was the only way to help the others survive long enough to slay this beast.

Only then would he worry about whether he'd ever walk again.

"Ronan!" Bast rushed to his side, looking like he was about to be sick.

"Don't worry about me."

"Don't tell me what I'm allowed to feel," the blond man snapped, performing a quick inspection before wrapping an arm around the uninjured side of his body and helping him to a seated position. "You nearly went up in flame saving my life. So you will excuse me while I do everything in my power to keep you from dying. If only to save myself the crippling guilt."

It was such a *Bast* thing to say that Ronan choked out a laugh despite the pain.

He'd lost track of the pirates while splitting his attention between what Shadow was doing and how he could assist from the ground. A quick glance showed them on the other side of the clearing, their gazes trained to the sky as the nightdrake flailed in earnest.

"Here it comes!" Jagger called at the same time Shadow's shout rang out, "Watch out!"

She must have finished tearing through enough of the wings that the creature could no longer keep itself airborne. It was falling fast, and there was no way to control its descent as it careened straight for them.

This entire battle had been a series of half-cocked plans and dumb luck. It was time to stop reacting and make a real fucking move.

"Everyone get down!" he roared.

Eyeing the nearby trees, Ronan dove deep into the heart of his power, draining himself almost entirely as he sent all of it pulsing through the earth. Dirt and leaves flew into the air. The ground shook, as did everything else in contact with it.

He knew the combination of Earth and Air was the right play when the trees shuddered and split, their trunks severed by the blast of his power. Without the proper support, they began to fall, tipping to the side with the aid of a bit more Air and creating an entire row of spikes to act as the nightdrake's landing strip. He still couldn't be sure it would be enough, but with the speed of the drake's fall, he was hoping the wood would pierce whatever part of the creature it came into contact with.

The gamble paid off spectacularly.

Three of the five spikes impaled the throat, middle of the belly, and what might have been an armpit were the creature human. The night-drake was dead before it finished sliding down them.

But even more impressive was the way Shadow jumped from its back and expertly caught a nearby branch before swinging herself down into a crouch. She made the acrobatics look so easy, he almost believed the feat an easy one until his eyes tracked the distance she'd flown through the air and his vision went spotty.

"Bast—"

"Shut up, Ronan. You've done enough."

"If I—"

"Do *not* give me the 'If I don't make it' speech. I'm supposed to be the one with the flair for the dramatic. Get yourself together."

"Tell her—"

"Tell her yourself, dammit."

Ronan didn't get the opportunity to bicker further. The spots had turned to a full-blown fog, and it was impossible to keep himself upright. He tipped backward, caught by a strong pair of arms before he hit the ground, but there was no way to know who they belonged to. The pain he'd worked so hard to suppress would no longer be ignored, and the only way his brain could deal with it was to shut down.

He couldn't be sure he wasn't imagining it when a soft voice whispered in his ear, "Sleep, Ronan. You've earned it. But if you think you're getting out of those promises you made by dying on me now, you have no idea who you're dealing with. I will find a way to bring you back just so I can kill you myself."

He would have laughed if he had any control of himself. But then the fierce whispers continued, and he had no desire to laugh at all. Weeping was a distinct possibility, though. For the words, while bittersweet, brought with them a tidal wave of relief.

"You do not get to make me fall in love with you only to leave me before we get to do anything about it. So rest, but then come back to me." There was a beat when what could have been a kiss was pressed to the center of his forehead. "Please come back to me."

When oblivion finally claimed him, there was a smile on his lips and a delirious refrain looping through his mind.

She loves me.

CHAPTER 21

SHADOW

*I*t was as if everyone waited for Ronan to fall unconscious before giving in to the worry they were feeling. Bast let out a heavy exhale, Caly shot pointed glances at her crew, and Shadow slumped over his still form.

Calling the fight sloppy would have been a kindness. She'd witnessed better battle strategies involving broken liquor bottles and slingshots. To be fair, there hadn't been much of a strategy. Just fervent prayers and a reliance on instinct she hadn't needed to employ in nearly a decade. It was a vast difference from the sort of careful choreography she usually employed. There'd been none of her usual finesse, just a desperate need to protect the people who'd only found themselves on the receiving end of Erebos's wrath because of her.

True, it wasn't her fault she was here, but the High Lord never would have gotten involved with any of them if not for her. It wasn't fair that they should die due to sheer proximity.

Right, Shadow. Because proximity *is the only reason he's hunting you and Ronan. It wouldn't have anything to do with jealousy. Or the fact that he wants you to be his Lady, and instead, you've all but thrown yourself at your captor. Or would-be captor. Does it still count as kidnapping if you don't mind the fact that you were stolen in the night?*

Shut. Up.

She did not have time to get into an argument with herself right now. Part of her recognized that panic was the reason for her mental tangent. It was easier to focus on nonsensical details rather than the very real threat looming over them all. Ronan could quite literally be dying in her arms, and she didn't know how to save him.

When he'd started to topple over, she'd only just reached him by sliding across the forest floor on her knees. It wasn't like he'd had far to fall, seated as he'd been, but she'd simply reacted without thinking. Now the bulk of his upper body was supported by her arms, and she was loath to release him. At least like this, she could feel the still steady beat of his heart against hers.

"What do we do? Is he going to make it?" Sebastian's face was creased in a deep frown, his gray gaze stormy when it met hers over Ronan's shoulder.

Shadow tried to keep her voice calm. "I don't know. We don't have access to a healer, let alone the kind of supplies to deal with a wound this serious." If they were back in Glimmermere, she would know exactly how to proceed, but out here in the middle of No Man's Land? She hadn't a clue.

"This is all your fault."

She jerked back, her arms curling protectively around Ronan's torso. "My fault?"

He waved his hands around, reminding her of birds taking flight. "If you hadn't taken my little speech quite so literally, this never would have happened."

"Maybe you should be less convincing next time," she snapped. Because fuck it all, it had been his words she'd heard when she'd stared up at the trees and a plan had taken shape. She didn't know where the instinct to climb had come from, only that her body had known exactly what to do. She'd felt at home in the trees in a way she couldn't recall ever feeling in the palace.

A shudder worked its way down her spine as another forest super-imposed itself over the trees before her, the tropical fronds replaced with ancient conifers. She blinked, Sebastian and the others' worried faces swimming back into view and rooting her firmly in the present.

"Bast, that's not fair," Calypso chided gently. "Shadow's quick thinking is likely the only reason we survived. We were not remotely prepared to battle that creature."

There was a flicker of something in the back of the captain's gaze.

"What aren't you saying?" Shadow asked.

"The whole thing just seemed odd to me. Why sneak up on us and then just watch and wait? It's like the thing wanted us to come up with some sort of strategy first."

"It was reporting back."

"How? Why?"

Shadow didn't know exactly how Erebos controlled his creations, only that he was linked to them in a similar fashion as Buttercup and Jagger. What they saw, he could see. What they heard, he could hear.

"He's playing with us," she realized, speaking the thought aloud at the same time it occurred to her. "Erebos wants me back. Alive. So these monsters he keeps sending, they're a distraction—"

"Monsters? You think he was behind the Lusca attack?" Caly asked.

"It tracks," Bronn said quietly. "Both creatures had the ability to shadowmeld. Have you ever known a Lusca to do so?"

Jagger and Calypso shook their heads.

"It's his specialty," Shadow admitted, thinking of all the other times she'd seen him craft fantastic beasts out of nothing more than twilight. "It's how I realized he was behind it."

"He likely won't stop until he has you. If he can manifest a Lusca and drake . . ." the captain trailed off.

"This is just the tip of what he's capable of," Shadow confirmed. "But he doesn't actually want to hurt me. Maybe if I turn myself over, he'll leave the rest of you in peace."

"Shut your mouth. Ronan did not sacrifice himself so you could turn around and give up on him now," Bast said, though not unkindly.

"I'm not! I'm trying to save his life. All your lives," she quickly amended.

"Well, stop it. He wouldn't want that. Since he can't voice his veto in his current state, I shall do it on his behalf."

Shadow bit the inside of her cheek, oddly touched by Bast's fierce support of his friend. "Fair enough."

"He's not waiting long between raids. These came within days of each other. More will be on the horizon," Bronn pointed out, crouching down to inspect the savage burns lining the better part of Ronan's left side.

They'd barely made it through the first two attacks; how would they survive another? Brushing some hair off his brow, the truth crashed into her. They wouldn't. Especially with Ronan in his current state.

Shadow couldn't let her gaze drift past his profile. The sight of all that charred flesh had her stomach twisting in knots. If she focused on the thick fringe of his eyelashes and the way they went blond at the tips, she could pretend he was just sleeping.

"Is there a healer or someone who has access to medical supplies in town?" she asked.

Calypso bit her bottom lip. "Yes, but . . ." The captain didn't need to finish the sentence; it was written all over her face. She didn't think Ronan would make it that long.

"Well, you heard Sebastian. We aren't giving up. If I have to carry him there myself, I'll do it. Just point me in the right direction."

Jagger moved silently, coming to stand behind her so he could rest his hand on her shoulder. "There might be another way."

"How? Tell me."

"It would be easier to show you."

"But Ronan—"

"We've got him," Bronn assured her. He and Sebastian already getting into position to carefully lift him off her so they could follow.

She wasn't thrilled with the idea of letting him out of her sight, but Sebastian and Bronn could manage much more quickly than she would attempting to carry him on her own.

"Lead the way," she said, giving Jagger a jerky nod.

Buttercup took off, heading to the west but never straying too far so the others could easily trail behind. It wasn't long, perhaps twenty minutes at most, before the trickle of water reached Shadow's ears. And then another five before the waterfall came into view.

The protector had brought them to a magical oasis. It was stunning. There was simply no other word to describe it. The water was an aqua so bright and translucent it seemed lit from below. All around the edge of the lagoon, bioluminescent flora grew, only adding to the glittering effect. The plants were unlike any she'd come across, from the navy and claret-colored vines growing along the rocks, to the bulb-like center of the turquoise flowers, with their spikey petals and glowing bits of pollen lazily floating just above them.

It was enchanting, romantic even, in a way that was completely lost on her, given their situation.

Buttercup let out a series of musical trills, finally pulling Shadow's attention back up to them when they began to perform a combination of spins and dives above the deepest part of the pool.

"You want me to get in the water?"

Another soft chirp she took as affirmation.

"But I'm not the one injured. How is my getting in the water going to help him?"

Shadow wasn't sure if it was pity or exasperation that finally had the protector speaking in her mind. *"He's unconscious. He's going to need you to keep him afloat."*

"Well, why not just say that in the first place," she muttered, kicking off her boots before paddling out into the water.

Bronn and Sebastian were right behind her, Ronan's large frame towed between them.

It didn't take long to realize the water had healing properties. The little aches and twinges she'd grown accustomed to after days spent on her feet and pushing herself to the limits vanished. The scrapes and cuts on her hands and forearms from her climb up the tree knit themselves back together before vanishing entirely.

She gasped. "How?"

How did you know this was here? How did you know what it

would do? The end of the question didn't matter since the answer was likely the same.

"We have something similar back home," Jagger replied. "Places like this . . .They have a heartbeat. My kind is drawn to them. We feel them even if we've never been there before."

My kind. Shadow had suspected the boson wasn't exactly an Empyrean native, but this was the first hint he'd provided that seemed to confirm it.

"And home is . . ."

"The Wildes." He didn't elaborate, but given the sharp glance Calypso shot his way, it was more than he should have revealed.

"And the water can heal him too?" She'd seen the proof of its abilities for herself, but she was afraid Ronan's injuries might be too much for even this place of power to undo.

"It already is."

Shadow's gaze returned to Ronan. Inky black smears were rippling away from him, like the charred skin running along his left side had just been a bit of mud.

"Thank you," she breathed, her voice huskier than usual, but if anyone noticed, they were too nice to comment on it.

"Here. Why don't you take him," Bronn called, likely reading her sudden need to touch him in her expression.

She waded through the waist-deep water back to where the men were holding up her red-haired warrior. He was mostly floating, but she wove her arms beneath him anyway. As she tucked him against her body, she happily noted that color had returned to his face and his breathing was even once more.

"How long does he need to remain in the water?"

"It takes as long as it takes."

"It could be a while," Jagger answered out loud. "Perhaps all night."

"You should return to camp then. Try to get some rest. I'll stand guard."

"I'll stay with you," Sebastian offered.

"No, that's all right." It wasn't that she didn't appreciate the offer, but after the chaos of the last few hours—days, really—she longed for a bit of peace. And Bast was many things, most of them good, but peaceful wasn't among them.

"Come on, puppy. You're with us," Bronn said, curling his arm around the other man's neck and pulling him away.

"But what if he needs me?"

Bronn slapped a hand to his chest. "Trust me, the sorts of needs he'll have when he wakes aren't the kind you can help with."

Bast opened his mouth to argue but then seemed to reconsider when he looked back at Shadow. He lingered only long enough to shoot her a glance that promised retribution if harm befell his friend, but his parting words were a tart, "I suppose there's a first time for everything."

She really couldn't help but admire anyone who could manage to be so fiercely protective and seemingly frivolous in the same breath. Bast wasn't what he appeared on the surface. She'd stake her life on it. There was simply too much intention behind the way he acted for his buffoonery to be entirely organic. Maybe the flirtatious fuck boy had been *exactly* who he was at one time, but not any longer. Now it was a part he played. A mantle he donned as easily she did her own.

Who are you really, Sebastian?

The others silently filed out of the hidden oasis until only Jagger remained. "Buttercup will keep watch. If you need anything . . ." Instead of finishing the thought, he gave her a slight dip of his chin and wandered off.

If she thought Bast was a riddle, that man was an entire book of them. Just when it seemed she might be making headway, he retreated back into himself. If she had the time or mental energy to take on anything else, she'd attempt to unravel the mysteries surrounding her companions. But her hands were full. Both literally and metaphorically.

Shadow waited until she and Ronan were well and truly alone—minus the finch circling languidly overhead—before glancing back down at the man in her arms. For once she was able to greedily look her fill.

The usually severe lines between his brows and bracketing his lips were smoothed away, revealing a fainter set of creases beside his eyes. She'd seen Ronan smile and laugh plenty of times, but the acts were almost always tinged by an aura of grief. The evidence that hadn't always been the case was bittersweet. She couldn't help but wonder what it might be like to spend time with him when he was relaxed and truly happy.

Her gaze trailed lower, down the slope of his nose with its light dusting of freckles, along his cheeks tinged red from their days spent in the sun, and down to his full lips. They were lightly parted and framed by several days' worth of thick stubble. The deep auburn scruff matched the ends of his hair bobbing along the surface of the water.

From there her eyes wandered lower, down the tanned column of his throat, over the bare shoulder with its thick black swirls and what appeared to be a series of hidden symbols. She itched to trace the markings with her fingers, to ask him about the meaning behind the tattoo. So far as she could tell, it was the only one he had. And given the prominence of its position—climbing across his broad chest and up over his shoulder before spiraling down to his elbow—it must be significant.

She lost all track of time as her visual feast continued. Her thoughts alternated between appreciation for his potent masculine beauty and curiosity about the man beneath the attractive trap-pings. And then all thoughts flitted away as she focused on the freshly healed skin peeking out from the scraps of clothes clinging to his left side. She hadn't realized how badly the garments had been damaged until she spied all the sun-darkened flesh on display.

It was a wonder he had any shirt to speak of at all. In truth it was little more than a right sleeve with a scrap wrapped around the bottom half of his toned stomach to hold it together. His pants hadn't fared much better.

Not that she was complaining. At all.

The tattered clothes gave her an excuse to visually traverse the peaks and valleys chiseled into existence by all those hard-earned muscles. She didn't realize her mouth had gone dry until her trail came to a disappointing end at the waistband of his trousers.

"Well, Butcher, I can't say this is exactly how I imagined seeing you naked for the first time."

"Oh?" he rasped, startling a cry from her lips.

Heart racing from the shock of hearing his voice, she jerked away. Ronan dropped like a stone, submerging himself completely in the water before surging back up in a riot of sputtering coughs.

"Mother's tits. Haven't I nearly drowned enough for one lifetime?"

"I'm sorry, I didn't mean . . . that is, you weren't supposed to . . . they said it could be all night."

He wiped a hand down his dripping face, brushing away water and long strands of his hair. "Well, don't leave me in suspense. How *did* you picture it?"

She blinked at him, her mind still scrambling to play catch-up. "Picture what?"

"Me." He gave her a lopsided smirk, his eyes luminous beneath his spiked lashes. "Naked."

"I didn't." The blurted lie was a reflex, but the seductive curl of his lip told her he wasn't going to let it go.

"I'm afraid the cat's out of the bag, *kitten.*" He prowled forward in the waist-high water until he stood mere inches away. "I heard you admit it quite clearly. In fact, I seem to have collected quite a few of your confessions."

Shadow gulped, her pulse skyrocketing at his proximity. "Oh?" She aimed for casual disinterest, but the breathless quality of her voice betrayed her.

"Mmhmm." He nodded slowly, his eyes locked on hers.

The heat she found in them positively seared her with its intensity. *How is it possible something the exact color of ice has the power to burn?* Even half-submerged in the cool water, her body was on fire. Lit from within by whatever it was he was doing to her with a mere look.

"People say lots of things in the heat of the moment."

"But you're not *people*, are you, kitten? You don't say anything you don't mean."

Shadow bit her lower lip. That wasn't strictly true. She'd lied to herself and Erebos plenty. Ronan, too. Though not, perhaps, in the way he meant.

"I'm known for being direct," she said eventually.

She couldn't look away from him. There was something about being in this place, surrounded by its beauty and power—and him— that was tearing away the last of her inhibitions. It was impossible to focus on anything other than how close he was standing. How if he'd only dip his head down, they'd be kissing.

What she should be doing was checking his injuries to ensure they were properly healed, or perhaps insisting he lay down and rest for a while. That's the whole reason they were here. Instead, her attention was singularly locked on his mouth and what might come next.

When he spoke again, his voice was barely more than a rasp, and she felt the vibration roll over her like the brush of a fingertip along her most sensitive skin. "So, did you mean it?"

"Mean what?"

He took her face between both his hands. "That you love me."

For a second it felt as though the floor dropped out from beneath her, but the warmth of his palms on her cheeks held her steady. She might be falling, but he was right there, ready to catch her.

You wanted to stop running, Shadow. You wanted to know what would happen if you gave in. Now's your chance.

There might be a million reasons this was a terrible idea. She could think of a certain blond one in particular, but she didn't care. Lying about it now wouldn't make what she felt for him any less real. It would only delay the inevitable.

And if the last few days had taught her anything, it was that *they* were inevitable.

Denial hadn't gotten her anywhere, and she was tired of running away from the things she wanted. It was time to find out what happened when she stopped running and finally took the leap.

So she jumped.

"Yes."

CHAPTER 22

RONAN

*H*e wasn't sure whether she'd actually said the word aloud, or if he'd just prayed to hear it so desperately that he hallucinated it leaving her lips.

A soft disbelieving laugh escaped, and she raised up on her toes until her eyes were almost level with his. "I said, yes, damn you."

All the breath left his lungs as he stared into those glittering green irises. "Yes?"

"Yes! Now, what are you going to do about it?"

The air grew charged as they continued to stare at one another, and then, like a band that had pulled past its limit, they were the two overstretched ends snapping back to one another. They both exploded into action, Shadow jumping up and Ronan there to catch her, his palms finding the rounded globes of her arse and hauling her against him as her long legs wrapped around his hips. Their lips crashed together as her hands curled around the sides of his head and slid into the freed strands of his hair.

"It's about fucking time, kitten."

"Don't ruin this by talking."

"If you think talking ruins it—"

"Shut up," she growled, giving his hair a tug as she nipped his bottom lip. "I'm much more interested in what you can do than whatever you can say."

Nothing about this woman was expected, and he loved that even in her moment of surrender, she continued to challenge him.

Challenge accepted, sweetheart.

Flexing his hands, he deepened the kiss and rolled his hips into her, letting her feel what she did to him. Her guttural moan had him biting back a smile. Just because she didn't want him to talk didn't mean he wouldn't make her sing.

It had been only a handful of days since he'd tasted her last, but it felt like the first time. Maybe because, in a lot of ways, it was. For him as much as her. Shadow didn't remember the alcove, and besides an extended courtship—if one could consider a year spent flirting and fighting side by side followed by five more tearing the world apart searching for her a courtship—that stolen moment was the only one they'd shared. In all that time, Ronan hadn't been with another. She was it for him. The ultimate prize. A love worth fighting for. Who else could possibly compete with that?

He'd been praying for this since she'd mended the shattered pieces of his heart. He thought he'd been in love once, but now realized what he'd experienced then didn't hold a candle to everything this woman made him feel. She inspired him. Frustrated him. Fucking owned him.

And she loved him.

Not time. Not distance. Not even a total loss of self had kept them from finding their way back to one another. So even if the sky started to rain down around them, Ronan wasn't about to let anything else keep him from making her his.

"Do you have any idea how much I fucking love you?" he growled against her mouth, needing to give her the words back. He knew how much it meant to hear them. He didn't want her to ever doubt his intentions.

"Show me," she breathed, her eyes fluttering closed as she reclaimed his lips.

A rumble of pleasure vibrated through his chest. Never had he been quite so eager to obey a command. Still kissing her, he slowly walked them out of the water, pulling back briefly to ensure the path was clear.

He hadn't had a chance to take in their surroundings; the only thing he'd had eyes for when he woke was the woman whose husky voice had lured him out of the darkness. But seeing it now, he couldn't have asked for a better place to make love to his woman. Between the cascade of water falling from the wall of moss-covered rocks, the glowing flowers with their luminescent pollen, and the privacy afforded them by a copse of trees, it looked like a glen Luna might craft for her own use.

He'd certainly made do with worse. And he supposed if they had to wait six years to have each other, at least it was going to be fucking memorable.

There wasn't much of a beach, just a subtle transition from water to sand to grass. But the patch of grass looked thick and soft and more than spacious enough for two people to roll around on. Angling them in that direction, he continued his slow walk. Savoring the feel of her lips opening beneath his, the press of her slick body against his, the way her center brushed over his cock with every step.

Reaching the edge of the little knoll, he slowly dropped to his knees, gently untangling her from his body and laying her back so he could drink his fill. Her silvery hair spilled around her like a halo. Her eyes were hooded and glassy with desire, lips already swollen from his kisses.

She was the most breathtakingly beautiful woman he'd ever seen.

"Ronan," she protested, reaching for him.

"Hush, love, let me look at you."

There was no embarrassed squirm or virginal flush. Instead, Shadow held his gaze and shifted so she could remove her clothes. She started with her borrowed shirt and a scrap of lace he almost asked her to put back on. Pulling both over her head, she tossed them to the side, then lowered herself back down and began working at the fastenings of her pants.

"I might need your help with these," she said, her lips curling into a siren's seductive grin.

"I live to serve." His fingers hooked into the sides of her damp leathers and peeled them down her thighs. She lifted her hips to help him, and he nearly swallowed his tongue as her body was bared to him. From the pillowy mounds of her breasts with their dusky rose nipples to the toned slope of her belly and flare of her hips, she was perfection. Every inch of her.

"You undo me," he rasped, hands trembling with the need to touch her.

Her answering smile was pure sin.

"Your turn," she demanded as he tossed her boots and pants in the same general direction she'd thrown the rest of her clothes.

His shirt, or what was left of it, was barely more than rags. He tore it easily from his body and let it fall to the ground. His pants were a bit trickier, requiring him to get back to his feet so he could shove them off.

When he was finished, he raised to his full height, staring down at her splayed body as hungrily as she raked her gaze over his. She lingered on the heavy weight of his erection, her tongue darting out to wet her lips. He had to take himself in his hand and squeeze the base to keep himself from spilling then and there. But he wasn't the only one affected. Watching the way her body responded, her nipples pebbling and a gentle flush stealing across her skin, he worked his palm up and down his shaft. A whimper escaped her, and she rubbed her thighs together, seeking the same friction he granted himself.

"You're so beautiful," she whispered.

"I think that's supposed to be my line."

"Don't make me beg."

"What if I want you to beg?"

She lifted her eyes to his, her breath hitching. "Please, Ronan."

Unable to deny her anything, least of all his body, he knelt between her legs, positioning himself with his shoulders bracketed by her thighs.

"What are you doing?"

"What I've been dreaming about since the first time you held me at knifepoint."

"Oh," she breathed when he swept his tongue along her seam with an approving rumble.

He repeated the move, this time sinking two of his fingers inside her tight sheath and sucking on the swollen bundle of nerves at the top.

"Stars," she panted, thighs clamping hard on either side of his head.

Ronan grinned and then really went to work, varying the pressure and intensity of every suck, lick, and teasing bite, depending on her reactions. It wasn't long before he'd mastered a combination that had her shuddering beneath him, her moans desperate and the fingers laced through his hair gripping tight.

"Darkness above, Ronan. Stop playing with me."

He peeked up at her, smirking. "Do you want to come, kitten?"

"Yes!"

"Shall I use my mouth?" He feathered a kiss over her dripping center. "Perhaps my fingers?" He curled the two fingers still inside her. "Or do you think you're ready for my cock?"

Her lips parted in a soft 'o', and his smile stretched.

"I told you talking doesn't ruin it."

"Ro—" Her exasperated groan tapered off as his thumb circled over her clit.

"I'm waiting."

"Cock," she panted. "Stars, I need you inside me, Ronan. Now."

"Thank fuck."

He'd have been happy to bring her to release however she wished, but his balls ached with the need to find his own, and he'd be damned if he came anywhere but planted deep inside her.

Rising to his knees, he lined himself up with her entrance, pulling a moan from them both when he ran his crown through her slickness.

"Say it again."

Momentary confusion furrowed her brow before it cleared, and she gave him a soft smile. "I love you." Then in customary fashion, her smile turned impish. "Despite all better judgment."

A laugh was torn from him. "Doesn't matter if it's a technicality. You said it, kitten, and I'm not letting you take it back."

"I don't want to."

"Good, because I won't lose you again."

Holding her gaze, he sank into her, inch by tantalizing inch. His jaw was clenched, and sweat trickled down his nape at the control required to not drive straight home. It was worth it for the look of wonder on her face alone.

He took her thighs in each hand and hauled her up, lifting her hips off the ground so he could slide in that extra bit. Her inner muscles fluttered and then gripped him tight.

"Fuck," he gasped, his eyes nearly crossed at how good it felt to be buried to the hilt.

"More, Ronan. I need more."

"Just . . . give me . . . a second," he gritted out, the climax that he'd been keeping at bay since their kiss in the water dangerously close to the edge.

She squirmed, her body instinctively seeking the friction she needed.

His fingers dug into her skin with the effort it took not to come. "Please, sweetheart. Stay still."

"Why?"

Strained laughter met the question. "Because I'm trying to make this last."

"Why?"

"What do you mean, why?"

"Who asked you to draw it out? I want to come, Ronan. With you. Right now."

Far be it for him to question the lady. But before he could give her what she asked for, she twisted her hips and pushed her body weight into him, flipping them over so she was seated on top. It was a move she'd used on him in the arena, but not one he'd ever expected to experience while inside her.

He saw fucking stars.

"Fuuuck," he rasped, the pleasure so intense it bordered on painful. Then she flexed her inner muscles around him, clamping down and squeezing him until another hoarse groan escaped. "You're killing me, kitten."

She smirked. "That *is* my specialty. Let me show you how it's done, Butcher."

"Ronan. Call me by my name when I'm inside you."

She leaned forward, her hands pressed against his chest and her hair a curtain around them. Her lips brushed over his as she whispered, "Whatever you want, Ronan."

Then she rolled her hips, grinding down on him as she began to ride.

As much as he preferred being the one in control since it allowed him to set the pace and dole out pleasure, there was undeniable beauty in watching Shadow chase her climax. The perfect slide of her along his shaft, the play of emotions across her face, from her furrowed brow to the flash of her teeth biting into her lower lip, and the soft cries falling from her throat. All of it was a seduction that beckoned his own.

He met her thrust for thrust, heart thundering, eyes alternating between her face and the place where they were joined.

"Ronan, I'm close. Come with me."

He'd never had a woman demand his orgasm before. But then, with her, everything was a first. He didn't even know if it was possible for him to come on command, but then she came with a shout of his name, and it was as if he'd been waiting for her.

As soon as she clamped down around him, his climax crested, and he spilled inside her. It was so intense his vision went black at the edges, and he had to clench his eyes shut. The thundering of his heart in his ears was the only thing he was aware of until she shifted above him. In case she thought she was going anywhere anytime soon, he tightened his grip on her hips.

"Stay," he grunted.

It was all he could manage.

"Ronan." There was an uncertain note threaded through his name. One that didn't belong after the way she'd been screaming it only moments prior.

The realization cleared his mind of its pleasure-drunk fog. "Yes, kitten?"

"You found me."

His body went utterly still, his breath leaving him as if a fist had just been slammed into his lungs. His eyes snapped open, finding hers peering down at him. There was a new weight to her gaze, a recognition that hadn't been there since he found her in the marketplace. A low hum started in his ears as electric tingles raced just beneath his skin.

Could it be?

Terrified he was about to make a heinous misstep, especially after how she reacted last time, but unable to ignore what his gut was screaming at him, he hesitantly ventured, "Reyna?"

Her answering smile was tremulous, wobbling at the edges as tears misted her eyes. "Hi."

Everything slammed into him at once. Joy. Disbelief. Gratitude. Shock.

She remembered.

After all this time . . . Reyna was back.

CHAPTER 23

REYNA

*T*he return of her memories wasn't the momentous occasion one might expect. It was akin to stepping across a threshold. One second, she was outside the gate; the next, the entirety of her past was laid out before her. There was no disorientation or shock. She knew who she was, who she'd been, how she'd gotten here and everything in between.

The fact that their return was heralded by the most explosive orgasm of her life, well . . . maybe there'd been a bit more fanfare than she realized.

Ronan sat up, the shift reminding her he was still very much buried inside her. She had to bite her lip to fight a moan as he took her face between his hands, his eyes searching hers.

"How?"

"I'm not sure."

She'd let Ronan believe he was responsible for her sudden recovery—after everything he'd done to save her, he deserved to be the hero. And there was no denying his presence these last few weeks had gone a long way to breaking through the fog, but a quick flick of her eyes to the lagoon on their right told her it was a more likely culprit. With the pool's miraculous healing properties, it only made

189

sense the water had undone the years of mental tampering Erebos had performed on her.

Or maybe it was a combination of the two. Ronan's soul tugging on the threads of hers and the water there to wash away whatever barriers the High Lord had left in her mind.

Whatever the reason, she was beyond grateful.

She ran the tips of her fingers through his hair and feathered her lips over his. "Must be because of you, I guess."

An awestruck grin lit up his face for a second before he laughed and shook his head. "Well, I'll be damned. He was right."

"Who?"

"Bast. He told me saving you required true love's kiss."

Heat that had nothing to do with embarrassment crept into her cheeks. "We did a fair bit more than kiss."

"Aye." His smile returned. "That we did, love. Perhaps he simply mistranslated."

Reyna laughed. Being with him like this made her giddy. She couldn't remember the last time laughter ever came so freely. "Are you trying to say that there's such a thing as 'true love's fuck'?"

His arms wrapped tightly around her waist. "I don't need to say anything. I'm holding the truth in my arms."

"You think quite highly of yourself, don't you?"

"Well . . . I mean . . ."

Another laugh slipped free. The man always had been confident to the point of arrogance. She would have loved to bring him down a peg or two, if only for the sake of everyone else who'd have to deal with him now. But . . . she couldn't. They deserved this moment of unadulterated bliss.

"Erebos . . ." she started. There was so much to say, so many things he needed to know, but Ronan stopped her with a kiss.

"Please don't say that bastard's name while I'm inside you, kitten."

"But we—"

"Need to talk. I know. And we will, but can we just enjoy this fucking miracle a while longer before ruining it? It's been five years, Reyna. Five fucking years. Do you have any idea . . ."

"I'm sorry."

"Mother, don't apologize. What happened isn't your fault."

"I know, but I'd have spared you the pain if I could."

A dark cloud rolled through his eyes. "There are a lot of things I would go back and do differently if I could. But loving you isn't one of them. So what if it hurts? At least that means I know it's real."

"Love shouldn't hurt, Ronan."

"You misunderstand. Loving you doesn't hurt. It's the easiest thing I've ever done in my life. It was losing you that nearly did me in. I wish I could say I was a good man, that I was worthy of you, but—"

This time it was she who stopped him with a kiss. "My hands are far from clean, Ronan. We do not need to compare sins. I know all that I need to know. And knowing what I do, I can say with complete certainty, there is nowhere else I'd rather be than right here, with you."

A shudder ran down the length of his body, and he squeezed his eyes shut, a ragged breath leaving him. "Reyna, I—" He opened his eyes, and what she found staring back at her took her breath away. "I missed you so fucking much."

She pressed her palm to the soft scrape of his beard. "I missed you too. Five years is a long time."

"For you, I'd wait a hundred."

"Really?" she teased. "You don't think you would have eventually moved on?"

"Moved on?" He looked so offended by the implication she couldn't help but laugh. "Reyna, the only thing that would have made me give up on finding you is learning you were already dead. In fact, it nearly did. And do you know what happened? I didn't *move on*. I tried to join you."

Her heart shattered. "Oh, Ronan. I wouldn't have wanted that."

"I know, but . . . I was hardly in a place where I could think past my pain. The truth is, kitten, I don't want to exist in a world that doesn't have you in it."

The raw honesty, his heartbreak, it slayed her.

"You are mine, Reyna," he fiercely vowed. "My woman, my mate, my future. There is no adventure, not even death, that I will not face by your side."

She'd fallen in love with him long ago. Somewhere between him waltzing uninvited into her forest and kissing her scars when she'd nearly lost her sight to Rowena's war. But here, in this moment, she finally understood the depth of it.

Reyna didn't realize she was crying until Ronan brushed a tear off her cheek. This time their kiss tasted of tears, but also hope. So much hope.

"I love you," she breathed.

"I love you more."

"I didn't realize it was a competition."

"With us? Sweetheart, it's always a competition. That's half the fun."

She had to laugh, because fuck if it wasn't true.

There was one last question she couldn't help but ask. The rest would come later, but this one she selfishly needed the answer to. "What about Helena?"

His lips twisted. "We really have to teach you not to bring up other people while we're naked together, kitten. Especially a woman I consider my sister."

"You started it with Bast—"

Ronan groaned and finally slid free of her.

She dropped an apologetic kiss on his nose. "Last time, I promise."

He sighed good-naturedly, his large palms roaming up and down her back. "What about Helena?"

"She's the Kiri. You're her Shield. You are life-sworn to her."

He lifted a shoulder. "So?"

"What do you mean 'so'?"

"Loving you doesn't suddenly make me incapable of protecting her. If the last few years have been good for anything, it was proving that." His gaze grew tender, and one of his hands slipped up to curl around the back of her neck. "What is it you're really worried about?"

"I don't want you to have to choose between us. I know what she means to you. What being one of the Circle means to you."

"After everything I've endured to find you, you're worried *that* will be the thing keeping us apart?"

It sounded silly when he put it that way. But Ronan was a man of honor, and he'd given the Chosen's queen his vow. It wasn't something he'd walk away from lightly. She needed to know he was sure. It would break her heart to only lose him in the end.

He must have read the uncertainty in her expression because the fingers around her neck dug in gently. "Helena knows where my heart lies. If being yours means I must relinquish my title to be with you, then I will. But that will be because of your obligations, not mine. I already told you, kitten. Where you go, I go."

Her heart gave a happy flutter. "My obligations?"

"You're the Night Stalker's queen."

Her bark of laughter was harsh. "In name, perhaps."

"Only name?"

Reyna ached at the thought of all the friends and family she'd loved who were lost to her. The ones she'd unknowingly left for dead. She didn't think she'd ever be able to forgive herself for that, even if she'd been helpless to stop it. As much as she wanted to explain, she didn't know how when so much of the answer involved Erebos's betrayal, and he'd asked her not to speak of him.

"A queen requires subjects to rule. I fear few, if any, Night Stalkers remain."

That seemed to be enough of an explanation because his eyes shone with empathy. He knew exactly what she was referring to.

"Then we find the ones who are left and begin again."

"You say that as if it's going to be easy."

"Easy? No, probably not. But if that is your path, we will walk it together."

"Ronan."

So much was wrapped up in that single word. Sentiments she couldn't begin to convey. But because it was Ronan, he understood all of it.

"Do you doubt us? In the last two days alone, we've fought and bested literal leviathans. I think a rescue mission would be child's play."

"First, I'm not sure we can claim to have bested the Lusca. Second, you're forgetting a specific monster we've yet to deal with."

His expression shuttered. "Erebos is naught more than a man with a god complex."

It was so close to the truth and so hilariously wrong that she laughed. Loud and long.

"What's so funny?"

So much for saving this conversation for another time. "My love, Erebos isn't just a man. Not even close. And if he has a god complex it's because he is one."

"What?"

"Ronan . . . think about it. How did Kieran accomplish all that he did?"

"He's a slimy, manipulative bastard."

"Maybe so, but what are the odds he'd find the correct prophecy, bring down the citadel, and break out of the Kiri's palace? A *man* would never be able to accomplish all that."

"And yet he did."

She gave him a little shake. "Do you really believe a single man could best the entirety of the Keepers? Kieran was never the one pulling the strings, Ronan. It was Erebos. Kieran is as much his puppet as I was, but in so many ways, he had it worse because Erebos didn't just use him. He took over."

"What are you saying?"

"You know what I'm saying." Reyna held his confused stare, giving him time to process all she'd just dumped in his lap.

"It's not just a new identity."

"No."

"Kieran is a Vessel."

"Yes."

"The same way Helena is."

"*Yes.*"

"This whole time . . . we've been dealing with a god?"

"Maybe not the whole time, but most of it, yes."

"How?"

This was the part she didn't fully understand herself, but she gave him as much of the truth as she'd pieced together. "I suspect he used Kieran to break him free. Those markers he unknowingly helped come to pass were more like locks. With each one that broke, Luna's hold on Erebos weakened. Once he was freed, he was able to fully assume control of Kieran's physical form, not just manipulate him from afar."

"But why? What interest could he have in walking among us?"

"Revenge."

"Revenge? For what?"

"Luna imprisoned Erebos for centuries for his crimes against the Chosen. I can't imagine he was very happy about it. Do you remember when we found the prophecy referring to the *Tul Mort Jateh*? The creator of the Night Stalkers?"

Ronan nodded. "The Father of Dreams."

A shiver of foreboding raced down her spine. "Otherwise known as the Lord of Death."

"*That's* who we're dealing with?"

Reyna gave a wooden nod, throat suddenly dry.

"He's the one who's been stalking your dreams."

"Not just my dreams. He's coming for me, Ronan. For us."

She swallowed down a wave of nausea at the thought. She had no defenses against her creator. None. If he got his hands on her, she'd become his mindless Shadow once more.

Ronan's gaze, so warm on hers, hardened. It was as if she could practically see the wheels in his head turning as he started to put together all the clues he'd unknowingly collected these past weeks.

"If he created your kind, his power runs through your veins. He needs it back. Which explains why he came after the Night Stalkers first. Why he keeps you so close."

"And why he'll never let me go."

His hold on her tightened. "Neither will I."

It was such a Ronan thing to say. Equal parts brave and foolish.

She melted in his arms. "Ronan, he'll destroy you and anyone else who stands in his way."

Instead of heeding her warning, he grinned. "I've danced with death before. Turns out, I'm not very easy to kill. Besides, Erebos isn't the only god around. What do you think Luna has to say about this tantrum of his?"

Reyna let out a bitter laugh. "I suppose calling it a tantrum is one way to classify it."

"What would you call it?"

She held his gaze, her heart heavy. "War."

CHAPTER 24

RONAN

*H*ours later, Reyna's words continued to ring through his mind, the echo of them as menacing as their first utterance. How in the Mother's name were they supposed to face off against a damned god? And not just any god. The literal god of death.

Unless Luna had plans she'd yet to share, the outcome was dismal indeed. Which was why Ronan wasn't bothering himself worrying about it. If the conclusion was foregone, what was the point? This could very well be one of his last chances to spend with the woman he'd walked to the ends of the earth for. He wasn't about to waste it on impotent fear.

Instead, he watched over her while she dreamed, loving how peaceful she was in sleep. None of the worry that had lined her face the last handful of days was present.

Ronan stroked her hair, the silver-white strands all that remained to mark her time as Shadow.

He still couldn't believe Reyna was in his arms. After so many years of dead ends, it had started to feel like a fool's dream. He was afraid to close his eyes and learn that it was, in fact, just a dream. Which was the other reason he was still awake long after she'd fallen asleep.

After their talk, they made love again, this time taking things slow so they could explore and savor one another. It had been as mind-blowing as the first time. As much a chance to play and learn as it was to show off, coaxing each other to the edge of climax and then demanding more before allowing themselves to free fall into pleasure-induced oblivion.

He'd never known a lover like her, and he never would again. Completion such as this, the uniting of two souls who'd recognized the missing pieces of themselves in the other, it was a once in a life-time merger. It was the very reason he'd nearly lost himself to madness without her. When a man discovered his soulmate, he did not simply learn to live without her. He moved heaven and earth to be reunited with her. She was the axis his world revolved around. The reason his heart beat and he continued to greet each day. That's what love was. A constant battle to be together. A yearning without end. A hunger that could only be sated in the presence of the other. Anything less than everything was unacceptable.

Reyna made a soft sound, somewhere between a whimper and his name, drawing his attention back to her. He leaned forward, pressing his lips to the slight crease between her brows.

"I'm right here, kitten."

Her eyes fluttered, the long ends of her lashes tangling together as she blinked them open. There was no mistaking the relief in her glittering gaze as she reached for him. "I thought I dreamed it all. I was afraid you wouldn't be here when I woke."

The near-perfect echo of his own fears had him huffing out a laugh. "It was the same for me."

She skated the pad of her thumb beneath his eye. "You didn't sleep at all, did you?"

Turning his head, he pressed a kiss to her palm. "I didn't dare close my eyes. I don't think I could bear to wake up and find you gone."

Her sleepy expression softened. "Come here."

He obeyed, shifting so his body was no longer beside hers but on top. Brushing his mouth to hers, he rasped, "Well, kitten, you wanted me. Now what are you going to do with me?"

QUEEN OF WHISPERS AND MIST

"Everything."

Her wicked grin had his cock jerking to attention. She kissed him, winding her body around his and weaving her hands through his hair. A growl rumbled through his chest when she scraped her nails lightly along his scalp and then tugged on the thick strands. It was a move she'd done often the night before and one that made little shivers race across his skin. He wasn't sure which of them enjoyed the act more.

She pulled back, drawing a mumbled protest from him. "But unfortunately, I think everything is going to have to wait. We should get back, check on the others."

"Why? They're grown-ups. They can look after themselves," he murmured, kissing a path down her neck and collarbone.

Her body shook with laughter as she countered, "Even Bast?"

"He passes for a grown-up."

"Look what happened last time he went off without you."

"You're not playing fair," he grumbled, resting his chin just above her heart so she could appreciate his scowl.

"I rarely do, handsome. That's why I always win."

"And here I thought I was the one with the perfect record."

Her gaze went molten. "You certainly won last night. And this morning."

"Which is precisely why I'm much more interested in this *every-thing* you speak of than returning to the others. I'm aiming to beat my personal best."

"Mmm, that does sound like fun, but . . ."

"No. No buts. Unless it's yours."

She smiled as she cupped his cheek, applying upward pressure until he moved so that his face hovered just over hers. "You'd never forgive yourself if anything happened to them."

The fact that it was true didn't make the pill any easier to swallow. "Fine," he groaned, flopping over onto his back. "Have it your way. Just . . . give me a second to course correct."

Reyna's eyes trailed appreciatively over his torso, lingering on the jut of his swollen shaft.

"Keep looking at him like that, love, and we'll be here all day."

She reached across him to take his rigid length in her hand. "I suppose it's only fair I help you take care of this first."

A moan slipped free as she slid her palm up, using her thumb to gather the pearly bead at the tip before corkscrewing her fist back down. Then she was moving, the ends of her hair trailing over his skin as she replaced her hand with her mouth. She worked him like she'd been born for it, her mouth and hand applying the perfect combination of pressure and suction. It wasn't long before the warning tingle of his impending orgasm crept up on him.

"Fuck, kitten. You have no business being so damned good at that."

She released him with a wet pop. "Are you really complaining about my skill?"

"No. Fuck. I—" She lightly dragged the edge of her nail along the underside of his shaft, and he hissed in unexpected pleasure. "You just make it so fucking good I can't—"

"Can't what?" she asked, wrapping her other hand around his balls and giving a firm tug.

Think. Breathe. Exercise a single ounce of control.

But all that left him was an incoherent grunt when she slipped her lips over him and took him straight to the back of her throat.

"Reyna—" He broke off on a strangled groan when she hummed. The flutter of vibration, along with whatever she was doing with her hands, sent him skyrocketing over the edge.

He should have been embarrassed she'd made him come faster than a green lad holding his first tit, but when she sat back and offered him a sultry look as she licked her lips, he just couldn't find it in himself to care.

"Better?"

He could barely hear past the roar of his pulse in his ears, but her smirk said it all. Surging up, he caught her by the hair and pulled her mouth to his. "If you're asking if I enjoyed myself, I think you can still taste the answer on your tongue. But if you're asking if my need for you has lessened, then the answer is no. It will always be no."

Flipping them over, he moved until her thighs were up over his shoulders.

"Ronan."

The breathless cry of his name had him tossing her a smug grin of his own.

"Shh, love. It's my turn."

"Is holding my hand really necessary?"

"Yes."

"Afraid you'll get lost?" Reyna teased.

"Not me. *You.*"

"Me? Ronan, I was born amongst the trees."

He grunted and squeezed her fingers tighter when she tried to pull free. "The last time you and I traipsed through the woods alone, you wandered off, and it took me five years to find you. I won't apologize for wanting to ensure it doesn't happen a second time."

Her gaze was soft and dreamy, and she leaned in close so she could rest her head on his shoulder. For several seconds, only the sound of their mingled breaths and the crunch of leaves accompanied them before she tossed out, "If you tell anyone about this, I'll deny it with my dying breath."

"I'd expect nothing less, killer," he said with a laugh.

"Killer?"

He pulled away to look down at her face. "I've always called you that."

She smoothed a hand down his chest. He hadn't bothered putting what was left of his shirt back on, so the play of skin over skin made him shiver. "I know, it's just . . ."

He tipped her chin up with his free hand. "You like it when I call you kitten?"

"Darkness help me, but I do." Reyna smiled, color tinging her cheeks. "If Ryder and the other Night Stalkers could see how soft you make me, they'd never let me live it down."

"Huh. And here I was thinking about how hard you—oof."

She elbowed him sharply in the stomach, making him laugh

through the burst of pain. He ran his thumb along her cheekbone, holding her in place when she made to keep walking. "You're not soft, Reyna. You're in love. There's a difference."

She made a contented sound in the back of her throat, giving him a quick kiss before pulling away. "I suppose so."

"You're still as savage and bloodthirsty as ever, I promise," he said with a slight wince, discreetly rubbing at his aching ribs.

Pleased with his verdict, they resumed their trek back to the campsite, still hand in hand.

"Do you think the others will be worried we were gone so long?" she asked.

"No. Buttercup stayed with us most of the night. They'd have let Jagger and the others know if we were in trouble."

She made a considering sound, her eyes narrowed.

"What is it?"

"Hmm? Oh . . . it's probably nothing."

Reyna was the last person he'd accuse of overreacting. If something felt off to her, he trusted her instincts. "Out with it."

"It's just . . . it seems odd to me that we haven't seen or heard any sign of them yet. I know we're still a little out from the campsite, but sound carries. Even if they were all asleep, they should have heard us by now or at least come to investigate the source of the noise after the attack last night."

"You're wondering why they haven't come to greet us?"

She nodded. "Bast especially. I don't know Calypso and her crew well, but they don't strike me as the sort to stand idly by. And Bast..."

"Say no more."

Ronan hadn't really stopped to consider it one way or the other. His thoughts had been too filled with her, but now that she mentioned something, it *was* completely out of character. Bast would have been the first one to gloat and demand details, not wait patiently in his cabin.

"Do you still have your daggers?"

Reyna shot him an incredulous look as she pulled two gleaming blades free. "As if I'd leave them behind."

He gestured for her to pass him one since the blade he'd gotten from Jagger hadn't made the journey to the lagoon with him. She handed it over without question.

"I could—"

"You better not be about to suggest we split up."

"But, I—"

"I said no."

Reyna spun, the tip of her dagger kissing his navel. "I don't remember asking permission, Shield."

He should *not* be hard right now.

"The Shield stayed in Elysia."

"Fine, *Butcher*. But the point stands. Don't expect me to suddenly be subservient because I told you how I feel about you. I'm not that girl."

"I never expected you to be."

"Good." She raised up on her toes and licked his lower lip before stepping away. It was all he could do not to take her by the hips and haul her up against a tree. "Now, as I was saying. I could cloak and scout ahead, make sure it's safe before we head straight for another trap."

"Cloak?"

"It really has been a while, huh?" she asked with a small smile, holding her hand palm up and curling her fingers. As each one rippled, so did the air around them, until her entire hand was obscured by shadow.

Reyna's memories weren't the only things that had returned. So had her powers. He'd almost forgotten about the Night Stalkers' ability to cloak themselves in shadow and blend into their surroundings. He reached out, holding his hand above her and then letting it fall until it met her warm skin. It was a trip since he still couldn't make it out.

"Is this what the others referred to as shadowmelding?"

She dipped her chin in a nod. "The Night Stalkers were the first of Erebos's nightmares. Makes sense we'd carry the trademark of our maker."

He felt marginally better about her suggestion to go ahead since he knew she'd be safely out of sight. Though, as she'd pointed out, it wasn't like he got a say in the matter.

"How far would you say we are from camp?" he asked, trusting her judgment since she was the one who'd been conscious when they'd made the trip.

"Maybe five minutes? It's not far."

"All right," he said, mind busy strategizing. "The nightdrake's corpse should still be there. If you still don't see signs of them by the time you reach it, I want you to turn and come back. You understand me?"

She grinned and gave him a mocking salute. "Sir, yes, sir."

"Technically it's commander," he murmured, liking the sound of the honorific on her lips far too much.

"Be right back, *commander*."

She started to call on the shadows, but a little prickle of awareness had him calling out.

"Kitten?"

"Hmm?"

"You better fucking come back to me."

CHAPTER 25

REYNA

*S*he hadn't counted on the overwhelming sense of nostalgia when she called on the mist. When she'd been younger, she'd thought of it as becoming the wind, for that's always what it seemed when her mother and her guard would cloak themselves in shadows and leap down from the Crow's Nest to the forest floor below.

It had been so long since she'd had the ability, or knowledge, to do the same that she'd forgotten about the whispers. Those indistinct voices chittering just out of range.

She used to be so afraid of them until her mother explained that they were her ancestors there to guide her way. What she hadn't understood at the time was that what her mother really meant was that they were the voices of the dead and that calling on the mist was a way of walking two realms at once.

For an assassin, she supposed it was a fitting gift as much as a warning. Be careful of those you send to the Father, for they are never truly gone, merely lying in wait. Her mother had never confirmed it, but Reyna had the sense that if she allowed herself to give into curiosity and seek out the ones the whispers belong to, she just might become trapped in this in-between place.

And since the Night Stalkers were a superstitious sort—how could they not be given their creator—it was also believed that the clearer the voices, the closer you were to death.

In her youth, Reyna had taken the lack of a distinct message as a sign that her missions would be a success. Now she knew the truth. Death had been caged and unaware of her existence. But not any longer. Now he walked free, and he had his sights locked on her.

Which is why she should have known he'd be waiting for her the second she crossed into his domain.

"Ah, there you are. How nice of you to visit."

Ice trickled through her veins.

"I've been waiting for you."

Her heart picked up its pace.

"You can run, moonbeam, but never hide. For you are the beacon that lights my path."

She was afraid to think lest he could hear the thought, so she focused on keeping her breathing steady, eyes closed, and mind empty.

"It won't be long until we're together once more."

Fear sat heavy in her stomach, the taste of it thick in the back of her throat.

"See you soon, Shadow mine."

It's Reyna! she wanted to shout, but she didn't dare correct him. On the outside chance he hadn't yet realized his hold on her was diminished, she didn't want to be the one to give away the secret. Instead, she dropped her hold on the mist and returned fully to the forest.

"Back so soon?"

She was coated in a fine sheen of sweat, her hands trembling. "I—"

But what could she say, that Erebos hunted them? That he was close and coming closer every day? Ronan already knew that. And if the High Lord was still on his way, then it meant he wasn't quite here. Therefore, he wasn't an immediate problem. Not like finding the rest of their party.

"I guess I'm a little out of practice," she joked lamely.

It was clear from his expression that Ronan wasn't buying the excuse. Before he could press her on it, she started off toward the camp.

"We should hurry."

"Rey!" he whisper-shouted. "Get back here, dammit . . . Reyna!"

But now she was running, her heart thundering beneath her ribs.

How could she have been so stupid? Why had she thought the mists would be safe when they were part of what *he'd* gifted her?

In truth, she hadn't been thinking. She'd been too excited about the prospect of reclaiming another lost piece of herself. That, and the mists were all she had left of her mother. The day she'd taught her to call on them was the last lesson they'd ever shared. Her mother, Regina, first of her name, died in battle the following day. There was much she would give to ask the woman who'd been her idol how she was supposed to protect herself and her friends from the wrath of a vengeful god.

She was still berating herself when she came upon the battle site from the night before. The nightdrake was no less terrifying in the sunlight. Its corpse was still impaled, but the blood that had dripped free had burned away most of the spikes holding it as well as the earth below, meaning that it had slid down until it was suspended just above an acid-made pit.

"Lovely."

She turned as Ronan drew up beside her. "We should probably burn it or bury it."

He grunted. "Why bother? It seems halfway through burying itself."

She shook her head, unable to dispute the logic, and allowed her gaze to drift to the houses beyond.

The obviously empty houses.

"They aren't here."

"Bast? Caly?" he shouted, frowning when no answer came back.

"Didn't believe me?"

He shrugged. "Doesn't hurt to check. Maybe they didn't want to take a chance Blind Willie over here would wake up and continue his reign of terror."

She snickered even as her gut told her it wasn't that innocent. With Erebos's warning still fresh in her mind, she couldn't mistake their disappearance as anything other than foul play. They wouldn't have moved on without leaving word of where they'd gone or sending Buttercup to collect them, at the very least.

Reyna crept closer to the abandoned cabins, her eyes constantly scanning for any sort of clue, the tension crawling through her growing more urgent with every passing second.

"Something doesn't feel right."

He jerked his thumb toward the corpse. "Besides him?"

She bit down on her lip and nodded. "The others should be here. Or at least nearby. Where would they have gone? And why did they leave without us?"

Ronan's expression was grim. "Maybe they didn't get a choice."

That's what she was afraid of.

She'd known this was a possibility, obviously. It was the entire reason she'd insisted Ronan leave their private oasis and come back with her. But part of her had hoped the instinctive urge prompting her had been a false alarm. That it was just her subconscious being overcautious after the last few days.

Reaching the end of the little village, she knelt down, her fingers skimming the packed dirt.

"What are you thinking?" Ronan asked, joining her.

"There should be a trail, right? It rained almost nonstop for a full day. The earth is still damp, perfect for prints. But look, no boot prints. Not in either direction, except for ours."

Ronan's brows dropped low as he looked back the way they'd just come, his eyes following the fresh marks they'd left. "Our tracks from last night should be here too."

She nodded.

But the tracks, just like the rest of the party, were missing.

"Do you think someone went through and cleared them?"

"Like who?"

"Maybe those riders came back for Bast, found the others, and nabbed them as well?" Ronan suggested.

"Hmm . . . maybe. It's certainly possible."

"But you don't think that's what happened?" he guessed.

She couldn't put her finger on it, but Reyna had the feeling they were missing something crucial.

As if sensing her mounting frustration, the wind whipped through the trees, sending a few leaves tumbling to the pockmarked ground. Another gust sent the leaves rolling along the dirt.

Squinting, Reyna eyed the smooth stretch of earth left in its wake, the little divots left by falling drops of water cleared away. She gasped as an idea took shape, and she darted for the nearest pile of leaves and a similarly rough bit of terrain.

"What is it?" Ronan asked, following her.

But she didn't have an answer for him yet. Selecting one of the leaves, she drew it along the ground, her suspicion confirmed when the patch was returned to the same undisturbed state as the village.

"Ronan," she said carefully as she stood, her eyes lifting to the trees. "I don't think we're looking for a someone."

"Then what are we looking for?"

The snap and crack of branches overhead had her reaching for her dagger.

"Some*thing*."

CHAPTER 26

RONAN

Tracking with Reyna was always an experience. He considered himself fairly skilled, but there was no question her knowledge of the forest far surpassed his own. She may not have grown up here, but her knowledge of the earth and trees was unmatched, and her eyes noted details he couldn't begin to detect.

When she'd cocked her head to listen to the wind and then dropped into a crouch, he knew better than to interfere. When she picked up a fallen leaf to draw it across the ground, he realized she'd figured something out. And when she tensed and reached for her weapon, he followed suit.

"Ronan, watch out!"

But even her warning wasn't enough to prepare him for what happened next.

As one, dozens of vines dropped from the branches above them. Some serpentine in their movements, others shooting out like whips. They were thicker than normal vines, their stalks as wide around as his wrist, the leaves jagged on the edges calling to mind the image of little saws. There were also a series of furled buds on them about the size of his head.

"Don't let them touch you."

"Wasn't planning on it," he muttered.

Wishing for his axe, Ronan lunged out of the way of a vine making its way toward him and used his power to heat the blade of his dagger so he could better cut through the thick stalk. An inhuman shriek rent the air as the vine fell. It wiggled and rolled across the floor like an animal before finally turning a sickly gray and shriveling up.

As if in retaliation, three more vines shot his way, their slithering movements synchronized as two aimed for his feet and the third his neck.

"Reyna, I think they might be sentient."

"You think?" she snapped, her hand impossible to track as she lashed out at a vine currently attempting to wind itself around her wrist.

Ronan was about to ask her what a fucking plant would want with a bunch of humans when one of the buds on the closest stalk unfurled, revealing a set of teeth that would have made the nightdrake envious.

"Mother's heaving tits. Carnivorous plants? Are you fucking kidding me? What the hell is wrong with this realm? Why does everything want to kill you?"

Reyna darted past him, taking care of the vines near his feet while he dealt with the one by his face. "You're starting to sound like Bast," she panted.

Maybe Sebastian was onto something.

"Mark my words. I'm never picking a bouquet of flowers again for fear of retribution. I already know my dreams tonight will be filled with images of being eaten alive by a field of damned daisies."

He caught her grin as she spun and threw her dagger, cutting down a dangling fucker sneaking up behind him. Taking up position at his side, she said, "Flowers are a useless gift. Decaying bits of floral genitalia? No thanks. If you're ever of a mind to buy me something pretty, Butcher, make it something that lasts. A weapon would do nicely."

He paused in his attack only long enough to ask, "You want me to give you a weapon in place of a romantic gift?"

"A weapon *is* a romantic gift."

His answering laugh was cut off by the sharp sting of teeth piercing his shoulder.

"Fuck this," he growled, reaching for his Fire as five more vines made their way for him.

"Ronan, no!" she shouted as a ball of molten flame grew in his palm. "This whole place will go up like a tinderbox. We still don't know where the others are. They might be trapped up in the trees, unable to escape."

"Trapped? You think these Mother-cursed weeds had the where-withal to hunt *and* store their next meal?"

"I don't think we know near enough to make any assumptions. But what I do know of predators is that they wouldn't waste fresh meat. Especially if they haven't eaten in a while."

"Dammit."

Not knowing what else to do, Ronan began shouting Sebastian's name, sometimes alternating with one of the others as he continued to hack and slash his way through the never-ending waves of creeping vines. But there was no answer.

"We're never going to get anywhere at this rate," he grunted as a fresh row of vines replaced the few they'd just severed.

"Have a better idea?" Reyna asked, her eyes fever bright as she risked a glance his way. She looked as fierce as he'd ever seen her. Had they been fighting humans, the dirt and sap smeared across her face would have been blood, and he loved that she treated this threat as seriously as any other foe.

"We need to determine if our friends are in the trees. Think you can manage to sneak up and do a bit of scouting if I draw their atten-tion?" It was essentially the same plan as the night before, but reversed. This time, he'd be the distraction.

"What are you proposing?" she asked, suspicion heavy in her voice.

"You won't let me use my Fire, but they don't need to know that. Sometimes the fear of being burned is enough."

Tearing a branch off the nearest tree, he set the other end ablaze and swept out with his torch. As expected, the wall of vines parted and drew away from him in a symphony of god-awful shrieks.

Using his Air, he continued to feed the flame and blow the smoke in the opposite direction. It wouldn't do them any good if he sent her off to scout only to immediately obscure the treetops with a dense cloud of gray.

"Reyna, go! Before they catch on."

~

REYNA

NOT WASTING A SECOND, she took off at a sprint, spying a branch thick enough to support her weight that was far enough from the continuous fall of vines for her to climb around them.

That was the hope, anyway. She had no idea what was waiting for her in the boughs.

As she shimmied her way up, she worked her way from tree to tree, climbing higher as she went, until she was roughly above the place where Ronan continued to fight with the monstrous flora.

It was impossible to know what she was looking for. She hadn't exactly come across an enemy such as this one. But she'd dealt with her fair share of monsters, and there were universal truths she'd learned that should apply to this scenario. If the vines were a collective or some sort of hive mind, there'd be a shared place for them to protect their food supply. It would need to be easily defensible but also easy to reach. More importantly, they wouldn't stray too far from it, lest another predator happen upon what was theirs.

A hiss of pain was torn from her as her palm slid over an unexpectedly sharp bit of bark. She froze, afraid the soft cry might alert the creatures below to her presence, but after several thunderous heartbeats, she determined it was safe to continue.

Reyna was just about to move into the next tree when she caught it. A thick coil of vines—these ones unmoving—protectively wrapped around a bud similar in shape to the ones taking bites out of them below. But that's where the similarities ended. This bud was darker, the seams clearly visible and as thick as two of her fingers. It was also significantly larger, big enough to contain a fully grown human.

Gotcha.

A quick scan revealed several others sprinkled throughout a cluster of nearby branches, all positioned in the vee of two conjoining boughs, though no more than one pod per tree.

Let's hope we're not too late.

Knowing she'd need to work fast, that there was no distraction that would prevent the hunters from coming back to protect their hoard if they realized it was under attack, she gave Ronan the only warning she could.

"I think I found them!"

She had no way of knowing if he heard her, and she couldn't wait around to find out. Dagger in hand, she raked it through the seam, her stomach giving a happy flip when the two pieces of foliage parted easily. She repeated the action on the next seam until a wedge-shaped piece fell away, revealing the contents within.

Jagger.

The boson was curled in on himself, his protector cradled protectively in his hands, their foreheads touching. A flurry of dark-colored dust floated out, and Shadow instinctively covered her mouth as it drifted down. As soon as the dust cleared and fresh air reached the boson, he took a shuddering breath.

Buttercup gave a tentative chirp and then flew out, their wings lightly grazing Reyna's face in what must have been thanks.

"We need to get the others," she whispered.

The finch flew back to Jagger as if to say, 'Go on, I've got him.'

Moving quickly, no clue what was happening below, Reyna darted over to the next pod. This time she spied the telltale remnant of dust and kept her mouth and nose covered by pulling up the neck of her shirt as she sawed away a section of the prison. When its inhabitant was revealed, her heart leapt in relief.

Bast.

Unlike Jagger and Buttercup, who came to as if they'd just woken from sleep, Sebastian was a flurry of flailing limbs. He threw himself at her, catching her off guard as he fought tooth and nail to defend himself. It was no novice reaction, either. His moves were calculated, aimed at the parts of her body that would cause the most damage.

"I will not fail now. You will not keep me from knowing the sweet taste of vengeance, you pathetic—"

"Peace, Bast. It's me. It's Rey—Shadow," she corrected, realizing he might not be familiar with her true name.

He froze, his expression comical as he drew back. There was a flash of something in his eyes, a lightning-quick decision being made before his expression settled back into its normal courtly veneer. "Where the hell have you been?"

"That's how you thank your rescuer?"

"What did you do with Ronan?"

"He's below, dealing with some rather aggressive vegetation. Come on, let's free the others, and you can see for yourself that your friend is hale and whole."

"Shadow." He stopped her with a hand on the shoulder as she made to turn away.

"Hmm?"

"Sorry for that." He gestured sheepishly at her cheek, where a trickle of warm blood made its way to her jaw. She'd barely registered the injury until he pointed it out.

"Never apologize for protecting yourself, Sebastian. Sometimes the only hero you can count on is yourself. There may come a day when Ronan and I can't be there to save you."

Her words caused another flash in the back of his gray gaze. An understanding she wouldn't have expected given his rakish persona. Since this was hardly the time or the place to ask him about it, she nudged him with her elbow and added, "Thankfully today is not that day, so what do you say? Ready to go play hero for the others?"

RONAN

"GIVE UP ALREADY, you demented fucking weed!"

He waved the torch, buying himself and Reyna a few more precious seconds, but his deterrent wasn't going to last much longer. He might be able to use his gift to sustain the flame, but he couldn't do much about salvaging the wood.

Ronan supposed he could make a second torch, but that would require him to split his attention, and he was already dangerously surrounded. Without the aid of Reyna's dagger to help cut them down, the flesh-eating pests had swelled in number.

Until now, the damned rodents they'd faced off with in Bael had been the most shameful loss he'd ever suffered, but he was starting to fear 'carnivorous vine' would soon replace lajhár in the top spot.

If this is your work, you really have a sick fucking sense of humor, you know that?

Perhaps taunting the Mother wasn't the smartest idea, but this attack didn't have the stink of Erebos on it. That arsehole tended to be a little more direct when sending a monster after them. And perhaps even more telling, so far as Ronan could tell, these pesky plants— while undeniably the creation of a madman—lacked Erebos's signature shadowmelding ability.

He let out a savage hiss as his torch began to sputter, the vines growing more aggressive as the flames died down. Ronan debated tossing it altogether when something—several somethings—crashed through the trees above him.

"Heads up!"

Ronan would have laughed at Reyna's wholly unnecessary shout punctuated by Bast's high-pitched screams if not for the fact that it heralded their safe return. They dropped to the ground in a shower of leaves and limbs, some landing more gracefully than others.

The vines, Ronan had quickly realized, didn't react to sound so much as movement. It wasn't until the others displaced the air that the deadly tendrils seemed to realize they had company.

Sebastian let out a colorful curse as he rebounded from his undignified sprawl and popped up to his feet. Brushing away a few lingering twigs and tenacious leaves, he gave Ronan a wide grin. "Miss me?"

"I was too busy trying not to die to miss you, Bast."

"Trying not to die . . . sure, that's what we'll call it." He gave a lascivious wink.

Ronan couldn't help but grin, relieved Sebastian was unharmed despite all statements he'd made feigning indifference. The dandy really had grown on him. Like a rash.

Knowing his traveling party was now accounted for, he couldn't care less about burning this entire fucking place to the ground. It was cursed. They should have just kept walking instead of being lured in by the presence of the abandoned buildings.

"Everybody back!"

Bronn curled an arm around his captain, using his body to shield her obviously injured one while they dodged the snaking vines. Jagger followed, hauling Bast up by the back of his shirt when he didn't move away fast enough. Reyna was close on his heels, staying only long enough to give him a meaningful look.

Hurry.

Once everyone was safely clear, Ronan summoned a huge wave of Fire. He threw it outward, catching all the remaining vines in the spray. The shrieks were terrible as the thick stalks withered and died. Most dropped to the ground, where they turned to piles of ash, but the singed ends of others retreated up into the safety of the canopy.

"Good riddance," Ronan muttered, keeping an eye on the blaze as he carefully backed away. When he determined he was a far enough distance, he spun on his heel and jogged over to the others. "Can we please get the fuck out of here?"

Then spying the nightdrake's corpse in his periphery, he lobbed a ball of Fire at it for good measure.

"I hate this place."

CHAPTER 27

RONAN

*T*he night's revelries were in full swing. There was nothing quite like a reminder of your mortality to make you eager to celebrate still being alive. And since this was the third time in as many days they'd had to face that particular lesson, the need to blow off steam was high.

"Do you think anyone would miss us if we went for a walk?" Reyna asked, her eyes darting meaningfully down the beach.

After the attack from above, no one felt comfortable with anything less than full visibility, so they'd made their way to the shore to spend the night under nothing but open sky and stars. The detour would add another day or two to their journey north, but peace of mind was priceless.

Ronan looked over to the other side of the fire he'd made using driftwood and magic. Currently, Bast and Bronn were busy trying to one-up each other with their exploits while Caly laughed at them both and Jagger watched on with an unreadable expression, his protector curled up against his neck.

"As long as we don't stray too far, we're probably safe."

"Good. Come on." Reyna stood and held out a hand for him.

There was no stopping the smile that stretched across his face as he accepted her offering. It hadn't even been a full day ago when she would have shoved him into the fire as soon as willingly hold his hand. The knowledge meant he'd never take such small displays of affection for granted.

As their skin slid against each other, he noted that while her palms were as callused as his, they still managed to be soft. It was an intimate detail he tucked away, fully intending to collect a dozen more before the night was through.

Lifting their joined hands to his lips, he brushed a kiss over the back of hers. "Lead the way, kitten. You already know I'll follow."

The second they rose, Sebastian shot to his feet. "Where do you two think you're going?"

"For a walk."

"Is that wise?"

"We're not going far. We'll be within sight the entire time."

Hopefully Reyna was up for a little exhibitionism. He'd been desperate to get his hands on her again the second they'd left the oasis this morning.

Bast narrowed his eyes, not remotely reassured. "I don't like it."

"How 'bout this? If we're not back in an hour, you have my permission to come and get us."

Reyna's brows flew up in surprise, but she didn't contradict him.

Bast huffed but ultimately relented. "All right. One hour. And don't get too close to the shore either. No telling what might leap out at you."

Wasn't that the fucking truth?

"We'll keep him entertained until you get back," Calypso promised.

He tossed the captain a thankful grin. It wasn't that he was eager to split up again so soon, but now that Reyna was back, he didn't want to miss out on the opportunity to be alone with her either. A walk down the beach hand in hand sounded like the perfect compromise. They'd be far enough away to hold a private conversation and steal a kiss or quick cuddle, but not so far as to leave either side vulnerable.

"I mean it, Ronan. One hour. Then I'm coming after you."

"We'd better hurry, kitten. Something tells me the hourglass is short on sand."

"I think you're right," she murmured, smiling at Bast and giving the others a small wave as he tugged her away from the fire.

They fell into a companionable silence, the flicker of flames quickly replaced by the soft crash of waves.

Once they were out of earshot, he asked, "Well, we've survived a sea monster, a miniature dragon, and man-eating weeds. What do you think the morrow will bring?"

Reyna shrugged and pursed her lips as she considered. "Perhaps plague, maybe famine."

"It really does feel like the end of the world, doesn't it?"

"I prefer to think of it as we've gotten the worst out of the way. Maybe it's all smooth sailing from here."

He squeezed her hand, neither of them believing her hopeful words.

"That would be a nice change of pace. I could do with a bit of boring. Find a quiet place to put down some roots, hang up my sword for a while."

"You? I don't buy it for a second. You'd be back out adventuring before the first sennight."

A low laugh rumbled through him. "Probably. I guess you'll just have to give me plenty of reason to stay home in bed."

"Oh no, just because you're ready to retire, old man, doesn't mean I am."

"Old man? I'm only a couple years your senior."

"What can I say, Butcher? They were rough years."

"You weren't complaining about my age last night."

Her grin was flirty. "That's because I didn't realize how feeble you truly were."

"Feeble? I'll show you feeble!" He bent down and grasped her around the knees, picking her up in a seamless move and taking off down the beach, her squeals of laughter floating on the air behind them as she collapsed over his shoulder.

"Ronan!" she wheezed between bouts of laughter, pounding on his back. "Ronan, you made your point. Set me down."

He continued to jog until she slid the tips of her fingers beneath the waistband of his fresh trousers. Thank the Mother, they'd had the foresight to grab a couple extra pairs of clothing when they'd raided the smuggler's cave, else he'd have been wandering around in little more than a loincloth. And while they were a bit short, not to mention tight, especially at the moment, at least they covered him from arse to calf.

"You sure that's what you want?"

"Yes!"

He dropped to one knee, flipping her over and onto her back in the sand, knocking the air from her lungs. Silent laughter continued to quake her shoulders.

"Do you still think me feeble?"

She rolled her lips together, looking as if she was about to say yes, before quickly shaking her head. Running her hands up his stomach and over his chest, she murmured, "You're quite virile for a man of your years."

"At least this time you speak true," he murmured, planting a hand by either side of her head as he leaned down over her.

She greeted his lips eagerly, her kiss tasting of sea spray and the bottle of wine they'd scavenged. It was a heady combination, and he was soon lost to it. Neither of them noticed the fog rolling in off the sea.

"How long before Bast comes for us?"

"What did I tell you about mentioning others while we're together?"

She poked him below his ribs. "We're neither naked nor are you inside me. Since those were your only two conditions, I believe I've followed your rules regarding speaking other's names."

"A gross oversight on my part. Allow me to correct my mistake." He reached for the fastening of her pants. "And to answer your original question, not long, so we'd better hurry."

"Good, because I need you."

His hand moved between leather and skin until he cupped her slick sex. "How much?"

"More than anything."

His heart gave a happy lurch. "More than . . . your daggers?" he whispered, feathering kisses over her jaw as he worked her with his fingers.

"Mmm . . . .that's a close one. My daggers are just so useful."

He pulled back with an incredulous laugh. "You little minx."

"Well, if this isn't just the most precious and nauseating display I've ever seen." Erebos's cultured drawl turned the sensual fire in his veins to ice.

Ronan shifted as best he could so that his body was between the High Lord and Reyna's, instinctively creating an invisible shield out of Air and reinforced with Earth. The interloper stood less than an arm's length away, his hands resting over the center of his chest, a sneer curling his upper lip.

"It practically warms the cockles of even my blackened heart."

Ronan tried to call out, his eyes darting down the beach to where the campfire and reinforcements should be, but all his eyes found was a thick wall of gray and black mist.

Fuck. So much for staying in sight.

"Come here to me, Shadow mine."

"The lady's name is Reyna."

Erebos's eyes flicked between the two of them, but he did not acknowledge Ronan's fierce declaration. "Things will be so much worse if you make me ask again."

Behind him, Reyna pushed to her feet.

"Reyna, don't."

"I have to. It's the only way to save you."

Erebos laughed, and it cracked through the night like thunder. "How naïve you are thinking there's anything you can do to protect him from me."

A cloud of black smoke in the shape of a taloned hand shot out, grasping Ronan about the neck and cutting off his oxygen. Not even the shield he'd created was strong enough to block it. It may as well have not been there at all for all the good it did. But what could he really expect when it was not a man he faced, but a god?

"Please," Reyna whispered. "If you promise not to hurt him or his compatriots, if you promise to let them walk free, I'll come with you. Willingly." Her gaze darted to Ronan's, pleading with him to understand. "I love you," she mouthed.

"No," he rasped, but the hand around his throat only crushed harder, causing spots to dance in his periphery.

"Deal," Erebos said, his eyes locked on hers.

Ronan could have told her it was an empty promise. The power flowing through her veins held everything he needed. The bastard would say whatever she wanted to hear if it got him his way. It didn't mean he had to follow through with any of it.

"Lies," he tried to warn her, but there wasn't enough air left in his lungs for the word to be more than a croak.

Reyna took a fortifying breath, and even though it was surrender, she walked to her creator like a queen. Shoulders straight, head held high, not a single ounce of fear evident in any part of her. He was so fucking proud of her strength, even as she ripped out his heart with her sacrifice.

It should be him. He was the one who should be laying down his life to save hers. Not this. Never this.

He could barely breathe, let alone tell her so. Cut off from air as he was, he could do little more than make harsh rasping sounds. She risked a final glance back at him, her gaze filled with everything she couldn't say.

I love you. Please don't do this.

As if she could hear him, a tear beaded at the corner of her eye, but she blinked it away before taking that final step.

The second Reyna was within range, Erebos pressed the palm of his hand to her forehead, and her eyes rolled back in her head, body going limp. Erebos caught her easily, lowering her into an unconscious heap at his feet.

"Reyna!" The outraged shout was barely a strangled grunt.

"I'll deal with her in a minute. Right now, I think it's past time you and I had a talk."

Ronan tried to bare his teeth in something that might pass as a derisive snarl, but it was hard to convince his limbs to do much of anything. Even his fingers, which had been attempting to peel away the smoke crushing his throat, were sliding down. It was a struggle just to keep his gaze trained on the other man's face.

"From the day you set foot on my continent, you've caused me no end of grief. I overlooked your trespasses, admittedly not considering you—a broken, pathetic man—much of a threat. But then you took something that belongs to me, and in doing so, ruined years of hard work. And that I simply cannot forgive." He exhaled, his head slowly tilting to the side as he studied him. "I'm afraid I'm going to enjoy this more than I should. Far more than you, certainly."

Erebos stalked forward, closing the distance between them. The smoky hand did not release him until the Lord of Death grasped his cheeks between his thumb and forefinger. Such a slight touch shouldn't have hurt, but it felt as though a storm's worth of lightning shot directly into his heart.

Ronan convulsed in his hold, vision blurring as his eyes rolled back in his head and agony became the only truth he knew. The pain stopped as suddenly as it started, Erebos's cruel voice whispering in his ear.

"Do you have any last words, Shield? I couldn't care less about them, to be perfectly honest, but there's a certain poetry to the ritual, isn't there? Especially if my wife is out there somewhere, watching. I wonder, would you have remained devoted to Luna and her Vessel if you'd known this was what was in store for you?"

Ronan struggled to pay attention. To memorize the words so he could pick them apart and make sense of them later. Erebos didn't make it easy for him, either. Especially since he wouldn't shut up.

"I want her to know this was the moment she failed. Where all her best-laid plans went awry. Because at the end of the day, *you* were never a match for *me*. I mean, really, what was she thinking sending such a wretched, pitiable creature to finish the job she herself failed to do? Alone at that?" He pulled back to meet Ronan's gaze. "I suppose that's a question I'll simply have to ask her myself."

Blood began to dribble out of Ronan's cracked lips as another pulse of electricity shot through him.

"Oh, don't worry, Shield. I'm not going to kill you . . . yet. I fully intend to draw this out. Use you to keep my pet in line. For she is my favorite toy, and you are hers. She'd do anything to save you. Just as I would do anything to keep her. And to think, all this time, I should have been torturing you instead. How differently things might have ended up if I'd simply done that from the beginning. Ah well, better to learn one's lesson late than never."

Erebos squeezed harder, his eyes furious black pits and his smile carved of malice.

Every muscle in Ronan's body went taut as he fought wave after wave of blinding agony. This time when the pain cut off, he dropped to his knees in the sand, bloody spit dripping from his mouth as he fought to catch his breath.

"Oh, I got a bit carried away, didn't I? We were discussing last words."

"Fuck. You." His vocal cords may not be able to convey the depth of his loathing, but he knew the truth of his hatred shone in his eyes.

"What was that? I didn't quite catch it," Erebos said, crouching beside him and hauling his head back by the hair.

Ronan spat a mouthful of blood in his face.

Erebos wiped a hand over the red-tinged spittle, looking like a bored tutor rather than an enraged Lord of Death. "Now that wasn't very nice, was it? Manners, Ronan. They matter. I believe it might be time I teach you some."

This time when the lightning shot through him, the torment went on without end, Ronan's anguished cries ringing out into the night until his voice was too hoarse to create sound. Even then, they continued to bounce around in his skull, the unending echo chasing itself until he was lost to it.

He must have passed out at some point because later, when he was able to once again think past the pain, he peeled open his eyes. In that one final moment of awareness, the last thing he saw was Reyna's slumped form being dragged beside his in the sand.

No!

He couldn't let his monster steal her from him again.

Reyna. Reyna!

He couldn't form the words, but his heart screamed them.

This couldn't be happening. Even if what Erebos had said about Luna always intending for this to happen had been true, he refused to accept it.

This could not be how their story ended.

Not knowing if it would work, Ronan did the only thing he could. He reached down into the heart of his power and called on the one person left who might be able to hear him.

Effie!

CHAPTER 28

EREBOS

He was assaulted by a hurricane of enraged woman the second he set foot in his errant wife's moonlit garden. Prying her away by sealing his hands around her wrists, he crooned, "Luna, darling, I do so love these chats of ours. But this is hardly the time for a tearful reunion. I'm quite busy, as I'm sure you know."

Angry tears rolled down her beautiful cheeks, her eyes glittering like stars in the night sky. "What did you do?"

"What needed to be done, same as I always have."

Luna shook her head, her hair rippling out around her like mist above water. "No . . . this is a stretch, even for you. You've always been cruel, but this time you've gone too far. You're no better than your monsters. Does nothing good or decent remain in you? Have you truly forgotten how to love?"

"Me? That's rich, seeing as how you were the unfaithful bitch who swore vows of eternal love all while you schemed and plotted against me. How is what I've done any worse than your own sins, darling? At the very least, you must admit I've never pretended to be anything other than what I am."

"Oh? And what's that?" she sneered, straining to pull away from him.

He gripped her tighter, holding her hostage. "Your perfect match. The darkness to your light. Chaos to your order. The pain to your pleasure."

She shivered in his hold, her eyes dropping to his lips for one unguarded second before she tore out of his grasp. "The only thing you've accomplished is ridding me of all but the last of options."

"It amuses me to no end that you think you hold any cards, dearest. I have already won. It's over."

Even streaked with tears, her face was terrifying in its beauty. He would have taken a step back if he didn't simultaneously yearn to pull her closer. They always had fought as hard as they loved.

"When will you learn not to underestimate me?"

"Maybe when you learn that you will never best me. I am your counterpart, sweetheart, created out of chaos to be your balance in all things. You will never be rid of me."

"We'll see about that."

"What is that supposed to mean?"

"Your actions today have left me no choice. I've prepared for this eventuality, but I'd foolishly hoped your love for me would keep you from setting us down this path. Now there is no stopping what's coming."

She turned and walked away from him.

"And what's that?" he couldn't help but shout, as turned on by her display of defiant temper as he was worried.

His goddess didn't bother turning around as she answered.

"A mother's vengeance."

ACKNOWLEDGMENTS

I'm going to keep this one short and sweet.

To everyone who took time out of their busy lives to share a kind word of support or encouragement, or just to check in on me. Your faith in me kept me going through what felt like impossible deadlines and endless workdays. I had to put a lot of my life on hold to get this book/series to you on time, but knowing you were out there rooting me on makes the sleepless nights, and lack of days off worth it.

Thank you for believing in me.

THE CHOSEN UNIVERSE

THE CHOSEN SERIES: THE COMPLETE SERIES

(VON & HELENA)

A FATED MATES HIGH FANTASY ROMANCE

MOTHER OF SHADOWS

REIGN OF ASH

CROWN OF EMBERS

QUEEN OF LIGHT

THE CHOSEN BOXSET #1

THE CHOSEN BOXSET #2

THE KEEPERS: THE COMPLETE SERIES

(LUCIAN & EFFIE)

A GUARDIAN/WARD HIGH FANTASY ROMANCE

THE DREAMER (A KEEPER'S PREQUEL)

THE KEEPERS LEGACY

THE KEEPERS RETRIBUTION

THE KEEPERS VOW

THE KEEPERS BOXSET

THE FORSAKEN: THE COMPLETE SERIES

(RONAN & REYNA)

A REJECTED MATES/ENEMIES-TO-LOVERS

HIGH FANTASY ROMANCE

PRISONER OF STEEL & SHADOW

QUEEN OF WHISPERS & MIST

COURT OF DEATH & DREAMS

ALSO BY MEG ANNE

BROTHERHOOD OF THE GUARDIANS /
THE NOVASGARDIAN VIKINGS

UNDERCOVER MAGIC

(NORD & LINA)

A SEXY & SUSPENSEFUL FATED MATES PNR

HINT OF DANGER

FACE OF DANGER

WORLD OF DANGER

PROMISE OF DANGER

CALL OF DANGER

BOUND BY DANGER (QUINN & FINLEY)

THE MATE GAMES: WAR

A SPICY PARANORMAL WHY CHOOSE ROMANCE

CO-WRITTEN WITH K. LORAINE

OBSESSION

REJECTION

POSSESSION

TEMPTATION

ABOUT MEG ANNE

USA Today and international bestselling paranormal and fantasy romance author Meg Anne has always had stories running on a loop in her head. They started off as daydreams about how the evil queen (aka Mom) had her slaving away doing chores, and more recently shifted into creating backgrounds about the people stuck beside her during rush hour. The stories have always been there; they were just waiting for her to tell them.

Like any true SoCal native, Meg enjoys staying inside curled up with a good book and her cat, Henry . . . or maybe that's just her. You can convince Meg to buy just about anything if it's covered in glitter or rhinestones, or make her laugh by sharing your favorite bad joke. She also accepts bribes in the form of baked goods and Mexican food.

Meg is best known for her leading men #MenbyMeg, her inevitable cliffhangers, and making her readers laugh out loud, all of which started with the bestselling Chosen series.

Made in the USA
Middletown, DE
27 November 2022

16209383R00151